Hamish Macfarlane

THREEPLAY

The Thriller Club
T.003

Aspire Publishing

An Aspire Publication

First published in Great Britain 1998

ISBN 1 902035 13 5

Printed and bound in Great Britain by
Caledonian International Book Manufacturing Ltd, Glasgow.

Typeset in Palatino by Kestrel Data, Exeter, Devon.

Cover design by Larry Rostant

Aspire Publishing – a division of XcentreX Ltd.

For Lindsay

Acknowledgements

Patricia Hawkes, for showing no mercy in editing; David Edwards, for pointing me in Aspire's direction; Caroline von Schmalensee, my email buddy, for illustrations and Web savvy; Christian and The Orgasmic Alphabet Orgy in Toronto, for their inspiration and friendship; Robin McKelvie, for providing some competition; Alan Parker, for his encouragement and humour; and my parents, for their faith and love.

Act I

GETTING WORSE

1

Launching The Missile

A woman whose face was torn open in an attack by a Rottweiler has postponed her wedding.

Susan Addison (21) was due to marry next month, but will now wait until her wounds have fully healed. She needed ten stitches in her cheek following the attack outside her brother's council flat in Wester Hailes on Monday.

Police are trying to trace the unmuzzled dog and its owner, who wrestled the animal away from Ms Addison before walking off . . .

– *Evening News*

ROGER:
I have tabloid-fever tonight.

And if I sleep, I know I'll dream of some awful disaster. My nightmares used to be abstract fear-scapes: a metaphor of my insecurities. For the last month, however, they have seemed utterly real. No more fantastic monsters. I see my family trapped in blazing fires. I feel myself savagely beaten by men speaking a foreign language. I know I am dreaming, but the terror remains. I read somewhere that lucid dreaming was very healthy, but I feel more unstable than ever. I should stop reading the *Evening News*. Too awful, human beings, they really are. But I can't help myself. I read the stories of destruction and

11

despair, looking for clues to my fate. My fear of life. My guilt upon waking each morning. Day to day existence is proving increasingly difficult.

Rebecca
I bought a one way ticket to Planet Stupid the night I told you the lie. And it was a lie: I would never do anything like that, please believe me.

Come home. I miss you like mad, and Fat Cat does too.

I love you.
Roger

In the letters I never send her I can tell her that I love her. But face to face, I suffered from a verbal paralysis. The moment would come. Some cuteness, beauty, sex. And then it would pass, the words left unsaid. I adore you. I am besotted with you. You mean everything to me. I could not tell her I loved her.

That's not the reason she went home to Hampstead. Well, not directly. I said something stupid, although I thought I was being cunning at the time. My fault. I just had to say the love words, and we could have moved forward. Instead, I concocted a wicked lie designed to put our relationship on the line and force the pace. These are the mistakes we make, trying to see life in black and white.

It was a typical Saturday night. Boring video, boring take-away, boring life. Becky rested her head on my shoulder as we watched some American dross (how anyone can watch T.V. at an angle is beyond me.) I could smell her hair and I tingled with pleasure. It made what I told her next all the madder.

'Becky?'

'Yes, Tiger?'

'Do you remember that party we went to last month? The one in the country?'

'Oh yes, they had the nicest French windows. Do we have any more beer?'

'It's in the fridge. Do you—?'

'You're so clever, Tiger.'

The Beckster got up and went into the kitchen. She wasn't meant to do that. She was meant to listen to me, and I would watch her eyes grow wide, then fill with tears as I made my terrible confession. But she was getting bottles of Dutch lager from the fridge.

She skipped back to the settee, and I tried to stay on track. 'Becky, do you remember when you didn't feel very well, and had a lie down in one of the guest rooms?'

'Mmm. Those hors d'oeuvres were definitely suspect. Budge up. God, you're tense.'

The girl I adore put her hands around my neck and massaged my terrified shoulders. I could have stopped talking, couldn't I? I could have just shut up and enjoyed her touch. No. I had to follow the script. I turned around to face her.

'The thing is Becky, while you were lying down, I met an old friend, and we kind of got talking. And there was so much to drink that we kind of got pissed.'

Becky smiled, waiting for the punch-line. Waited for me to tell her that we stole a painting from the drawing room, that we threw up in the cloak room. When I tell her stories she smiles and laughs as if I'm the funniest man alive.

I looked straight into her eyes and launched the missile. 'And we kind of had sex.'

There's a devil living inside of me. It makes me say things just for effect. I call him Georgy Porgy.

It was an imaginary affair. I expected Becky to shout for a bit, cry for a while, and then I would beg her forgiveness, tell her I loved her, and we would screw like stallions until dawn. Yes, I would have to say that I loved her, to save the situation. And after I had said it the first time, I could say it again and again. We would move on, and we would be happy.

I had a fair idea that the cunning plan had not worked out when I found myself standing in the rain outside my flat. Becky shouted, cried, but also ran out into the Edinburgh cold, telling me to "kind of" piss off and die.

I did not tell her I loved her. I stood in the rain, trying to work out what had gone wrong. Reading this, do not condemn me for my stupidity. Perhaps for you love is straight-forward. I stayed with Jay that night, went round to his plush flat and cried on his shoulder. He was, as always, very supportive, and I felt a lot better about things by morning.

When I returned to my flat Becky was not there. I went next door, but she wasn't there either. And neither was any of her stuff.

I telephoned one of her friends only to be told that 'Becky knew exactly who I had slept with and she would never forgive me'. How could she know, who could have told her about an event that didn't exist? And *Chloe*? Why would I sleep with her? But the who and why didn't really matter. More importantly, our relationship had crumbled because of a sexual mis-demeanour that never happened. The punishment, without the pleasure. Damn you Georgy!

You must think me mad. But stay close, and I will explain my life.

2

A Passionate Moment

There are a growing number of studies on the reasons why some organisations are more successful than others. All make it clear that the clarity of strategic direction and its relevance to a changing environment is critical.

The wiser researchers and writers realise, however, that it is not possible to reduce the explanations of how this is done to simple do's and don'ts. Rather, successful organisations are those that are able to sense the critical forces at work around them and change by building a capability for organisation-wide learning and adaptation.

It is the ability of managers to relate to their external environment, their internal culture and the people around them, that will ensure success.

– *Business Strategy in the Twenty First Century*

JAY:
Oh dear. Poor Roger seems a trifle confused. Weighed down by his romantic neuroses he's jumped straight into the middle of our little tale. Roger's lack of artistic style will be the death of us, I swear.

I can see that I shall have to take you back to the beginning, to avoid further confusion. Not only that, I must clarify a point fudged so recklessly by the exaggerating, hyperbolising Roger. Our little jester did stay at my residence after darling Rebecca tossed his limp form into the street (I gave him due attention after making a discreet telephone call.) But his post-scuffle hysteria was brought on not by love by but embarrassment. The lad does not love our cherished Rebecca, he is merely upset at losing the relationship game, a sport he plays appallingly badly.

Sweet Rebecca is not a truly loveable girl, and Roger, fickle beast, is incapable of any emotion higher than infatuation. Yes, Roger (I love him like a brother you know) is like a child hankering after the latest toy, the most fashionable piece of Japanese plastic. And just like a toy, the girl loses her sparkle soon after acquisition.

But fear not. I, Jay, his best friend and confidante, will endeavour to cure him of this tired affliction, his chocolate broken heart. I shall direct him to greener pastures, where he can play to his ventricle's content.

So the beginning. Let us adjourn to a month before Roger's little *faux pas*, to a delightful party, where I shall show you how the business of "love" ought to be conducted. So come with me, ladies and gentlemen, and watch and learn. Watch and learn.

'Sorry!'

The usually resilient frame of the delectable Rebecca pushes feebly past me and makes a tortoise dash – half crawl, half scuttle – to the downstairs bathroom. I lick spilt *Pouilly Fumé* from my slender fingers and cast a concerned eye at my dear friend Roger. 'Your luscious Rebecca looked a trifle green. Too much of the old champers and caviar?'

Roger shakes his head. 'She's been on Budweiser and sausage rolls all night.'

Well, no one can accuse the voluptuous Rebecca of being a *snob gastronomique*. I tell Roger this, as a precursor to my erudite discourse on the connection between diet and party political allegiance, but before I can start, before I can even begin to expound, Roger grips the sleeve of my Valentino shirt and says, 'I'm kind of in a fix, actually Jay.'

'A pharmaceutical fix?' I ask, delving into the chemical treasure trove that is my trouser pocket.

'No. Well, I could do with some Charlie if you've any spare, but it's about Becky and I.'

Becky and *me*. Hasn't he heard of accusative forms of pronouns? I sometimes question whether English is Roger's first language. But he looks most downcast, so I forgive his grammatical confusion and slip a coke wrap into his sweaty paw, then lead him away from the noise and heat of the party and into the dim relaxation of the conservatory (a room to which only the select few have a key.)

I stroll over to a geranium and inhale it's heaven-scent. 'So tell all, Roger, tell all.'

'Well, I think Becky's the cat's pyjamas and everything, I mean she's absolutely the bee's knees, but I'm worried that she doesn't know how I feel. I mean I'm totally in love with her, but I don't think she gets it.'

'Well, Roger, this may sound like a crazy plan, but why don't you just *tell* her?'

'That's just it. We've been going out for two years, and it's going to sound weird if I just say pass the milk and by the way I love you. She'll probably think I'm having an affair or something.'

'Well, how have you said it before?'

'I told you, I've never said it before.'

17

'Before Rebecca, how have you told a girl you loved her?'

'I haven't.'

An appalling silence. An *appalled* silence. How did Roger get into Rebecca's pants in the first place with this lacklustre attitude? But as usual, I shall get him out of trouble. You see how hard I try to cure him? You see how strenuously I work?

'Look Roger, I'm going to make this very simple for you. The next time you're alone with Rebecca, and you have an intimate moment, just open your mouth and let the words fall out.'

'An intimate moment?'

'That's right.'

'You mean sex?'

'Don't be so unimaginative. I'm talking about dancing to your favourite song, feeding the ducks, Hell, just something, when you're alone together, and you have that moment before you rush back home to your little ghetto and break the mattress.'

Direction enough, don't you think? But no, Roger can turn the simplest concept into brain surgery.

'But,' he whines, 'but what if one of these moments doesn't happen?'

'For goodness sake, Roger, just make one up! The bigger the better. Say you've been having an affair with her best friend, tell her your mother has just butchered your father with her Sabatier bread knife. Make it something spicy, because in the heat of the moment, Roger, we can say anything.'

'Isn't that a little deceitful?' whispers Roger, concern shuddering across his ample features.

'Means to an end. Once you've said 'I love you' the first time, it's a veritable piece of cake. You can say it again and again and you and Rebecca can make the bedsprings squeak with joy.'

'Wow,' says Roger. There's a tear in his eyes, I hope to God it's the alcohol. 'Thanks, Jay. I really appreciate this, you're a real mate.'

Well, no one's disputing that.

This is a proper Edinburgh party. A party with breeding, no trainspotters here. This is high society. Behave, and I may let you stay.

You have to understand, this is a party of success, as well as excess. The guests either have a lot of money, make a lot of money, or look as if they're about to. I fall into the first category, by the by, while Roger is sandwiched firmly between the second and third.

The guests at this party are in control. And they affect you. Bought some shares recently? Your broker's at this party. Been to the theatre lately? A cast member is present (perhaps he's screwing your stock broker.) Do any drugs this week? Both your doctor and dealer are here, their professions aren't so different, both in the business of alleviating pain and—

Excuse me? Am I a dealer? No, silly, rewind, retract, rescind, go and find the theatre programme you kept. Look, I'm the director! And Roger's the producer! Now don't you feel better, knowing what we do? Isn't that cosy? But enough. Let's mingle.

Ah, perfect, there's Marianne. I'd know her laugh anywhere. But she's talking to Alasdair, as per usual these days. Alasdair. The perfect name. Alas, indeed. While I create theatre, it's Alasdair's chosen profession to criticise it. I'm sure that illustrates the intellectual gulf between us more than adequately.

Dear God, he's wearing his mock-victim face, and Marianne is giggling. There's nothing worse than a victim *pretending* he's a victim. Don't bother with

19

your self-deprecation, Alasdair, we already know how hopeless you are.

Oh dear, he's said something else (he's clearly infatuated with the poor girl, why doesn't he just grit his working class teeth and get the embarrassing pass made and over with?) and Marianne roars once more (what does she see in him, even platonically?) Marianne doesn't laugh like a model, but she is. Her laugh has no poise, however, it stumbles down the auditory catwalk, the Army Surplus Store of fashion laughs.

But we're wasting time. I turn my carnivorous gaze away from the throng and catch sight of my prey. A lady in red, smoking an obnoxious looking cigar, curled up cat style in a magnificent fat armchair. I smooth myself and select a suitable script. Then I waltz on over and invite her to join my dance. Her eyes sparkle, I've saved her from herself, and she holds a trembling hand to my face.

It's important to know one's limits, don't you think? The girl knows that the plot has already been worked, the playwright has edited and submitted, there can be no last minute alterations. We play the subtlest of games. She pretends not to know who I am, and I pretend to know who she is. But I know she's a player, and she knows I'm M.V.P. Then she adjusts to my rhythm. I proffer the bedroom key and we dance away, the crowd oblivious to our smoke-screened exit.

I pause at the doorway and glance over at Marianne. Ah yes. Divine Marianne. I shall have to have her, and be quick about it, for her beauty has a transient quality. Her hazel eyes whisper 'I am but a falling star, catch me if you can.'

3

The Condition Starts with an 'H'

. . . the entire scene, comprised as it is of jive, mambo, frenzy, and over-heated sex-anger-aggression, is framed by dance, and the dance itself is its own motivation. The Buddies stage explodes with the energy that the young characters must expend and contain, the tension between the two impulses giving the scene its genuinely thrilling charge . . .
– *The Scotsman*

ALASDAIR:
I've been feeling slightly sick for the last few days. Just the vaguest hint of fever, it swaddles me during random moments; taking the shuddering number twenty three bus to work, snatching an unremarkable microwave meal from the chilled section in Scotmid. I think I could be coming down with something. I think I could be on the verge of something awful. I'm taking paracetamol for the fever and spearmint Rennies for the upset stomach. But it's not enough to quell this raging, if somewhat sporadic, nausea.

I should go to the doctor. Ask him for the magic potion to take away my queasy disposition. Trouble is, my local GP doesn't seem to take me seriously anymore. He is obsessed with 'visible signs of illness,' and he can never find anything wrong with me. Well, I'm no physician, but it's obvious that he's just not looking hard enough. Where are the CAT Scans, where are the marrow biopsies? I know what I've got. Everything, everything under the dying sun. But there's no name for my cumulative disease, not enough letters in the alphabet to spell out the malaise. I've looked up my symptoms, read the books in the Central Library, but I'm ahead of a trend, the medical texts haven't caught up with me yet.

Unbelievably, on my last visit the doctor was positively irritable. Said that I was the healthiest person he'd ever examined, that *I* was wasting *his* time. Now isn't that the sick joke? But it's not his inability to cure me that's so upsetting. It's the dishonesty. If only he'd come clean and say 'Dear God, I've never seen anything like this, I'm afraid there's nothing we can do.' That would be fine, because then I could simply nod sagely, adopt an air of manly resignation, and begin to put my affairs in order. But he won't even do me that simple favour.

Fuck the National Health Service. I'll save my money and go private. I'm sure that if I paid BUPA enough they would be able to put a name to my condition.

The last time I felt 'okay' was two weeks ago, in Negociants with Roger and Jay. It was a relative feeling of well-being, brought on in relation to the madman who interrupted my usual neurosis and made me feel happy and sane.

It was Wednesday lunch-time, mid-week hell. I was shattered already, it was only through the hot chocolate sitting in front of me that I could have faith in surviving until Saturday. Jay was on his usual

Stellas and Peter Stuyvesants. I looked at his face, screaming health from every ivory pore, and casually wished him sclerosis and cancer. But the bitter truth is that Jay is most likely immortal, and I, guilty only of sitting too close to the action, will succumb to both killers. Never mind passive smoking, it will be passive drinking on my death certificate.

Jay took a break from his poison and gave me an admittedly dazzling grin. 'Thanks again for the review, Alasdair, it did some serious good.'

'Don't mention it,' I replied. 'If the show had been shitty, I would have said so.'

'But of course,' said Jay, and his grin acquired epic proportions.

What an asshole. Jay knew full well that I would never have slated his play. Ever since we met, a lifetime ago, we've had a critic-director understanding. Never trust a theatre review because odds on it's loaded, based on favours past and present.

I turned my attention to Roger, who was simultaneously leafing through the *Evening News* and inflicting serious damage on a Monster Bean Burrito (Mexican beans and yellow rice wrapped in a flour tortilla served with salsa crudities and sour cream, the menu alleged.) Roger normally looks happiest when he's eating, but that day there was a maudlin quality about the way he attacked his grease-pile, and I guessed that he was still suffering from a broken heart.

Jay stubbed out his cigarette and plucked a neglected celery stick from Roger's plate. 'Why Roger, that's only your second burrito and you're clearly struggling. Sure you're not still hankering after the delectable Rebecca?'

'No,' said Roger, 'I mean yes! I mean, fuck, of course I am.'

Jay raised an eyebrow. 'Well, at least we're clear on that.'

'Fuck! You know, if it comes down to it, if it's the only thing that'll work, I'll go down to Hampstead, sort it out, doesn't matter how long it takes. Oh God.' Roger took a half-determined, half-hopeless bite of his burrito, leaving Jay a little tenser than before.

'I can't have you skipping out of town before the show, Roger, that won't do at all.'

Roger, his mouth full of monster, shrugged miserably and turned to the *Evening News* football results.

Jay snorted his imperial distaste. 'And I wish you'd stop buying that bloody newspaper. We are not going to find the road to commercial success in the local tabloid, are we?'

Roger managed a bulky swallow, perhaps he was about to launch a heartfelt defence of the Evening News, but before he had a chance to draw breath, a smartly dressed man jumped into the seat next to me and banged his empty pint glass down on the table. His attention grabbing demeanour implied that he was a friend of Jay's, so I turned and gave him a thin-lipped smile. Then he said something weird.

'You think I'm feeling sorry for myself, don't you?' he said. 'And that's suddenly a war crime? Jesus, I'd worry if I *stopped* feeling sorry for myself. Think about it, deconstruct the phrase, and you'll find that it's a positive sentiment. It's saying hey, you've had a bad day, you've had a bad taco, whatever's happened, show a little self-empathy. Realise that you're having a sad time. And that's the key, stopping to think about your place in the world, because when things are going well, you don't stop, you keep on going, until crash! You're in the shit with no idea how you got there. You have to feel sorry for yourself sometimes, you have to take stock of your life.'

I looked at Jay, waited for him to tell his friend to shut up, but he wasn't even paying attention, just fiddling with his Zippo. Roger was now engrossed in the lonely hearts page, so I was clearly the only uncomfortable person at the table.

Then the man snatched the newspaper from Roger and slapped it down in front of us. 'A story in the rag today. A woman in New York is killed by an enthusiastic car thief. Nothing unusual in that, except the woman managed to record the last fifteen minutes of her life using a dictating machine in her jacket pocket. Now that's a story, that's a real Grand Theft Auto! A real-life murder, recorded for CNN, c'mon, don't you wanna hear it?'

'Maybe,' said Roger, his ears pricking up at the sound of tabloid bullshit. 'It's only natural to be interested in death.'

'Oh you're so right. But tragedy of tragedies, the tape ran out seconds before she died, so we never hear her last gasp, her last grasp at life.'

'Your point being?'

'The point, the *point*, is that no one cares about the woman, they just want a techno-thrill, an audio turn-on. Rubber-necking on the motorway so they can see the latest carnage, so they have a story to tell their family during dinner. Any accident, any murder, whether they see it in the flesh or on TV, it's a charge, a boost. They want to know everything, and when we find out how many people died, is it ever enough? "Words cannot express," isn't that what they say? Words cannot express, then they spout their story anyway, for the tabloid that's still listening. But nothing's shocking. Nothing's truly shocking anymore. The rape and the murder, it switches off with a point of the remote control.'

'That's not fair at all!' cried Roger, turning to Jay

for support, but he was still lost in his lighter.

'Oh really?' sneered the stranger.

'Yeah, really,' replied Roger, incredibly on the verge of losing his appetite, a rare and frightening moment.

'Friend, I have some late-breaking news for you. Everyone puts themselves first. They want a spouse, a child. "He has your eyes, don't you think?" Damn you, he has his own eyes! They want these things for themselves, to satisfy their own desires. Nature is so honest, humanity has damned itself by pretending to have higher aspirations than the survival of the species. There is no higher order, no higher calling. The call of the wild.'

Exhausted from his speech, the man gasped for air, then smiled warmly, revealing brilliant white teeth that reminded me of Colgate commercials, and said:

'Have a great day.' Then he stood up and walked briskly out of the bar.

Roger pushed his plate away.'That guy was really mad, Jay, why didn't you tell him where to go?

It was Jay's turn to shrug. 'I assumed he was a friend of Alasdair's, it wasn't my place to interfere.'

Christ, how wonderfully insane. I couldn't help but smile. The more I thought about it, the broader my smile got.

Jay looked at me, bemused, then just annoyed. 'And what the hell, Alasdair, are you so happy about?'

I'm the last one by the way. If you're wondering that is. There are no more after me. Just the three of us, playing our game. Perhaps you don't care. But I thought you should know.

4

Tart Dog Woman

A cheating husband used a lonely hearts column to con his way into women's beds while his wife was working for the Salvation Army.

Arthur Hurdman (63) met more than twenty middle-aged women in his attempts to satisfy his lust for sex – and ended up raping six of them.

Hurdman, a former taxi driver, offered 'tender loving care' in his newspaper ad, but the violence of his last attack left his victim – a sixty-year-old widow seeking company after the death of her husband – confined to a wheelchair with a damaged spine.

Yesterday Hurdman, of Leith Walk, was jailed for seven years after a jury at Edinburgh Sheriff Court convicted him of . . .
– *Evening News*

ROGER:
Tabloid-fever runs and runs, its blinding savagery matched only by my hangover on Saturday morning. Becky's still in Hampstead, and the virus remains, loyal to a fault. But yes, I know, some things were meant to be suffered.

At first friends tried to buck me up with comments such as:

She is a tart

She is a dog

She is a woman

You are far better off without her. Why everyone thought that condemning Becky in front of me would make me feel better at first left me in miserable confusion. But eventually I understood: they didn't realise I loved her. They didn't know she meant everything to me. They didn't know because I never told them! Their words were double blows, and I cried all the harder.

My ignorant friends took me out to pubs and clubs. Plenty more fish in the sea and all that. But every song on the jukebox would remind me of the Beckster, every pair of lovers on the dance-floor would make me whimper with self-pity. Even the bar snacks would remind me of her. I never used to cry in public. But now tears would spring to my eyes at the most inconvenient of moments. At a dinner party, during a rehearsal, it was getting out of control.

But no, why should you care? I haven't told you enough about Becky, you're not in love with her, are you? If you met her, though, she'd knock your socks off, no doubt about that. Oh God, I want my cat's pyjamas back. I want my bee's knees.

When I graduated from the University of Edinburgh, my parents gave me the deposit for a flat in Marchmont, a reward for my academic adequacy. The place needed a little work, but Mum was ready and willing to help with the scraping and painting.

One night, soon after moving in, I was sitting at my desk doing some theatre accounts. I had left the front door open to help the paint fumes escape, and lost in Excel, I didn't notice the cat enter my flat. Sniffing the air, the cat must have padded down the hall and into the living room. Looking for attention, looking for a new snack supply, the cat walked up behind me and jumped up onto the desk.

'Wuh—!'

Startled, I drew back and almost fell off my chair. Then, as my heart began to beat once more, and the acid burn of fright had subsided into a manageable sting, I examined my visitor. The cat was grey. Grey, and huge.

'Hi, cat.' The cat sat on my mouse-pad and stared back.

'So, I guess we're neighbours, then.'

The cat made no response.

'You know, don't take this the wrong way, but you're the biggest cat I've ever seen. Is that muscle or fat? I mean, are you a body building cat burglar about to wrestle me to the ground, or just a maladjusted feline with a gland problem?'

The cat said nothing.

'Pen?' I held out my pen for the cat's inspection. He duly nuzzled it. I then scratched under his chin, and he began to purr cautiously.

'You cats, you're great. I can talk to you, and there's no misunderstanding. I could say the first thing that popped into my head, and there's no come-back. Let me tell you, if there were more cats in this world, life would run a lot smoother.'

I smiled benevolently at my surprise visitor, and the cat smiled back. At least I thought it did. There was definitely an up-turning at the corners of the mouth. Yes, we were certainly sharing something. Definitely having a moment, as Jay would say.

'Hey, if you like I can order pizza and we can watch TV. Have a real slob night. I'll even let you have the remote. Pepperoni? Anchovies? Whaddya say?'

There was a tentative knocking on my open front

door, and I felt the burn of surprise for the second time that evening. I got up from my chair to see a woman of around my age, wearing a sweatshirt and jeans, standing in the doorway. She had an expression on her face that reflected a mixture of embarrassment and amusement. I walked through to the hall, closely followed by the cat, who jumped off the desk with a thump and thudded over to the woman.

The human beings exchanged smiles, and the cat did a circle of eight between the woman's legs.

'Yours?' I asked.

'Yeah,' replied the woman. 'All of him.'

I ran my fingers through my hair. 'I suppose you heard me talking to him.'

'Uh-huh.'

'I suppose you think I'm absolutely nuts.'

'Oh no,' said the woman,' 'Everyone talks to Fat Cat. He has that effect on people. I've always thought that he would make an excellent therapist.'

'Appropriate name. But how did you know he was going to be so fat when you christened him?'

'Oh, he got me. He was fully grown when he came wandering into my apartment. He's stuck around so far, but he'll probably stroll along somewhere else one day.'

'Wherever he lays his collar, right?'

'Exactly right!' She held out her hand. 'I'm Rebecca.'

'Oh, right. I mean, I'm Roger.' I returned the gesture and we squeezed palms. There was silence for a few seconds. The kind that last for centuries. The kind that occur when two people consider whether they would like to have sex with the other. Her long brown hair was a mess and her face was make-up free. She was beautiful. She broke the silence, adding a smile that only added to my physical confusion.

'Well, Roger. I'll have the pepperoni.'

'Huh? Oh, sure. Come in, come in.' Rebecca stepped over the threshold and wandered down the hall. I closed the door and followed her into the living room.

So now you know the start. And perhaps I've told you the end as well. I hope not, because I'm terrible at being single. You need someone to shout at, someone to abuse. You need someone to buy presents for, to share good news with, to cuddle when the nightmares get too bad. You need to have a partner, life's far too tiring without one.

I have got a friend called Alasdair who never goes on dates, and the obvious result of this is that he never has a girlfriend. Jay nick-named him T.U., Terminally Unattached. T.U. has no points on the board, unless he's keeping very quiet about it. You don't invite T.U. to dinner parties unless you have an odd number. You don't ask T.U. for advice about relationships or sex.

My point is that I start to feel paranoid as the days roll by without Becky. Cast members go quiet when I walk into the dressing room. Why? Because they're talking about shagging, that's why. And as I've just been dumped, I'm not allowed to join in the discussion. So I start to feel a little sympathy for TU, but more importantly I start to feel sorry for myself. Being single is just not cool. When you're single and you have the Horn, you masturbate, and everyone knows it.

I need Jay's advice, as always, on how to get Becky back. Jay knows, well everything, I think, about women. They like him no matter what he does. And he is good-looking, yes, absolutely yes. And not fat. But there's more to it than that. Jay's always in control, always planning the next move. Look into his eyes, you can almost see the Pentium processor as it speeds along, calculating the next girl, the next score, the next bump. Yes. Jay certainly goes through them.

Sometimes I think that I should try to keep count of Jay's successes, but it would be too depressing, to lose count, to lose hope. I'm in the shadows, looking on as the Grand Master puts more and more points on the board. He shines beside me, finely cut and polished, and all I can do is watch and learn. In the seven years that I've known Jay, he's never crashed and burned. Never. It's not possible. It's like chips without brown sauce, it's like a Big Mac without meat: just not a viable proposition.

Bad news, you might think, standing by while Jay lays waste to Edinburgh's female population. And before the Beckster came along, if I had a lucky night out and found myself in some girl's bed, or floor, or street-corner, I couldn't help the question lurking at the back of my mind, has Jay been here before me? Is she a cast off, a shed skin, is she fucking me but dreaming of him? Mad mad mad, unless you know Jay. Sometimes, I swear to God, I'd be having sex with some girl who had decided that she liked fat men, when I would smell his after-shave on her neck, a faint glimmer of his juggernaut success.

Becky changed all that, though. After she and I got together (and I made damn sure that she'd never heard of Jay Wellesley), I listened to his stories without fear and trepidation. I could listen with good humour, safe and secure in a relationship that was life, the universe and everything. He could tell me anything, and it no longer shocked or frightened me.

32

He talked on, detail lapping against detail, and I would lie back and think of Rebecca.

Jay was pretty shocked, I think, when I got together with Becky. He was even more shocked when we stayed together. I was surprised myself, of course, as the weeks sped by without the Beckster bumping me for a slimmer, more sophisticated man. And there's a lot of them about, you know, these better versions of ourselves. I fantasised about putting blinkers on Becky's face, to stop her seeing all the possibilities as we walked from Buddies or her office to the flat we were lounging in that night. But she stayed, I relaxed, and Jay got used to her. In fact, Jay's never said one bad thing about Becky, never once put her down. But there was an atmosphere when the three of us were together, a thin veil of resentment from Jay that I was somehow letting the side down by staying so loyal to the enemy. He might have thought that he had concealed it, but I felt it all the same.

Jay chases women, you know that now, but he doesn't really like them. He has history, events in his past that have coloured his viewpoint. His mother—

No, I shouldn't talk about him like this, not behind his back, it's not fair. You have to look after your friends, don't you? And Jay's been fantastic since Becky left. More than I deserve, probably. He's always been there, saving me from disaster. But this time it's different. I have to sort this one out myself. Roger and Rebecca and Rebecca and Roger. It rolls off the tongue, we belong together. I'm going to stop complaining to Jay, I'll stop crying on his shoulder. I'll work this problem out on my own.

5

Helping Out With Lonely Hearts

JAY:

Oh Roger, what's going on in that little doggy head
of yours? What's your plan, what's your scheme? Or
have you just gone mad? The latter, I swear, is very
bad for business.

An excellent rehearsal on Friday, only mildly
tainted by Roger's now regular air of despondence.
He slouched – a deflated plastic producer doll – in
the first row, his singular contribution to proceedings
being a sporadic whimper of puppyish abandon-
ment. So I had to laugh for both of us, to let the actors
know when they had uttered an amusing line. I tell
you, by the middle of Scene IV I was practically
hoarse.

I tried to bring him cheer during a smoke break
with juicy details regarding my latest conquest (Tara,
third spear holder on the left in the talent stakes, but
with the breasts of a superstar. More on this later). No
reaction. Not even the merest hint of a tail wag. Well
really. It's been four whole weeks since the dynamic
Rebecca bumped him. What on earth is the problem?
And then, to top it all, when I'm generous enough to
offer him a drink in the World's End after rehearsals,
he tells me he's got a date!

Good news, of course, and I'm delighted to
hear that his libido has finally risen from the ashes.

Ecstatic that Rebecca has been taken down from the pedestal. But if Roger actually has a date, then why is he still carrying on like a whipped mule? Normally Roger is the most transparent fellow under the moon, but recently I've been both bemused and befuddled by his erratic behaviour. And now I have to put up with a tedious pint of British socialism with the stage manager. By the third beer (we've reached Atlee by this point) I can take no more, and flee the pub for the comforts of home, only to realise halfway there that I forgot to ask Roger for his notes. So I back-track to his place, feeling more and more like an ice-hockey puck: flat and bruised.

Roger's place. Sounds nice, doesn't it? Sounds like the place where you'd like to pop round for a cup of tea and a slice of cake. Well, I'm sorry to shatter your romantic delusions, but Roger's flat is a hole. Crippled acommodation. Liberals wouldn't let convicted rapists stay in such aesthetically displeasing conditions. Crimes against wallpaper, lighting and floor-space. Dear Roger, has theatre taught you nothing? He understands the Buddies sets almost as well as I do, so why is he such a miserable failure in the domestic arena?

But it's even worse than that. If it stayed as it was, with its mess of pizza boxes and acidic wine bottles, Roger could at least bring off the whole deal with a whiff of supposed masculinity. But then you have to consider his other half. You have to consider Rebecca. This woman, this imposition, she kept her next door flat (and isn't that sweet?) free from Roger's confused rubble, but saw fit to infect his flat with her hormonal influence, bastardising the little character that was there. Monet prints and ironic oven gloves (the closest Roger gets to using the oven is lighting cigarettes with the gas ring), she insisted on providing Roger with what he could never appreciate or use. And more than that, invading his space without apology, taking up wads of bathroom space with Body Shop fiascos; a Chinese aromatherapy candle here, an Ecuadorean loofah there.

The day after her ridiculous cat stormed Roger's bachelor barricades, Rebecca brought a plant into the flat. A spider plant! That horrid horticutural mistake, the kind of plant that has no sense of decency, no idea of when to stop growing. It sits there even now, revelling in the corner of Roger's living room, unaffected by Rebecca's departure, contemptuous of the cat's biting and clawing. It grows and grows, undusted and unwatered. It doesn't need food in the biological sense; it survives, it thrives, by sucking the atmosphere out of the room.

Oh I could go on, but you get the picture. The invasive Rebecca stepped over the lines and took Roger to planes he couldn't possibly have wanted to go. Now she's gone, and I intend to keep it that way. I intend to give the poor, bumbling Roger back his pride.

Take Jay's place. Now there's somewhere you can live. No tired greenery, no fusty potted organisms gasping for sunlight. I am the only being in my apartment. I vibrate and hum against a twenty-first century backdrop, a multi-media assortment of securities and entertainments. The door of the main building lets the select few up shining stairs, free of tramp and piss infestation, and onto the first landing, leaving the sordid hustle of the street behind. Perhaps, if you please me, I'll give you the four digit code into the building and into heaven.

My apartment is light and sound, darkness and silence. It is whatever the moment calls for, and there are an awful lot of moments. The male guests are delighted, the females are doomed. Ah, I'll bring someone we both know back to my place sometime soon and you can have a good peek. Just as long as you don't break anything, understood?

I have a key to Roger's little hovel so I ease gently in, just in case he has actually dragged his date back for a Mars Bar Supper. I pad down the hall and I am more than mildly surprised to find Roger comatose on his bathroom floor. Date? *Date?* Am I the only one confused here? I wonder for a split-second whether he has OD'd on some sensational chemical cocktail, then dismiss the notion with a thin chuckle. Suicide is far too dramatic for Roger, he gets quite enough theatre at work.

With no desire to rouse him from his nest, I walk through to the living room to get his folder, pausing only to almost break my neck on a half-empty bottle of Macallan. Recovered, I retrieve the folder and turn to leave when I espy a copy of the dreaded *Evening News* on the couch. I resist a familiar urge to set fire to the infernal rag with my Zippo, but then I see, horrors, it is open at the lonely hearts page (or pages; doesn't that tell us something about the average reader?)

Yet another plot twist, I'm even more confused, and where Roger's actions are concerned I hate to be in the dark. But I see a way to get back on track, to regain control of the runaway Roger 125. If he wants a lonely heart, I shall give him one. I circle an ad at random and slide through to the bedroom to call the mystery woman's voice mail.

What did I say? What does it matter, it was a magnificent message in any case. You see how I try to help Roger. He could never deliver a telephone performance like that. Truly the line of the century. I take my leave, pausing only to remove the Macallan from Roger's future clutches. I'm doing him a favour by taking it, he really does drink far too much.

6

Sleeping under the Bath

ALASDAIR:

'Anyone for tennis?' Marianne's door was ajar, so I shimmied on into her flat. 'It's me. You ready?'

No answer. A quick search around the property confirmed my suspicion that she was not in. I guessed that she had popped out to the corner shop, so I put my sports bag down in the hall and made myself at home.

There were a limited number of activities to indulge in as I wait for Mari – we're just good friends by the way – to return from her cigarette/ magazine/food quest. No television, which was obviously a bitter disappointment. There is a compact disc player, but she owns the grand total of three CDs, all played to death.

Defeated, I moseyed over to her magazine collection, her magazine mountain. I deftly selected three at random and retreated to the sofa. Mari – I swear it's not a sex thing, the last thing I want, really – hoards fashion magazines, which isn't that odd, I suppose. Her multitude of *Vogues*, *Tatlers* et al exceeds even Jay's porn collection in number, no small feat. Of course the ironic similarity between Jay and Marianne is that they both look at the photos rather than reading the words, except Mari has a professional interest. And I must say that I

39

prefer Mari's choice of reading material.

I never enjoyed porn magazines. I tried, I really did. When I was at school I had a Saturday job in a newsagent, and on breaks I would sit in the back office with a Playboy I'd taken from the rack. I'd sit there, and make supreme efforts to get a hard on. The pictures were nice enough, but I made a mistake reading the comments in-between:

So Trudy, any trouble getting ready for the shoot?

Not at all, I never get nervous. I just think of all those guys beating off to my picture, and I get all hot and excited.

Et cetera . . .

Awful. First of all Trudy's posing and thinking about the men and the men are wanking whilst thinking about Trudy. It just seems so anti-social, couldn't they at least have a drink first? Second, I realised that Trudy wasn't really thinking about all those men, otherwise she'd come to her senses and run a mile. No, I knew that the comments were lies, and the photographs were lies, and that was a tremendous turn off. I was just embarrassed, it all seemed too silly and degrading, for both parties, to be fun.

But I shouldn't talk about sex or pornography. I shouldn't give you the impression that I'm currently involved in either activity. Sex and I, we don't belong in the same sentence. And I'm not a prude, no matter what Jays says. Sex itself, I know how it goes, and I'd like some, thank you. The mechanics I understand, even some of the subtleties are within my grasp. It's the period before sex that's the problem. Not fore-play, I have no problem with that. Trust me, I'd be delighted to do anything with a woman if only they'd let me. No. It's the part before the foreplay. It's the threeplay.

This chitchat mating ritual, this ruffling of feathers,

why does everyone on the planet know how it works except me? Was I sick the day they taught it at school? Did I miss the movie when it was on general release? I asked at Blockbusters but they claim not to have heard of it (I'm waiting for the book to come out, it's bound to happen sooner or later, there's certainly a market for it). It's a conspiracy, I feel, late at night, lying between ice-cold sheets. You all know how to do it, but you won't tell me. Take pity, for God's sake, and show me how it's done.

I watch them at parties when I'm feeling deluded enough to attend, pairing off one by one, two by two into the Sex Ark. I hug the wall, watching, listening, yet learning nothing. I get close to threeplay sometimes. I can smell it, but the scent won't rub off on me. It remains a total mystery to me, and I'm home alone once more. Why can't I do it? What's so terribly wrong with me? Is it my job? Is it my accent? Is it my nose?

I walk the streets, watching you flirting and teasing, and it all looks like so much fun, it all looks so possible, until I remember my lack of threeplay knowledge. Admitting defeat, I find tepid comfort in buying a fish supper. I go to the Concorde Fish Bar, fight my way through the fumes of heart disease, and watch the girl behind the counter as she plies her trade. That girl really knows how to wrap suppers. Her fingers are a blur of cream flesh and paper folds, covering the imminent treasure of haddock, chicken, black pudding. And chips. I go to the Concorde whenever I can bear it, to seek a covert glimpse of her hands at work. I order whatever, whatever's there, and the man whose black Italian hair shines like his chips takes the fish, the pizza, the battered sausage, and puts it in front of the girl, who then works her dextrous magic.

'Two fifty,' the girl says to me. Looks at me and smiles!

'Ta,' I grunt. Put the money on the counter. Cup my hands for my change, and the girl drops the coins into my palms. Better that way: no skin contact. If she were to touch me, I might not be responsible for my actions. I take the fish, chicken, pizza supper home. I open the package up and dump the cholesterol stock-pile into the bin. I am utterly sick of the smell of fish suppers. I am utterly sick.

Something has to change, don't you think? Something has to change, before I just burst.

'Nice peg top, huh?'

'Wuh?'

Mari appeared from behind the sofa, pointing over my shoulder at a photo in the magazine. A model wearing a skirt, which as the name suggests is wider at the hip than at the knee or ankle. I would have noticed if Mari had come through the front door, and concluded that she must have been in the flat all the time. Relieved that I hadn't spent my time playing with her underwear, I endeavoured to discover her hiding place.

'Yeah, nice. Where'd you spring from?'

'And look at her bob. I love that look, don't you?'

The model's black hair is cut just short of the nape, it looked pretty ordinary to me.

'Sure. I didn't hear you come in, Mari.'

'Some things never go out of fashion. The bob's been around since 1920. The guy who started it all, uh . . . Signor Raspani, he used to provide his customers with smelling salts, to help them get over the sight of their tresses on the floor, and the thought of their husband's wrath!'

'Yeah, the battle between the sexes started at the hairdressers in my opinion.'

'Exactly right!' cried Mari. 'Anatole France said that you could tell more about civilisation from women's fashion than from whole volumes of philosophy!'

Well, indeed. Marianne seemed very happy, and I was curious as to the reason. 'Mari, you're positively pink with perkiness. What's the reason for your rapture?'

'I just had a very nice sleep, that's all,' she replied.

'Where did this sleep occur, exactly?'

'Aha! I shall let you in on my wonderful discovery!'

And she took me by the paw to her source of rest and recuperation. It was the bathroom.

'I checked in here when I arrived, Mari, and it totally lacked your presence.'

'Aha!' said Mari again, and lifted the bath mat to reveal the wooden floor, from which she lifted two boards. 'Check it out!'

I got down onto my knees and peered down into the black hole. Madly expecting to discover a secret boudoir, I was rather disappointed to find merely a gap underneath the bath just large enough for someone to slip into.

'Isn't it great?'

'You sleep under your bath?' I tried desperately to think this through. Is it possible that everyone does this, that I've missed out on one of life's great pleasures all these years? I mean, if it's a well known fact, then I didn't want to sound like a total idiot.

'God yes! It's so warm and dark. I just plop the boards down on top of me and the only sound is from the water heater. It's just the snuggest thing!'

Okay, after a few seconds' reflection I decided that it's a weird thing to do. But she seemed so delighted I couldn't bear to bring her down. Besides, modelling is an artistic profession, she's allowed one or two eccentricities.

'That's . . . great,' I said. 'All you need is a kettle and an alarm clock and you're sorted.'

'Right! You can try it sometime if you like,' she offered.

'What a generous soul you are, Marianne.'

'Well, I believe it's my civic duty to share wonderful discoveries such as this.'

'You're a model citizen.'

'No,' said Mari, 'just a model.' And she went to fetch her tennis racquet.

Friday Night & Saturday Morning

ROGER:
So forty-eight hours ago I did something that I hadn't
done since I was fifteen. I pretended I had a date.
As expected, this declaration relieved some serious
social pressure. Of course that didn't stop me feeling
like a complete idiot.

On Friday night at about nine o'clock, after a
terrible rehearsal, I couldn't go to the pub because of
my insane idea of pretending I had a date. I decided
to stay home with an *Evening News*, bad Chianti, and
a pizza supper, determined to prove that my own
company was a veritable joy. Further plans included
rounding off the evening with a monkey spank so
energetic the neighbours would complain. Of course,
drinking when depressed is not a good idea. And if
you drink when depressed and alone, there's no one
to tell you when to stop. So you don't.

I woke up yesterday morning on my bathroom
floor. It took only a few seconds for me to realise I
was lying in my own vomit and urine. Minutes
passed as my brain searched for a solution to the
latest dilemma.

Heal thyself. Yes, of course. I made a valiant attempt
at sitting up, only to bang my head on the underneath of the sink, setting off a headache so ferocious
that decapitation would have been an agreeable

alternative. I whispered a scream and lay back down.

At 7.15 my clock radio clicked into action, and the tinny music drifted through from the bedroom, interrupting my stream of self-pity. I managed to get to my knees and wrestle four ibuprofen from the bathroom cabinet. With the medication clenched in a determined fist, I crawled through to the living room. There were three bottles lying by the coffee table. Chianti, Diet Coke and the duty-free Absolut Citron. No sign of the eighteen-year-old Macallan: I mean the actual bottle had just disappeared. Jesus. My drinks cabinet was crippled and all I had to show for it was a stained shirt. I took the bottle that still had content and swallowed the pills. Then I made one final Herculean physical effort and climbed onto the sofa.

Thirty minutes later the headache subsided to a dull roar, and I had enough energy to remove the newspaper I had been lying on and toss it to the floor. I lay back down again, but not before I noticed that the paper had been open at the lonely hearts page. The last resort of the Terminally Unattached. I closed my eyes, dimly noting that my life was over.

One fuck-awful nightmare later I was woken up by the postman. The arrival of mail is always a cause for delight, regardless of the current situation. I got up and stumbled my way to the front door. Scottish Power cheerfully asked me to ignore this letter if I had sent them payment in the last seven days, but if I hadn't, they would cut me off. Crude but effective. Greenpeace request my help in saving the Whales, and Victoria Wine thanked me for my sensational customer loyalty, which was nice. No letter from Becky. I trudged mournfully into my foul smelling bathroom and had a little cry.

Fortunately the bathroom also contains a shower,

and ten minutes later I emerged pink, fresh and righteous. My hangovers never last for too long, with is rather handy. I shaved, combed, rinsed. Yes I feel better, yes I am a good person, yes I deserve to be happy. Life is beautiful. I strode manfully into my bedroom, got dressed with gay abandon and opened the curtains. Brilliant sunshine blasted into the flat and warmed my soul. Smiling to myself, I went into the living room and picked up the *Evening News*. That is when I notice one of the lonely heart ads is circled. The sun beat a hasty retreat behind a dark storm cloud and I felt a distinct chill in the air.

Let me explain about the *Evening News* lonely hearts section. If you see an ad you like the sound of, you ring their number and leave a charming piece of voice mail. This means that there were two key possibilities:

I circled the ad, and did nothing.

I circled the ad, and did something.

If it had been by mail I would have been safe. There's no way I would have had the competency to write and post a letter. But by telephone it was entirely possible that I left some message on the poor woman's voice mail. I cursed my parents for having unprotected sex twenty-six years ago, and had another little cry. Afterwards I sat down at the kitchen table with coffee, Snickers Bar and cigarette and examined the ad in question:

Unconventional Vegetarian
Green thirty-something female
seeks sensitive soulmate for tears
and laughter, hugs and spiritual
togetherness. Strict veggies only
please! City. Dial XXXX

My coffee sat cold and forgotten, and the cigarette burned down to the filter unaided. Because I knew I left a message for this woman. I wouldn't have been able to restrain myself from letting rip. Not because I would have found her attractive. On the contrary, she sounds like utter hell.

Green? Probably more to do with the condition of her skin than any political allegiance. Thirty-something? Doesn't she know her exact age? For spiritual togetherness, read religious cult. And what the hell is an unconventional vegetarian? Does she eat meat in that case, or what?

As I sat at the kitchen table, the sun laughed at me from a once more clear blue sky. I had obviously left a message for the Psycho-Veggie. I said something unintelligible, illegal, or worst of all, something really stupid. And of course there is no doubt I told her my address. I lit another cigarette and glanced nervously towards the front door, expecting a gang of eco-terrorists to break it down at any moment. I would be made an example of, a ritualistic sacrifice to the Great Nut Cutlet in the heavens, for the heinous crimes of not recycling my glass and turning off the T.V. with the remote control. Doomed. Any minute now.

RING RING

It's her. It's the monster. It's the monster with the perfect sense of timing. I can't move.

RING RING

What have I got myself into? I'll never drink again.

RING RING

I'm going to be stuck here for ever. The 'phone will never stop and I'll die in my own kitchen. The Police will find me with a look of terror frozen on my dead face. The 'phone will still be ringing and without understanding why they'll be too afraid to answer it as well.

RING RING

How ridiculous. I broke the spell and walked through to the bedroom, sat on my bed and looked down at the ugly piece of push button plastic smirking up at me.

I'll pick up the telephone and it'll be her. She'll say *I know where you live*. Then I'll be in big trouble.

I pick up the telephone.

'I know where you live.'

It's all right. It's Jay.

'So you should do. You've abused yourself in my bathroom often enough.'

'I've abused your mother in your bathroom, Roger. Everyone has. She loves it.'

'Fuck you, fuck your children, and fuck your children's children.'

Jay took this very well. There was a momentary lapse in banter as he lit a cigarette, and I could hear Tara, his latest and remarkably untalented girlfriend, giggling in the background. Jay exhaled happily and I hated him for a split second, as I had left my fags in the kitchen.

'Anyway, how was last night?'

This was of course Jay's reason for calling. I remembered the lie and looked at my decidedly clean bedsheets. The only thing to do, of course, was to embellish the initial falsehood a little.

'First class honours.'

'Excellent, my good man! Put her on, I want to hear those dulcet tones you were raving about.'

Oops. Let's dig ourselves a little deeper. 'Sorry. She left for the airport at seven. Paris. Business. Executive. You know?' *Oh dear God.*

'Points on the board, Roger! You'll have to tell me all about it.'

Yes indeed.

'Roger, we're having some technical difficulties down here. When are you coming down?'

Oh yes, work. 'I'll be there by two. Roll one for me, will you?'

'Rest assured, compadre. Tell me, was she a dyed blonde then, or the real thing?'

'Pardon?'

'You know, Roger, Down Below. What's her true colours?'

'See you later, Jay.'

CLICK

Jay's a dirty bastard, that's why I love him.

That's better. What was I getting worked up about? There was no problem. I'd go to the theatre and do what I'm paid to do. I'd do it brilliantly as usual. And we'd drink coffee, smoke some dope, and listen to some seriously rockin' music over our magnificent sound system. Excellent. I lit a cigarette, grabbed my jacket, wallet and keys and headed for the door. Even better, I'd go via Pound-Stretchers and get some major cleaning products. Then tomorrow morning I'd clean the flat, the bathroom would no longer smell of vomit and urine, and I'd invite a girl back to my little palace. She would immediately fall in love with me and my fantastic hygiene habits, and I would be happy.

And I won't think about Becky.

Outside the flat I turned the key in the lock.

RING RING

Damn. I unlocked the door and went back in. I'd picked up the telephone before I had a chance to ponder who the caller might be.

'Hello?'

It's the monster.

8

Buddies

JAY:
Welcome to one o'clock on Saturday afternoon. Welcome to Schubert's Fourth Symphony. Welcome, ladies and gentlemen, to my theatre.

Welcome to Buddies.

I'm sitting in a dark, wooden fire-risk that serves as the tech box, smoking Peter Stuyvesants (extra mild, one has to look after one's throat) looking down at the stage. Lord of an empty theatre, I sit, smoke, and listen. And think. When I saw Buddies seven years ago, I knew that it had to be mine. I watched it struggle along, an artistic and financial cripple, with tired shows, confused actors, no promotion and the barest trickle of ticket sales. I waited and planned, and I watched it collapse. Then I got my graduation present. Thank you, Father. Thank you for my theatre. I told you I could turn the place around in four years, then I did it in three. Yes, I know, I'm a chip off the old block.

Boys and girls, do you know what happens in the theatre? Do you have the slightest idea? These dens of artistry, they come in many different shapes and sizes, but they all have one thing in common – they are all full of sport. You missed the excitement of course, too busy watching Roger's hangover to enjoy my Saturday morning activity.

But it's all right. Here's the action-replay.

Tara and I are lying on the bed. Holding hands, stage right, bathed in cool blue, surrounded by silence, save for the random traffic noise from outside; an ambulance this time, gnashing its teeth. What's the emergency? Slow down, old fellow, haven't you heard? Everything is under control.

'I bet you didn't know a theatre could be this quiet.'

'No,' she whispers, turning her blue-hued face to me. We look at each other, and I take her visage in. Her face is fine, there are no problems, this will be worthwhile.

'I normally spend Saturday mornings here alone. To reflect, you understand,' – she nods; yes, of course she understands, of course she does – 'to bring a little focus into my hectic life.'

'You must be awfully busy,' she says. Her warm breath smells of Silk Cut, Nescafe Gold Blend, and excitement. Or is it nerves? Ah, it's all the same thing, n'est-ce pas?

I give her the barest hint of a smile. 'Yes. Very little time for the simple pleasures, I'm afraid. But I wanted to show you around, show you what it's all about.'

She gives my hand a squeeze. 'I really appreciate it, Jay, I want to learn all about the theatre.'

'And indeed you shall, my dear.'

I rise onto one elbow and appraise her body. Unusually, almost uniquely, Tara looks better naked than fully clad. Her clothes, our clothes, are mingling in the stalls. I think her bra even made it to Row H; very athletic, I must say. Her curves and slopes, pale shadows and shining crescents, I soak her all up. They don't start to look all the same, the more you have; instead, you become a connoisseur, a collector and exhibitor, nothing fools you. Tara is fresh, she doesn't need to sneak any sagging blemishes past me.

'I've decided,' I say, stroking her face with an artist's fingers. 'Your audition showed such raw promise. Pure talent, I want to unleash you into the world. I'm going to make you a star.'

She smiles uncertainly, then decides to gamble. 'Do you really think so?'

More traffic from outside. A fire engine, indignant, then furious, looking for evidence, looking for incrimination. Where's the telltale smoke? Where's the fire?

'You have such a presence, you'd blow them away.'

'Do you really think so?' she says again, dazed, startled, a rabbit in the headlights.

I put a finger under her chin. 'Especially the men. Your sexual energy, Tara, surely you know this. No man can resist you, they'll come from all over just to gaze at your beauty.'

Tara takes hold of my finger and presses it against her lips for a moment of delight. And, encouraged, I let my hands off their leash. 'Face facts, Tara, no man could be satisfied with being just friends with you. Always that urge, sitting between – '

She gasps, re-appraising her past lovers in the light of this new experience, in the light of Jay Wellesley. They were nothing, those boys, with their clay hands and concrete tongues. This is a whole different ball game. Blood racing, heart galloping, and we're not going to fall at the first fence.

'Sitting between you, waiting for its moment to erupt,' I murmur. 'Just accept what you are, sweetheart, a walking—' She cries out; she hadn't wanted to, but there was no helping the outburst. She's an explosion, burst pipes, no going back. ' – wet dream. And just like everyone else, all I really, really, want—'

Etcetera. And it goes without saying, but I always get what I want. Fade now, fade back to the present, for we have more pressing issues to take care of. Tara doesn't really concern us. I direct her, she'll do what she's told, let us not spend any more time dwelling on such frivolities. Even Tara doesn't waste time dwelling on Tara, throwing on a minimum of clothing, stuffing her tights into her jacket pocket, racing out into the street. Clever girl, she's taking great pains not to bore me. Who knows, she might have a future in the theatre after all.

'Hi!'

At last. Here comes the Producer. Here comes Roger Brown. I couldn't have done it without ya, Roger, ole pal.

'Jay?'

I turn off Schubert, and call down to Mr. Brown.

'Techie Heaven!'

'Right!'

I light another Peter Stuyvesant, and Roger, who never has to be told something twice, clambers magnificently up the ladder and into the tech box.

'Hi, Jay. You really shouldn't smoke in here, you know.'

Don't panic, boys and girls. He's not actually telling me to extinguish Pete. We both know that I shouldn't smoke in Techie Heaven, and we both know it's my theatre and I can do what I want. That's why he said "shouldn't", not "can't". So it's all right, there's no mutiny. Roger, most definitely, knows the score. I exhale carcinogens with exquisite form and press the first lighting preset.

'One, two, three, four, five.' Lights positioned on

the ground upstage go from dead to brilliant white, casting a fantastic shadow on the back wall as the light finds the mannequin standing centre-stage. 'Gorgeous.'

'Yeah,' says Roger, 'if only your actors could find their light as easily as that dummy, this would be a breeze.'

Goodness, I know, such biting criticism. But it's okay, I can take the attack. Besides it was almost witty and I do all I can to encourage Roger's sense of humour.

'*My* actors?' I cry. 'I remember your sticking your nose in plenty during auditions.'

'Wrong. The cast belongs to the Director, everyone knows that. Along with their bitching, moaning and screw-ups. Whereas the Producer gets the real things. The set, the sound, the lights . . .' Roger reaches over with a chubby paw and presses the second preset. The footlights fade and a centre spot picks out the mannequin's face and nothing more. Absolute precision, the techie fellow has done the business.

'. . . And the props. Things you can fix when they break as opposed to the performers, who suffer nervous breakdowns if I ask them to stand in a certain place at a certain time so the audience can actually see them, instead of giving the performance of their fucking lives in the fucking pitch black!'

There now follows an uncomfortable silence.

Well, Gosh! Such an outburst, such passion. Careful Roger, careful. A man of your dimensions is just asking for a burst blood-vessel. What's gotten into him? Has he told you? Do you know? I don't have adequate information, I really don't. Embarrassed for poor Roger, I use the manual faders for the third cue, the white spot smoothly replaced by a soft blue that dusts stage right and the bed, that bed, that sits there.

So let's find out what the problem is, let's put the fib under the microscope.

'I thought you said you got laid last night?'

Roger looks down at the lighting desk, unable to lie to my face. 'I did.'

'So why are you so riled?'

'I'm not riled.'

'You are, you're livid, man. Did she laugh at your appendage?'

Confess, Roger, confess to father Jay. But no, he just will not "fess up". And I, like Alice, get curiouser and curiouser.

'The problem isn't my dick, it's your actors spending more time "bonding" than learning their stage directions. Yesterday's cue to cue was a shambles, the press night's in five days, and instead of using the stage our star performers are probably butt-fucking each other to death!'

He's not happy, is he? I am getting distinctly upset vibes here. Hardly an excuse for such disrespectful wailing but as I said, I can take it. I am not going to lose my temper. I prefer to reserve my rage for important moments, when a good bollocking is truly necessary; during a dress rehearsal, for example, when an actor claims he can only deliver the goods in front of a live audience. So I decide to humour my puppy producer. Soft voice, the barest twinkle in my eyes.

'Roger, the show is going to be perfect and you know it. Are you sure she didn't giggle when you dropped your pants?'

There. That is how to defuse a tense situation. That is why I am the Director. Take notes if you like. No, put your chequebook away, this one is on the house.

I bring up the house-lights, 'Schubert please, Mr. Brown,' and ladder it down into the auditorium.

Roger does as directed, and *presto vivace* thunders down after me. We walk through to the back office. Roger collapses in his rightful place, the Tatty Couch, while I, Lord of the Manor, take position, relaxed but with perfect posture, on the swivel chair behind the desk. I have intimidated the hell out of many an actor from this pole position. I've even made a few cry but they don't complain. Desperate actors will do anything for a role. But you knew that already didn't you? (Tara certainly does.)

Schubert leaks in under the door (he will not be denied; I am a fan, and a thief) and I retrieve my silver cigarette case from my personal drawer. I take out a pre-rolled joint and toss it over to Roger. He treats it like one of his cheeseburgers and *devours* it. That's a good pup. Soon the room has the smoke-filled atmosphere of a corrupt political meeting. Now, let us see.

'Next Saturday, Roger. What say we tunnel over to that Glasgow hole you like so much? What say we find us some sport? Or we can take Tara and Chloe, she's very keen to spend some quality time with you.'

'Chloe? Why her?'

'Why not? Give her a try, give her a shot. It's better than spending Saturday night on your own, and she really is very keen.'

'Right,' he says. 'Well, the truth is, I have another date next Saturday.'

'But I thought you said she'd gone to Paris.'

'Yeah, *she* has. This is a different woman.'

Liar liar, pants most definitely on fire. But he did not even stutter. Either Roger has become a consummate liar or he really has a date this time. Ladbrokes would not know where to go on that one (ladies and gentlemen, do you think that lonely hearts nonsense has paid off already?)

57

'You're out of control, Roger! Where are you meeting all these fabulous women?'

'Guess I'm just a babe magnet,' he replies.

Well, at least he hasn't lost his sense of humour. I make a mental note to call Chloe; she'll just have to wait a little longer. There's a wedding coming up, she can make her threeplay then.

Meanwhile, there's one more issue that needs clarifying. 'And dear Rebecca?' I ask the question casually enough, but I'm dying to know the score.

'That's in the past,' says Roger. 'Dead and buried. All she wrote.'

'Way to go Roger! Bitches and whores the lot of them! Art is our number one priority. Art and guilt-free shagging. Here's to a sex-cessful Saturday night!'

9

Tennis

ALASDAIR:

Sometimes I imagine myself, thirteen-years-old, seeing through the eyes I have now. I'm in a theatre, I can see that I'm watching a play. I have my notepad and pen, and I'm putting words on a page. And I wonder what I would think, this adolescent, seeing all this. Would I be pleased, happy to be a theatre critic? Perhaps it sounds interesting. Perhaps I would feel like someone who got things done, who people listened to.

But it would all be a mistake. That's what I think. It would be wrong for my thirteen-year-old self to think I had succeeded. He wouldn't comprehend the sheer boredom of most of my working day, the inane scribbles that my editor actually accepts, making me blush, making me cringe with embarrassment. I'm summed up in repetitious column inches; there's only so much you can write, only so much people want to read.

So what if my child looks through my eyes when I'm in The Merlin? I'm drinking hot chocolate with Marianne, we're talking, I'm looking at her, and my virginal teenager thinks hey, this must be my girlfriend. Beautiful, what a result, what a tremendous score. Surely all that pain, all that growing up horror, was worth it in the end. And would I be right? It's all a fanciful illusion for my child, and wouldn't he be so very disappointed to know the truth. That we're just good friends.

I've let myself down, with my tedious job and lack of meaningful relationships. I'm gliding through life, keeping things safe and predictable. And this is where I look back to my childhood, and like everyone else in the western world, blame my parents. But it doesn't pan out, because I was always this way, as far back as I can remember. I was always quiet, passive, inert. My parents never abused me, never divorced, never ran out of money. They were never rich, but we had cars, holidays, shoes on our feet.

Perhaps I need to go further back, to nightmares in the womb, to find the source of my problems. I have a brother, eight years older than me, a solicitor with the Scottish Office. He has a family of his own now; he is a success. I get the feeling that his progress took the pressure off me; my parents thought that it was all right to have one failure as a son. It is the eight year gap that gives me ideas. So long between children, no one ever plans it that way. It is clear to me that I was a mistake, an unexpected foetus that my mother was too gentle to abort. Any life at all is a bonus, you know, when you've narrowly escaped termination.

My brother Robert and I, we never had anything in common. The gap between us was too large to bridge. Our television and toys, our school days and weekends, we lived under the same roof but under different rules. If Robert had any empathy or advice to pass on regarding a lesson or bruise, he had forgotten it by the time I got there. Action Man and Scalextric, masturbation and 'O' grades, they were all distant memories. He left for university, another set of laws and logic, when I was ten-years-old. He still lives in Edinburgh, of course, and we see each other as a ritual once a month, at home for dinner with our parents. But he brings his wife and son with him, and we are strangers, taking turns to mock my father's choice of wine. I watch him at the dinner table, handling his little boy, and I want to ask him, how did you manage all this, how did you get so far? But it's too late to go to him looking for answers. I'm on my own, and big brother is not watching me.

In 1988 one of Robert's friends told me about the telephones. We sat in a booth at the Canny Mans down Morningside Road and Steve asked me if I'd ever smoked a joint. I lied. He took one out of his jacket pocket, lit it and passed it to me. I inhaled, did a bit of predictable coughing, and passed it back. Steve didn't laugh at me. Like my brother he was twenty four, and I was sixteen. He knew everything. He drank Becks and I drank Diet Coke. He wore a black leather jacket and I wore the blue cotton shirt my Father had bought me in Littlewoods. He smoked Marlboro Reds and I didn't. And he knew everything.

'You know the 'phone by the door?' Steve asked.

I said I did. I knew the one he meant. The one by the door.

'It's tapped,' he said.

I nodded. 'Right.'

He grinned at me, and we left.

The next night Steve and I went to buy some hash. I sat in the guy's living room, looking at the slab of resin balancing on his scales. It looked sweet, it looked a bit like a big bar of chocolate. The guy – the guy who was selling – crumbled a little of the hash, rolled a joint, and offered it to me.

'No thanks,' I said, smiling. 'I'm fine thanks.'

'He'll smoke it,' Steve said. 'He's my quality control.'

So I took the joint and inhaled, and did some coughing. Steve didn't laugh at me.

'How is it?' he asked.

I looked at him. 'Fine,' I wheezed.

Steve got up and paid the seller. He grinned at me and we left.

I didn't talk in the taxi back to his flat, but when we were on the stairs I asked Steve why he hadn't tried the hash himself.

'Like I told the man,' Steve said, 'you're my quality control.'

Once inside Steve cut an eighth, wrapped it in cling-film and put it in the pocket of my blue cotton shirt. 'That's for you,' he said. 'Services rendered.'

'Should I smoke it?'

Steve shrugged. 'Do what you want, man, it's your blow.'

When I walked in the front door and kissed my mother. I told myself she couldn't smell the lump of tightly wrapped hash in the pocket of my blue cotton shirt. She told me I looked tanned. I said it was just dirt, and she laughed.

A week later a bleached blonde who had played Lady Capulet to my Friar Laurence ended my virginity to the sound of the Platoon soundtrack: Helicopters, Charlie Sheen, Adagio for Strings, gunfire, Otis Redding, The Doors. *Hello, I Love You, won't you tell me your name?*

Lisa, like Steve, had a leather jacket, but hers was brown. She smoked Silk Cut and drank Bacardi and Coke. She was nineteen-years-old. She knew everything. I told her that I loved her. She didn't laugh at me.

One Friday night we went to the Dominion and

62

saw Eddie Murphy in *Coming to America*. After the film we met up with two guys Lisa knew. They complained they couldn't find any hash, so I sold them my untouched eight for fifteen pounds.

'You're a real big-shot!' said one of the guys, laughing and ruffling my hair. Lisa grinned at me, then she drove me home.

The next afternoon I waited inside the King's Theatre. *West Side Story* was touring from London, Lisa's favourite, so she said, but she was late. Just before the final bell she raced in, full of her own theatre. Her two friends had been caught smoking a joint beside the Waverley Shopping Centre; Scotrail had the whole thing taped. I didn't know that Edinburgh *had* security cameras.

'They're in big trouble now,' said Lisa.

I shrugged. 'It was their blow,' I said, 'they did what they wanted.'

We walked into the auditorium, and I felt untouchable.

In the month before Lisa left for London and English Literature 1, we saw a lot of each other. She read me her poetry, and I told her I loved her. She took me for country drives in her Audi Quatro, and I told her I loved her. I skipped school so we could have sex in her lunch hour, and I told her I loved her.

Two weeks after Lisa left, her mother came to my house to return a music cassette Lisa had borrowed. She stood in the doorway and I told her I loved her daughter. She laughed at me. 'No,' she said. 'No you don't.' Then she left.

I went up to my bedroom and played the tape. New Order Substance 1987. Lisa's favourite. I sniffed at the cassette case and it smelt of perfume and cigarettes.

*   *   *

I tell you these things to show that I have lived like most other people. Ups and downs, loves and losses, I'm not a blank page. I can't start from scratch, too much has happened. Do you like me more, knowing a few small pieces of my past? Does my vulnerability appeal to you? I need to be liked, at least a little bit, so you will listen to my side of the story. Jay can be charming, but don't let him pull the wool over your eyes. And Roger, usually blunt in his honesty, is also prone to exaggeration and theatre. I will tell you the truth, I will be the set text. I'm not amusing, definitely not exciting. But stay, please. Stay a little longer. Reserve your judgement until the curtain falls.

The morning after a failed suicide attempt is always spectacular, mainly because you're amazed that the sun is rising at all. Everything is new, fresh, a peach. Then the feeling . . . God! The feeling that comes, you remember what you tried! Why? And who knows that you tried it?

Okay, let's assume that you never tried to kill yourself, and I mean in a direct way. You could argue to the winds for all I care, that we are all killing ourselves, slowly, poignantly, with cigarettes, alcohol, pollution, cultural vanity and emotional insecurity. You could argue that, and I would answer, hey! My suicide, is going to be a conscious suicide, one where you actually make that life-shattering decision. Life shattering, that's good isn't it? Belongs in a TV movie, belongs sulkingly superior at the back of the class.

So say you never tried it. The point being, if you had, you would know the feelings mentioned above, the *whywhywhy*?, and then the *whowhowho*?

The dawning that someone knows, if you were un-lucky, that you tried. That's the worst. To try and fail, and for someone to know. And I'm sure you can get to grips with the concept, alien that it might be, because it's similar to the post-screw emotional holo-caust, when you're not feeling as wild and reckless as you did the night before, but instead you're a fright-ened squid, you don't want to talk about this right now, and your stomach is hollow, except for a burn-ing dot of fear, because he/she's just come around the corner, and now you have to talk about it. It. You have done the deed, and there's blood on your hands.

The comparison is made in retrospect, however, because I competed in the suicide game, played with the self-murder toy, when I was fifteen, before I discovered sex, drugs and the irrelevant rock 'n' roll. And looking back, I'm glad I didn't succeed in killing myself. Glad, in a calm, passive way. I'm still here, I did some things I wouldn't have done otherwise, and that's fine. And if I had died, I wouldn't have known Marianne.

'How bad is their dress sense?' asked Marianne.
    'Fucking bad?'
    '*Fucking* bad. I am astounded, I am amazed, by how little interest people take in their own clothes.'
    'You're amazed by a lot of things, Marianne.'
    'That's true, but I was amazed from an early age.'
    'Amazed by what?' I asked.
    'Nothing in particular. Everything. Just amazed. I was an amazement child prodigy. My mother said I was born with an astonished look on my face. I've gone through life, sliding between two emotional poles: bewilderment and perplexity.'
    'That sounds very tiring.'

'Yes, but in a positive way. It means I'm never in any danger of jumping off the bridge. If I'm ever close to the edge, I think to myself, what about the little things I'd miss? Private jokes, burnt toast, the rain, bubble bath. The little things, the lights, save me. The lights stop me jumping off.'

I looked at her. She did perspire during the game, but obviously not in an unattractive way. It was a hip sweat, a designer glow, that made her T-shirt cling to her skin, that made strands of hair stick to her forehead and neck.

I knew Mari was offering me information about herself. I liked to know about her life, I chased after these emotional morsels like a stray mongrel after scraps. The mention of suicide could have been a joke, a throwaway comment. I looked at her, trying to read her eyes, and I couldn't decipher her expression. But my need to know, my need for the suicide data, made me ask the question.

'Have you ever thought about it? Really thought about it?'

'Jumping off the bridge, you mean?'

'Yeah.'

'Hasn't everyone?'

The perfect answer. Transferring suicidal tendency from mental illness to something as normal as athlete's foot in a single step. And I'd never thought about it that way before. Hasn't everyone? I wanted to say yes, yes of course, everyone does, because then I'm not mad, I'm normal, it's normal to want to jump off the bridge occasionally.

'I don't know,' I said.

I wanted to tell her about my teenage attempt at taking my own life, my suicide screw-up. I had felt too ashamed, even after ten years, to tell anyone, to let them know how weak and loathsome I

66

was. But something told me that Mari would understand.

'I tried once,' I said.

No look of surprise. Instead she held my face in her hands and smiled. 'I guessed.'

'How?' I asked, horrified, mesmerised.

'You're a suicide survivor. I can spot them a mile off. It's all in the eyes,' she whispered, as she looked intently into mine. 'A survivor's eyes take nothing for granted.'

Mari let go of my face and reached into her bag for a cigarette. And I told her everything. About going to stay with my aunt and uncle in London for my fifeenth summer. About finding the bottle of Mogadon in their bathroom cabinet one day. About swallowing the pills a week later with gin from their drinks cabinet. And about my aunt, my insomniac aunt, wandering into the bathroom at 2 am, and discovering the theft, going into my bedroom and finding me, shaking me, slapping me, saving me.

'What was the trigger?' Mari asked gently.

'I can't remember. I know it sounds stupid but I can't. It was everything and nothing, going on for years. I just remember thinking, hey, here are some pills. It won't hurt, it won't leave a mess. It hadn't been the thought of my family that had stopped me before, it had been the thought that it might hurt. I know how weak that sounds.'

'How did your parents take it?' Mari asked, ignoring the self-deprecation.

'They took the train down to London when they heard. I lay in my hospital bed, and although I looked like hell, I mean, I looked fucking awful, my mother looked worse. My mother, who hadn't had her stomach pumped the night before, looked ten

67

times worse than I did. So I decided there and then not to try it again. And so far . . .'

'Yeah,' Mari said with a smile. 'So far you're still here.' And she leaned forward and kissed me. It was a strong kiss, a proper kiss. She held my head and slipped her tongue into my mouth, exploring the internal me. Closing my eyes, I got the ridiculous idea that she was searching for hidden treasure, a cunning pirate about to plunder my sparkling riches. What a way to go.

Mari took her tongue back and wiped her mouth with the back of her hand, even making that look like a stylish and chic act.

'Thanks,' I said stupidly.

'You taste of life. Let's keep it that way. Let's keep each other alive.'

Good deal.

10

Unconventional Vegetarian

A lovestruck pilot looped-the-loop over his girlfriend's house shouting "I love you" – and crashed to his death.

A wing of his Cessna clipped his sweetheart's chimney, sending his plane spiralling to the ground in Bahia de Salvador, Brazil.

The flier's grief-stricken lover said: "He was mad about me."
– *Evening News*

ROGER:
Her voice.

Looking back on events, and all that I can say against her, one thing's for sure: Elizabeth gives damn good telephone.

'You said some beautiful things in your message last night.'

'Thanks.' *And would you be so good as to tell me what I actually said, because I was out of my face at the time and I don't remember a thing.*

'I felt truly "touched", Roger. I felt as though I had sent . . . a message in a bottle out to sea, and you're my sea captain who sees something glinting in the water and fishes it out. We're just so . . . connected.'

At that moment I would have given my soul to find out what I had said on her voice mail. It was clearly the line of the century.

Velvet. She sounded like velvet. We talked on the telephone and she had her tongue in my ear. I was in boy heaven.

'I know this is going to sound very forward of me,' she said, 'but if you were to come around to my place next Friday for dinner, I just know we would have the most lovely time.'

The Most Lovely Time. How could I resist? I had to push my preconceptions of the Unconventional Vegetarian away in a second. Hesitate for too long and this gap in her diary might have snapped shut forever. I opened my mouth and ignored my balls as they shrunk with trepidation.

'That sounds . . . lovely,' I said.

She gave me a soft laugh, and I melted.

Tonight's technical rehearsal went better than I expected. The peptalk that Jay shouted at them seemed to do the trick. Shortly before the end of the first act I passed the pad and stopwatch to the stage manager, who gave me a questioning look as I made my way quietly out of the auditorium, and then smiled as he read my note: 'Nature calls. Consider yourself deputised, and I'll see you and Jay for coffee in Negociants tomorrow.'

Now even though I had changed my perception of Elizabeth to that of potential Superlay, I still kept her request for 'strict veggies only' in mind. Did she drink? Probably not. I nipped down to the Grassmarket and into the Aqua Bar with its blue metal stools and precarious tables, unable to bear the thought of having a totally sober blind date. Throwing my spare change into the Top Tenner one armed bandit, I considered other potential strikes against my lifestyle. Did she smoke? No way. I pushed the evils of the tobacco industry to one side and consumed nicotine until I was engulfed in a coughing fit that threatened to end with my lungs rocketing up my throat and onto the blue wooden bar. The bar man and his fashionable regulars, they glanced and smiled, bouncing along to the joyfully banal AOR: they knew where I was headed.

So my nicotine and alcohol levels were adequate, but that wasn't all. I crossed over from The Mound and down into Hanover Street, and I looked different. Taking advantage of the theatre's costume department, I had swapped my jacket, shoes, belt, wallet and watchstrap (all made of leather) for some more cow-friendly items. So I looked different. I looked righteous. I looked like a vegetarian. In fact, if it had not been for the Big Mac I was holding, my costume would have been perfect. I was ready for the performance of the century.

She smiled and put her hand on my knee. Just for a moment. But I felt truly blessed at that instant, and I was caught between the joy of the touch and the fear of losing control and just jumping her there and then. I thought about the starving millions in Africa, but the Horn wouldn't go away. I thought about watching cricket. The Horn wouldn't budge. In desperation I plunged into the last resort, and contemplated testicular cancer. That did the trick. The Horn subsided to a manageable scream and I could look Elizabeth in the eye without feeling as though I was drowning.

Elizabeth is beautiful. Should I describe her? The danger here is that if I say she's a brunette and you don't like brunettes, then you'll say, well, she's not beautiful is she? And you'd be so wrong. No, I can't take the risk. I can't break the spell. Invent her for yourself. Define beauty, and let Elizabeth appear before you.

I'll describe her flat instead. In a single hyperbolic word – it's fantastic. The kitchen, unlike the kitchens in most Edinburgh flats, is actually designed for cooking in. And she has some great equipment: steamers, electric juicer, a set of knives sharp enough to do serious damage to a vegetable caught in the wrong place at the wrong time. And she has a stock of such wonderful food: exotic fruits I've never seen before, spices, fresh herbs. The icing on the cake is that she can actually cook. The food she serves up is alive with flavours and textures, without an animal product in sight. I've always been a sucker for good cooks, so I'm putty in her hands.

But it gets even better. As if from nowhere she pulled out a bottle of red. Organic, of course, but it was still wine. So I could eat well enough that she could feel sure I liked her cooking, despite the Big Mac. And I oohed and aahed in all the right places. Anyway, we told each other about our jobs, families, and other such vital statistics. I liked the girl so much I even told her the truth most of the time.

But now the meal was over, we sat next to each other on her sofa and life threatened to get a little intense. As Elizabeth talked, I occasionally managed to tear my gaze away from her and look around the dimly lit room. Elizabeth knows her lighting – some soft white bulbs attached to the walls, their brightness masked by shades and giving the effect of gentle soft focus instead of a cave where you can't see your date and end up making a pass at the rubber plant in the corner. A subtle smell of incense, and ambient music swirls around the room. There were books everywhere, scattered on the coffee table, in piles by the wall. In a mad burst of generosity I decided that tomorrow I would go to Texas Homecare and buy her some bookshelves. The majority of the titles were related to the environment. Ecology, geography, energy, politics. Elizabeth had clearly done her homework.

'Everything we do has an effect on our environment,' she said. 'Heating our homes, building more roads, butchering animals. We're destroying nature's natural equilibrium, and those politicians are too stupid to see it. We're destroying nature, and we're destroying our own future.'

Elizabeth should work in advertising. She was selling me not just her views but her justification for living, and I found myself buying it. Because she's so utterly convinced of it herself. She has internalised the ideas, she's searched for ways to support them, and has ignored everything else. Talk about focus. I decided to buy dolphin-safe tuna. Or even stop buying meat altogether. If Elizabeth cooked for me I'd never need to eat "dead flesh" ever again. And I'd send money to Greenpeace. And write letters to my member of parliament. I even thought of producing an ecological play.

I'm normally so utterly cynical, but this time it was different. There was no hidden agenda, no secret power base. Elizabeth wants to save the world because it's the right thing to do! She's devoting her life to planet Earth. On top of that, I knew how happy it would make her if I agreed with her views. And what harm could it do? I would give her support, and she'd carry on working towards her goals. So I nodded and made little noises of approval. I listened to her and threw the words straight back in paraphrased nuggets.

Elizabeth talked about the Earth getting hotter, the fish dying in polluted waters, food being adulterated

73

by man-made chemicals. Poisoning our bodies, poisoning our minds.

'People think the environment is a marginal issue, but it's everything. The twentieth century is the first time that humankind has been capable of completely destroying the planet. Earth has to be saved from humanity. Oh, I look at people leaving Scotmid with their CFC-free hairsprays, their consciences clear. I want to run up to them, to tell them it's not enough, it's not nearly enough. Can't they see what's happening? Can't anyone see what's happening?'

She stopped. She had told me everything. We looked at each other, and I realised that she had asked me a question. Did I agree? Did I accept her? Was I like her?

I looked at her, and the Horn was worse than ever. Elizabeth was offering herself to me at that moment. All I had to do is say the words. What was the risk? What was I getting into? But none of this mattered because I'm a boy and she's girl, and if we could have sex, I really would be able to forget about Becky for an hour. I would be happy. I would feel like a man again. Silly puppy. The ambient music pulsed through me and my dick kept time.

I looked her straight in the eyes and launched the missile. 'I'm with you, Elizabeth. I'm completely with you.'

She gasped. A gasp of joy. I made her happy. That's not such a bad thing, is it?

'I knew you were the one, Roger!'

The scene was set. The lights were perfect, the props were in place and the music played on. Elizabeth had delivered her speech and I had delivered a performance of my own. By mutual consent we moved closer to each other. She stroked my cheek, and I tingled with delight. I moved my hands through her hair, something I'd wanted to do all night. Now I could touch and breathe her. No going back. All I could see was her face; I was lost in her. We moved the final inches and our lips brushed together, the slightest of kisses but I was on fire. Suddenly the impatience was gone, because I could taste her, and this would go on forever. I kissed her mouth, her face, her eyes, her ears. I sucked up her scent and our future was certain. Nothing else existed.

Elizabeth took the initiative and explored my face and neck. I felt her lips press passionately against my skin, and I felt her nose as she inhaled my smell. Her voice was muffled and I was lost, but she was asking me something.

'Roger, what's that fabulous scent you're wearing?'

I smiled at her question. Anything she had said would have made me smile. 'Egoiste.'

And everything changed. Elizabeth's entire body stiffened and I heard an entirely different gasp. One of horror.

'What's wrong?'

She didn't answer, but pushed me away and jumped off the sofa as If I had given her an electric shock. She stood facing the opposite wall, and she was shaking. She was shaking, and I was more than a little unclear as to what had gone wrong.

'Elizabeth, what's the matter?'

She clicked on the main lights and I flinched against the sudden brightness. She turned around, and she was not, as I had expected, crying. But her face was very different. She looked at me with venom in her eyes. I stood up and made a move towards her.

'Elizabeth?'

'Stay away from me, murderer!' She spat the words out as if they were poison in her mouth.

I was still confused as to my crime. 'Eh?'

She laughed, and it was not the laugh I fell in lust with. It was a laugh of contempt. 'Your precious cologne is made using animal products. They died for your vanity!' She shouted at me, and still she didn't cry. Her face was set like stone, frozen into an expression of hatred.

'Elizabeth, I didn't—'

'You have blood on your face! You're wearing a corpse!'

This was a bad situation. The Horn was nowhere to be felt, and I found myself wondering where the evening had gone. Suddenly I was facing a woman who looked as though she would blow me away rather than blow me, and all because I had made a poor choice of aftershave.

'Elizabeth, I didn't know, all right? Jesus, I'm sorry, but it isn't really that important compared to everything else that's happened tonight, is it?'

I didn't think that Elizabeth could look any more full of hate, but I was wrong.

'You . . . fucking . . . people. You're all the same. You live in ignorance, and then act all hurt when I . . . someone points out the truth. Well, you should have known. You should have made it your business to know. I thought you were different, but you're just like the rest of them.'

I suddenly noticed that the music was still playing. I went over to the hi-fi and pressed a button, trying to turn it off but switching on the radio instead. A DJ rambled on inanely, but it was better than that ambient rhythm that had started to sound like utter madness. I looked around the living room. Fully lit and without the music, it actually looked rather silly. It looked, in truth, like a complete mess. It looked like I felt. I needed a cigarette, I needed a drink, and my body was asking my brain some very loud questions, like why wasn't I screwing? I felt ridiculous, and I started to laugh.

Elizabeth uttered a strangled scream, and I had a bad feeling that at any moment she was going to come up with an alternative use for her sharp knives. I looked at her and offered a tired smile.

'I'm not laughing at you,' I said, 'I'm just . . . this is a little silly, that's all. How can you condemn me for one little mistake. Your values are all messed up, how can you live every day with such aggression?'

She said nothing. The DJ shut up and started to play some music. It sounded familiar but I couldn't name it. I tried again.

'Tell me, when you buy fruit from the cornershop, do you hate the shopkeeper for selling bacon as well? When you walk past McDonalds do you hate the kids sitting inside?'

Nothing. Frozen against the wall, only her eyes follow me as I go into the hall to get my jacket. I now understood what an Unconventional Vegetarian is. Someone who respects dead flesh but can't form a relationship with any living being.

'Your standards are too high,' I said. 'If you hate all who fail to meet them, how can you have affection for any human being? What happened to make you feel like this?' I still wanted to help her. I'd have killed for a cigarette, but I was willing to stay. If she let me in I would try to help.

Elizabeth spoke, and let me know that there was no way in. 'You're either with me or against me. You're either for the world or against it. I pledge my life for the planet. Everyone else is so selfish, they're so fickle, they just won't commit . . .' She paused, lost in some painful memory.

I listened to the radio song as I watched her tortured face, and the lyrics were crystal clear.

'Well, here we are again my dear
Pour yourself a drink
It's quieter now than it was before
But I still can't hear myself think'

I'm not one for taking gems of wisdom from pop songs, really I'm not. But at that moment I realised how mixed up I had been in recent months. My inability to tell Becky how I felt, the made up affair, and tonight. What a mess.

'She went upstairs to get undressed
The price she was willing to pay
It was morning when he found her gone
There was nothing left to say'

I felt a release. I felt as though I had suddenly received a flood of intelligence about my life that could save me from the disaster I have feared for so long. I'd been such an idiot.

'We're just trying to get by,' I said softly.

'Huh?' Elizabeth looked at me, her thoughts broken.

'Us. People. We're just trying to get by. This isn't important, not really,' and I dismissed her books with a wave of my hand. 'Don't you see? I want to have a family, I want to devote myself to people. I love Becky.'

'Who?' Elizabeth looked at me as if I was the mad one.

'Rebecca. She's all that matters. I've been scared of rejection all these years, but it's been pointless. If you take yourself too seriously, you become too scared to

78

live. I cut myself off, boarded myself up, and I drove Becky away. I'm not going to make that mistake again.'

I walked into the hall and opened the front door. Seeing that I was leaving, Elizabeth un-froze herself and ran after me.

'Wait,' she said,' 'What about the cause? What about the world?'

I touched her face, trying to pass on my realisation to her through my fingers. 'What's the point of living in a world without love? Without friendship? You shouldn't make yourself so many enemies, Elizabeth. Let people in, no one got anywhere by playing safe. Look – I have to go.'

I gave her a quick kiss on the cheek, then ran down the stairs and into the street.

I took a taxi back to my flat. It's now 7 am, and I can hear the milk vans making their way up the street. The sun is making its presence known and it looks like it's going to be a decent day. I'm going to take a shower before I go to Waverley Station. I'll call Jay from the station, he'll understand. Besides, I'll be back before press night, and I can rely on Alasdair to give us a decent review. What are friends for, after all?

Hey, did you notice? I said I loved Becky out loud. I did it! I'll go to her parents house in Hampstead. Then I'll tell her I love her, and then I'll ask her to come home. Simple as that.

Wish me luck, if you get the chance. I might just need it.

11

Waking Up In St Leonards

It has been acknowledged that the managers
of organisations have important obligations to
a variety of stakeholders and not just the share-
holders, and this should be reflected in the
organisation's statement of purpose, such as mission statements.

This raises the question of how the activities of
organisations affect the behaviour of individuals
and the values of society, and concerns important ethical questions about the role of managers
in the strategic management process.

Much of the initial discussion on these issues
centred on the social responsibility of organisations and was reflected in policies inclined
towards corporate social responsibility. More recently, the debate has widened somewhat and is
now more generally described as business ethics.
– *Business Strategy in the Twenty First Century*

JAY:
I wake up to the smell of someone's bed-farts. Feeling
the body-heat lying next to my own, I keep my eyes
closed.

The alarm clock which the inept Tara had forgotten
to switch off makes its horrified cry at 7:30 am. I leap

blindly but gracefully from the bed to the windowsill, tracing black plastic contours with my fingers, finding the button that magically soothes the electronic weeping. The alarm now pacified, I stand nobly by the window – a stretch here, a bounce there – and gaze pitilessly down at the St Leonards lowlife on the street below.

The road is wet, it rained during the night. It has rained all this month. What am I doing in Edinburgh? I should live somewhere warm and dry. Hot, even, but without any frightening insects. Where people sit around drinking red wine and smoking high tar cigarettes. Where people speak English but with exotic accents. Where everyone has a tan, dresses elegantly and smells of freshly made sex. Am I really asking too much?

I turn, turn like the worm I am (don't think I don't know) and look at Tara as she dreams. She is smiling in her sleep. I'm sure I don't smile in my sleep. I probably scowl. Or cry. Bad dreams will do that to you. But Tara does that a lot, that smiling thing. It clearly doesn't take much to satisfy her. Perhaps she's dreaming of engagement rings and positive home pregnancy kits, not necessarily in that order. She has a nice face, for what it's worth. And I do like her quite a bit, otherwise I would let her come along for the trip. The carnival tragedy ride. I look at her, and wonder what she's smiling about. Bump her. Bump her for good. She doesn't belong in your catastrophe, your Calamity Jane.

Tara opens her eyes and smiles. She draws up her knees expectantly to make room and I walk over and dutifully sit down on her side of the bed. I stroke Tara's hair away from her face, and she yawns at me, the little minx.

'I woke up,' she says, 'sometime, I don't know

when, but you were asleep, and you had such a serious expression on your face. It was like you were guarding me or . . . God, is it still raining?' Tara follows her brilliant deduction with a glance towards the steady drumming on the window.

'It rained all night,' I say, caressing my better half, my *raison d'être*, my *raison se raser*. Tara yawns again, but it is more gesture than symptom, and her alert left hand creeps over the duvet and into my silk boxers. She finds my penis erect and full of thunder. She strokes it with adequate know-how.

'How about a snuggle, honey,' she says. 'How about a roll in the hay?'

Honey? Too close, Tara, you're far too close. I lean over and plant a tasty tongue into her eager mouth.

'Like to, but I have to get a wriggle on. Coffee would be nice, though.'

'Oh,' she says, poor little waif. 'Right. Sure.'

I stand up and walk out of the bedroom with my mobile, leaving her husky and forlorn, just what she deserves for behaving so familiar with me. Really, all I did was stay the night.

'I'm just going to make a quick 'phone call. Milk, no sugar, remember?'

'Got it.'

First number on the list is my own. Three messages on the voice-mail; my father sharing some joke he'd read in the Telegraph, T.U. telling me he can't make Negociants (Why? What else could he possibly have to do?) and finally, a real blinder – Roger's caught the train to London. He's going to see the irrepressible Rebecca! Once upon a time Roger would come to me before making such a momentous decision, but he's becoming too spontaneous, too secretive, for his own good. How does he expect me to help him if I get all his declarations second-hand? Bad puppy.

I make another call just to keep my hand in the game. Then I throw some clothes on, flip in my contact lenses, and slap my face with some of Tara's moisturiser. I walk through to her unkempt kitchen.

'I'll call you later.'

'What about your coffee?' she bleats, holding out a cup of putrid Nescafe.

'Have to shake a leg, I'm afraid. See you.' I kiss her, a full-blooded tonsil-smacker once again, then I leave her, weak-kneed and aglow, and sprint down the stairs and onto the Edinburgh pavement.

The elevator stops. Not on the third floor. That's all right, no one wanted to go there. Not on the fourth floor. Shame, we all want to go there. The elevator stops halfway between the third and fourth floor. With the gentlest of thuds. No, not even a thud, more of a sigh. Yes, on Saturday morning in Jenner's the elevator *sighs* to a stop. And the doors don't open.

The start of my disaster, I think to myself with resignation. We'll hear a snap of cable, and plummet to our certain deaths. What a way to go, I didn't even get my cup of Earl Grey. This is definitely not the way I dreamed it would be.

I had thought that coffee and a sticky bun in Kinelli's would be the perfect place to plan next weeks press night. Instead I trip into Marianne and her permanent escort Alasdair, so we plump for the cafe in Jenner's, only to end with all three of us stuck in the lift.

The white light that indicates the location of the lift blinks out, out for the count, out for lunch, well out of order. That's about as violent as the mechanical fault gets. No snapping of cable, no plummeting to our certain deaths. No one could die in Jenner's, Edinburgh's oldest and most sophisticated department store. It's just not done. Nothing snaps, and no one plummets.

Suddenly several things don't happen. The door doesn't open, we don't leave, and we don't get on with the rest of our existence. Then, quick as a flash, several things do happen. Alasdair continues to actively look at the floor, really examine the carpet beneath our feet, I feel a mental ticking that signals the need for a cigarette, and Marianne declares that she really would like to go to the toilet. A minute crawls by, lost forever, doomed to be known as the minute when no one did anything. Then, filled with a sense of purpose, my mind's eye set on the ashtray in Jenner's restaurant, I take a majestic step forward and press button four. Nothing happens. Again. I turn around and faces my fellow prisoners.

'Houston, We have a problem,' I declare in an authentic American accent. Marianne utters her monstrous hawking laugh. I give her a smile, then move the discussion from Hollywood derivation to the mechanically obvious. 'I have come to the conclusion that we're stuck. Is that a fair assumption, do you think?'

'Uh-huh,' replies Marianne brilliantly. But I feel duty bound to turn to the third inmate for consensus.

'Are we agreed, then, dear Alasdair. Do we have a stuck situation, here?'

Alasdair shrugs miserably and continues to stare at the floor. I take that as a yes, then eye the alarm switch on the wall. Rubbing my finely shaped chin in contemplation, I consider our options:

'Now, we can switch on the alarm, and presumably they would come to our rescue. Are we agreed that our predicament constitutes an emergency?'

'Well, we *are* stuck,' says Marianne. Now who says fashion models are stupid? (But she is gorgeous, up

84

close and personal, she's the real thing, and I'm going to have her, just see if I don't).

'Yes,' I reply, warming to the subject, 'but we're all headed for the cafe, and I'm not certain if tea and cake is critical for survival. Besides, the alarm is going to be very loud, and it just seems, well, rude to set off an alarm in an establishment such as this. We might give some old dear a heart attack. Then there'll be trouble,' I conclude ominously.

'*The Scotsman* would have a field day, our reputations would be in tatters,' agrees Marianne, and we both laugh.

'Hey, I got it!' I reach into my jacket pocket and pull out my mobile 'phone. 'Moby to the rescue.' I call Directory Enquiries for Jenner's number. 'Hi, I'm sorry to bother you, but I'm stuck in your lift . . . mmm . . . How long will that take? . . . Right, the thing is, there's a pregnant woman here, and I think she's about to go into labour . . . yeah . . . thanks, that'd be great . . . appreciate it.' I put the 'phone back in my jacket. 'People management, they'll be as quick as they can. What?'

Alasdair's and Marianne's looks of horror are most puzzling.

'Why did you say that?' asks Marianne.

'Just thought I'd speed them up a bit. We'll be here all day otherwise.'

'That was really stupid,' says Alasdair, whispering for no apparent reason. 'That was just *mad*.'

'Ah!' I cry, feeling my pockets with an increasing frenzy. 'Oh dear God my life is over!'

'What?' asks Marianne in a panic, presumably forgetting her bladder for a few precious seconds.

'I totally forgot my cigarettes.'

Alasdair, full of his usual understanding, glares at me, then sits down in a corner, bringing his knees up to his chin and putting a white carrier-bag beside him.

'Have you got any cigarettes?' I ask Marianne, a suitably wild gleam of panic in my eyes. Marianne scrabbles around in her handbag and throws me a pack.

'Thanks,' I say, trauma over, but I tense again as soon as I see the brand. 'So this is what it's come to. Stuck in a lift with a pack of Silk Cut Ultra Low.' I sniff miserably, sit down, then open the pack. 'Can I have three?'

'Sure,' says Marianne, sitting down beside me and offering her lighter.

'Hey,' says Alasdair, sensing a threat to his proprietorial rights and moving into action.

'What?' I ask, breaking off the filter and putting the unfrayed end of the cigarette in my mouth.

'You're not really going to smoke, are you?'

I stare across at him, cigarette hanging from my lips, with Marianne poised uncertainly with her lighter. 'Is that a trick question?'

'This is a seriously confined space, and I'm feeling claustrophobic enough already,' says Alasdair as forcefully as he can manage, which isn't quite forcefully enough.

'Alasdair, you're right, this is a confined space, but I'm seriously addicted to nicotine. Right now I'm feeling pretty damn ratty and if you in any way attempt to stop me smoking this cigarette, I'll have to kill you. Just hold your breath or something. Now Marianne, light that bastard before I pass out.'

Marianne kindly obliges, and after a moment's hesitation, lights one for herself as well. Alasdair sits opposite us, seething quietly. Carcinogens flow down two sets of lungs, and the world gradually begins to look like a less hateful place to be.

I exhale joyously, and put my hand on my smoking partner's knee. *And she does nothing to remove it.* Perhaps she's used to our fondling and groping, perhaps she isn't aware of such physical slights anymore. Perhaps, just perhaps, I could fuck her, here and now, without her even noticing. No. Not yet. Timing is everything, and Marianne is no trivial lay.

'Marianne, my dear, when this frightful ordeal is over, I shall whisk you by taxi to the City Cafe, and I'll buy you a proper pack of cigarettes. Then we'll sit next to the entrance drinking bottles of imported beer and laugh at the dress sense, the dress non-sense of passers-by. The perfect Saturday afternoon.'

'Okay,' said Marianne, then she winced. 'As long as I get to go to the ladies' first, I think I'm about to burst.'

'Well, that would certainly be unpleasant,' I say. 'Are you normally so reckless as to get into a lift without going to the toilet first? I know I went before I came. I bet Alasdair did,' and I give Alasdair a glorious smirk. Poor Alasdair looks away, no doubt wondering why this shit always, always happens to him. But we know why, don't we boys and girls; he was placed on this earth just to have shit happen to him.

Meanwhile, Marianne crosses her legs with renewed desperation. 'It's a . . . lady's problem; I have to go a lot at the moment.'

'Really?' I say, with the slightest of interest. 'And which of the plethora of ladies' problems would this one be?'

'Cystitis,' says Marianne gravely, feeling the pinch that was more than an inch.

I put an arm around her shoulder. 'Ah, but that's not strictly a ladies' problem, because gentlemen can get it too.'

'Really?' says Marianne, looking up at me hope-fully. Typical woman, the idea that men could get cystitis seems like a very nice one.

'Oh yes,' I continue sagely, 'it's just that as ladies' bits are packed closer together, it's easier for infection to spread, so they get it more often than men.'

'Wow,' says Marianne softly, impressed, delighted, delirious. 'I never knew that.'

I break the filter off another cigarette. 'You ought to get yourself a bag of frozen peas,' I say discern-ingly, stroking her arm, moving down the pass making checklist like an Evening News hack with a copy deadline.

Startled, Marianne gazes into my eyes, stunned at my erudition. 'How did you know about that? I only found out about that on Thursday!'

'An ex-girlfriend mentioned it during one of her sleep-talks. One of her sleep-rants. I tell you, she could never have been unfaithful because she would've sleep-raved about it at some point. I think I learnt more about her when I slept with her than when I *slept* with her, if you know what I mean.'

'I just didn't realise it was so universal,' says Marianne.

'Frozen peas?' I ask, smiling my killer shark smile.

'Mmm.' Marianne rests her head on my shoulder.

'Well, I'll tell you what,' I say smoothly, 'we'll go to Tesco's on the way to the City Cafe and get a little bag, then we can sit drinking and smoking, and no one will know you have a bag of frozen peas sitting on your—'

'Hey!' Alasdair made his first important contribu-tion to the discussion. 'Do you mind?'

'What's the problem, Alasdair?' I ask innocently.

'Your conversation. It's absolutely *disgusting*,' he

says, somehow managing to put the emphasis on all three syllables.

'Disgusting?' I say. 'Well, that's an interesting perspective. Totally erroneous, but interesting. So what would you like to talk about?'

'Nothing,' he pleads, 'Just nothing. This is a nightmare.'

'Alasdair, this situation is whatever you want it to be. Now come on, we'll talk about whatever you like. Say, what's in the bag?' I point my Silk Cut at the white carrier-bag at Alasdair's feet. Alasdair blanches and grabs hold of the bag.

'None of your business,' says Alasdair quietly.

'Don't be like that, man,' I say, wounded to the core. 'What do you think he's got in his bag, Marianne?'

Marianne shakes her head with a smile. 'No idea,' she says.

'C'mon, take a wild guess, a reckless stab in the dark. Alasdair can tell us if we're getting warm or not.'

Marianne grinned in contemplation. Beautiful teeth, go figure. 'A bomb?' she suggests, with mock excitement.

'Alasdair? Are we hot or cold?' I ask.

Alasdair sighed and closed his eyes.

'Hmm, I guess not, then. A bag of cocaine?'

'A gun,' offers Marianne, smiling into my shoulder. (I can feel her lips. And I want to feel them again sometime. And I will).

Alasdair says nothing. Nothing out loud.

'I don't think we're even close,' I say. 'I think, I firmly believe, that the bag contains' – I pause for dramatic effect – 'A book!'

Marianne gasps with excitement. 'A book?' she mouths breathlessly.

'A book,' I repeat, with chilling certainty.

Alasdair opens his eyes. 'It's a magazine, all right? It's a fucking magazine.'

I raise an eyebrow. 'A *fucking* magazine? Now we're talking. Is it a "How To?" Is it traditional porn? Playboy? Escort? Or does it have a more international flavour? Asian Babes, perhaps?'

'Do you ever stop?' asks Alasdair miserably, 'Do you ever stop talking shite?'

'Don't be shy,' I say, 'Let us in on your fetish. We're both pretty open-minded people, I mean, as long as it isn't the Mothercare Catalogue I think we can handle the kink-factor.'

'Ow!' cried Marianne, 'Don't make me laugh, I'll wet myself!'

'Here!' Alasdair threw the bag across the floor. 'Now shut up!

'Oh, joy,' I say softly. 'Treasure.'

I light the third Silk Cut, really smoking now at last, and Marianne opens the bag.

'Ooh' she says, 'I didn't know you were interested in poetry.'

'It's for work,' says Alasdair, looking distinctly sheepish.

'You're kidding.' I grab the magazine, incredulous, and it really is a poetry rag. Has Edinburgh gone mad? Why are the people I know doing all these strange things? 'Now what could a crude philistine such as yourself want with poetry?'

'You are one rude motherfucker!' Alasdair shouts for no good reason, and Marianne and I share a bemused glance. I open my mouth to answer, to tear his life apart, but at that moment there is an abrupt mechanical jolt as the lift slides upwards.

'We're moving!' says Marianne with delight.

'Action stations,' I say, getting to my feet. 'Come on, dear lady, relief is at hand.'

We stand to attention as the lift halts. We breathe in, then breathe out as the doors open and we see the fourth floor. We step, okay, jump, out of the lift, and find a well dressed man with a plastic smile waiting for us.

'I'm Ian the duty manager,' Ian the duty manager begins, 'And I would just like to say how terribly—'

'Sorry!' yells Marianne and she pushes past him and sprints to the Ladies. Ian the duty manager looks after her as she runs, and a question appears in his shop-assistant mind.

'I thought she was—'

'Indigestion,' I say. 'Sorry, my mistake. Now I presume you were about to offer us complimentary tea and cake, and lots of it?

'Ah . . . of course,' says Ian the duty manager.

'Of *course*,' I say, and walk in the direction of the cafe.

Ian the duty manager looks questioningly at Alasdair. I glance back in time to see his scowl before he follows me to the cafe.

'Tell me Alasdair, when was the last time you got laid?'

Dear God. I can't say it. I can't write the words. It's too fantastic. No, I really can't say. He's joking, *peut-être*. Please, let him be kidding.

'No, seriously, when was the last time?'

'Seriously, that was the last time, Jay.'

'Good grief. If I went without sex for that length of time I don't know what I'd do. Something violent, anyway. Good grief . . .'

I pale at the mere thought of it. Then I pour myself some Earl Grey and start the game. 'I'll set you up with someone. You can have Tara, she's rather a Klingon, but is blessed with fine physical attributes.

It wouldn't be a problem, in fact it would be my pleasure.'

Alasdair's face heats up from his usual deathly pallor to an almost human white. 'Jay, I appreciate the—'

'And if it's an impotence problem you've got, then all the better, because no one's easier to screw than an actress.'

'Actually I'm not—'

But I'm on a roll. 'Now I know I've said that all actresses are psychotic bitches from hell and should be avoided at all costs, but that's precisely where the advantage lies if you're having erectional difficulties.'

'Jay I don't—'

''Cause you see they can't stop acting, even in bed, so it's like you're both performing roles, and it's much easier to act out a part than commit yourself to the emotions of sex, and hey presto, you're hard as nails!'

And what is Alasdair's response? Well, a simple thank you would suffice.

'Jay, I'm not impotent, and I don't want one of your deranged cast-offs, so leave me alone, okay?'

But no, most rude. I'm glad Tara isn't hear to take this abuse. All in all, Alasdair deserves what's coming to him.

Marianne. Now there's a prize worth fighting for. I could tell in the elevator that she wanted me, written all over that amazing face. So let's try some threeplay: let Alasdair, love-sick fool that he is, finally make a pass at her, then I shall come forward to claim my trophy while she's still crying with laughter. This one is just too easy. Are you learning yet? Do you get the picture? Do you see how easy it is to get on?

'Marianne's nice, isn't she?' I say, dropping an single cube of sweet calories into my tea.

'Yes,' Alasdair says, pink-faced, picking the allergy-threatening almonds off a fruit slice.

'I can tell she likes you.'

'I don't think so.' Voice distinctly croaky. Face pink to red.

'Now Alasdair, how can you say that? There I was raving like a lunatic fresh out of the asylum, crumbling under the pressure of our little predicament, and you sat there cool as a courgette, the strong silent type. I tell you, if you actually came on to her, she'd go for you in a big way. She was very impressed.' I reach for my cigarettes, remember that they aren't there, and sigh.

'Really?' asks Alasdair.

I nod emphatically. 'You were a tower of strength. Milk?'

A minute later Marianne arrives, looking radiant with relief.

12

Not Tom Hanks

Nobody could level the charge of subtlety against Buddies' latest production. Indeed, the director would have done well to read his own programme notes about plausibility. The pratfalls and heavy-footed chases through which he puts his cast elicited some stony silences from the first-night audience.
– *The Scotsman*

ALASDAIR:

I should have known better of course. You don't live a life like mine without developing an invaluable cynicism. When I consider the sheer insanity of taking Jay's loaded advice on anything, I feel as if I've learned nothing since I left school.

I've shared a flat with a girl called Veronica since second year of university. She's an absolute terror and we have zero in common, but we can't seem to shake ourselves free of each other. Fortunately there's never any sexual tension in the flat, nothing that could disrupt our platonic relationship. Veronica and I have a tacit understanding: I never fuck anyone, and she fucks every man in Edinburgh except me. It's the perfect flat set-up.

Veronica works nine to five somewhere; it varies, it ebbs and flows. She takes sensational amounts of sick leave and then finds another nowhere job. Veronica's got it all figured out: she told me her master-plan during a hideously embarrassing soul searching session late one night, fuelled by Malibu and her bizarre belief that I cared what she did with her life. Veronica's cunning scheme is to find a husband. That's it. That's the plan. Someone really ought to tell her (not me, Christ, I'm hardly brave enough for that) that she's going about it all the wrong way. Please, someone, anyone, tell my flatmate she's heading for disaster.

I blame Veronica for one of the worst mornings of my life: a Sunday morning disaster in the middle of Junior Honours, when Essay deadlines were tight and domestic trauma was the last thing I needed. I'd actually spent the night before doing my own little rain dance, stumbling home dazed and confused, so I missed Veronica's entrance with her *homme de jour*. I got up early, feeling horrendous hangover guilt, and desperate for a piss. I stumbled through to the bathroom, only to find the door locked. I cursed my way to the kitchen, my bladder at battle-stations and insisting on a sink job, but Veronica was sitting at the table, dishevelled, strained and radiant all at once. I croaked a good morning, then set about finding a pint glass, so I could scamper back to my bedroom with guilty hands. But Veronica, two cups of coffee and an ashtray I hadn't hidden well enough sitting in front of her, wanted to chat.

'Ally!' A stage hiss, waking up my headache, making me see stars.

'What?' I leant against the cupboard and crossed my legs.

Veronica lit a cigarette, some pretentious brand that I doubted she could even pronounce. 'This guy is fucking amazing!'

'You don't smoke, remember. Is he?'

'He's . . . Christ, he's a total' – the bathroom door opened – 'Ssshh!'

I turned to see what the usual suspect looked like this time, planning to break for urinary salvation once he'd squeezed through the kitchen door.

'Ah! I thought this hole looked familiar.' Jay swept past me and took his place at the table, where Veronica was fumbling with the cigarettes and the sugar bowl.

'No, my dear, I'm sweet enough already. Don't you think, Alasdair?'

I looked at my feet, toes curling into the tiled floor.

'Isn't he a scream?' asked Veronica.

I walked, slow motion and grey, to the bathroom. Violated, I wanted to scrub myself clean. I wanted to shower in bleach. Instead I took a laser piss, got dressed, then crept out of the flat, burglar style, to find an open Paki shop and to get away from Jay. That's the thing about him, that's the essence. No-where's safe from his designs. Like a deadly virus, Jay Wellesley gets everywhere.

I returned, a bag of over-priced Sunday fat grams held in one hand, Veronica's *News of the World* in the other. She was still in the kitchen, with two cold cups of coffee and a full ashtray. She was crying, and I hated her for it. I hated her almost as much as I despised Jay.

'Oh, Ally, I wish my Dad was here,' she said between tumultuous sobs. I took my customary place beside her at the table, and she buried her streaked face into my jacket. Gulping and hitching, making an awful mess, Veronica came as close as she'll ever get to a critical assessment of her potential husbands.

'I don't know what I'm doing wrong. I always act

so nice, and I always let them stay, but they're always such bastards in the morning.'

We were in my flat, home territory, Veronica out skulking in Century 2000, when I decided to make my move. I've known Mari for three years. That's three years of lunches, coffees, tennis, all sorts of platonic pleasures. Christ, I've even gone bowling with her. And, of course, lots of theatre.

But no more. There was always a seed of hope, mainly late at night of course (when anything, good or bad, seems possible) that she might want to have sex with me. It had to come from her, you understand. I couldn't try to seduce a fashion model, that would be insane. Now though, Jay's words ran through me like electricity. If anyone knows women, it's Jay. He had to be right about Mari. But she was shy, that much was clear. And those boyfriends she'd had during our friendship; they'd only been crutches to lean on while she pined for me. So I had to make the first move. I decided to invite her round to watch *Sleepless in Seattle*, and after the film I would make the world a better place. Yes, this is what I really thought about late at night, tossing away another wasted Kleenex.

Roll credits. Boosted by the star-power that is Tom Hanks, I keep Jay's assurances running through my mind like a mantra, and turn to face Marianne. But she's already looking at me.

'You know what I like about you?' Mari asked.

Fuck! Perhaps she was going to do the work for me. Declare her own intentions, as it were. I decided to keep the situation light, just to make it easier for her.

'My dashing good looks?'

She smiled. Shook her head.

'My athletic prowess?'

She grinned. Another shake of the head. Okay, I thought, let me have it, give it your best shot, Mari, this moment is going to change our lives forever.

'I give up.'

'Even though you're a guy,' she said, 'you're so totally un-male.'

A pair of testicles slumped between my legs like forgotten leftovers even the cat wouldn't touch. I considered what she'd said, put the words on the coffee table. They lay there, festering between the *Argos Catalogue* and the remote control. They looked bad. They didn't look complimentary at all. With dying relish, the words peered up at me with malicious smiles. They knew me, everything about me. I'd given myself away to this girl, and the words told the story. My maleness unravelled before her. Penis? What penis? I had no concept of penis. Twenty years of testosterone washed off my psyche like cum off a duck's back. I felt the wound in my groin where she had gouged out my manhood with her blunt oral scalpel.

Mari saw me wince. 'No, don't take it the wrong way.'

Excuse me?

'I mean that you don't threaten like the rest of them,' she said. 'I'm ogled all the time, I make a living out of it. But you don't ogle.'

There's a certain amount of irony here, because I'm simply too much in awe to ogle Mari.

'I think you may be in the wrong business,' I replied dryly. How dry am I? I'm an Autumn leaf, that's how dry. And Mari laughed, my reward.

'And that, Alasdair, is exactly my point. In my private life I surround myself with gentlemen. *Gentle men*, the perfect foil to the business rogues and charlatans I deal with at work. I want my private life to be subtle. Quiet.'

'It's the quiet ones you have to watch out for,' I said with a weak smile.

'But you're a quiet one, Alasdair,' she replied.

Ah. She had me there.

'Exception to the rule,' I said, 'Trust me on this. The quiet ones are all sex demons waiting to pounce when you least expect it.'

'Apart from you?'

'Correct,' I replied glumly.

And Mari laughed again, what more could I ask for? Well, you know what. Me and Marianne. Marianne and I. She thinks I'm happy just being her friend, she thinks I'm different from the others. She thinks I'm nice. Don't think that I'm nice, Mari. I'm not nice. Truly, I'm not. I'm just another cock trying to get in.

13

Making Friends

ROGER:
How did we meet? How did we get to be friends? I
mean, the question has to be asked. What are the
three of us possibly doing in each other's pockets like
this? Me, Jay, Alasdair, what a team, what a posse.
What's *that* all about?

Jay would say it was organic. Or perhaps that's
what he would say, I've never actually asked him.
Although it's been on the tip of my tongue, countless
times, over coffee in Negociants, under pressure at
Buddies. I can't ask him, I can't ask Alasdair. Why do
you like me? Why do you stick around? What a
question to ask. I really don't like to invite frightening answers.

I can't remember when we first got together. You
might think I would recall my first glimpse of Jay, eye
contact across a smoke-filled room, and all that. But
to be honest, one day I woke up and we were best
friends, and I'm not at all sure how it happened. It's
the same with Alasdair. Maybe it was at Buddies,
maybe it was at the *Student* offices, I don't have the
rewind, I couldn't possibly say.

If I'm feeling cynical, then I'd say that it was purely
theatre that has kept us together. And it's true,
theatre's all we really talk about. For six years, from
the student newspaper and university theatre, to

Buddies and *The Scotsman*, we've been granting each other the same favours we always did. Jay wanted to direct a certain play, I wanted to produce a certain play, Alasdair wanted access and exclusives, and Jay and I wanted Alasdair to write those magic words in his column: *Don't miss it*.

But it's more than just business. I like them a lot, and I'd go well out of my way for either of them. Friends are pretty crucial, I find, to my standard of living. I spend so much time with Jay, the Buddies shift, and that's fair enough. But when we break for lunch, or hit a restaurant for dinner and drinks, everything changes. I can talk to Jay about things I'd never talk to other people about. My love, my sex, my intelligence. He asks all the right questions, and I'm more than happy to deliver the answers.

It's different with Alasdair, of course. No hot, sweaty chats about premature and late, about slap and tickle. Alasdair hides away from the passionate side of human affairs, but he knows so much about theatre. He's got a wider view of things, of the Edinburgh scene, at least. He knows all the venues, all the casts, what's going to shine and what's going to crumble.

Jay doesn't pay nearly as much attention to other theatres. It's partially this arrogance that accounts for Buddies' success. He ignored the status quo and drove ahead for his unique vision of how a theatre should be: young, innovative, and very hip. Of course having a ridiculously wealthy father didn't do any harm. But Jay doesn't take too much notice of the other companies, and it's Alasdair I turn to before the Edinburgh Festival, for a true SWOT analysis, for a reliable read on potential opportunities and threats.

What does Alasdair need *me* for? Just someone who won't have a go at him, I think. I don't push or shove.

You have to be gentle with a guy like that, or he'll jump back into his shell and never come out. But I'll be there when he finally wants to talk about the real things in life. When he wants to talk about the passion.

So have I got the best end of the deal? Alasdair and Jay are both much smarter than me, so much more clued in to art and theatre. But I have a few things to offer too. It's no idle boast to say that I've always had more friends than them. All through university, I hit Teviot Union on Friday night, out with the boys, out on the piss. Jay was there as well, of course, but he wasn't one of the guys. He would pick off the girls – the Freshers, the Goths, the English Yahs – and do the business, do the deed. All very impressive, but taking it too far didn't make him a favourite with the lads. You had to put your time in with the other, equally critical, activities. You had to eat a lot of chips, puke in a lot of taxis, steal a lot of traffic cones.

Being a lady-killer is all very well, but you had to careful, because all those broken hearts added up to a lot of disgruntled brothers. All that sex, never crashing and burning. Jay didn't even have the sense to *pretend* to fail. He scared the other guys off with his sheer success. Who wants to be friends with someone you have nothing in common with?

It's easy, on the other hand, to be mates with me. I don't ask for too much, I forgive people's mistakes, I don't go in for unpredictable behaviour. What you see is what you get. And I think that everyone needs a friend like that.

ALASDAIR:
I don't make friends very easily. I don't keep friends very easily either. The truth is, I'm pretty glad to have Roger and Jay on my side, and I intend to keep

them there, if I can help it. They're not perfect, of course. Roger, with his blokeish naivete, doesn't really belong in the theatre. And Jay, unscrupulous womaniser, self-centred nihilist, doesn't really belong on the planet. But I can't be too choosy, and I do like them. Roger's a good friend, an honest guy, and Jay's entertaining to be around, as long as he's not directing his venom at me.

How do people make friends? At parties, in business, waiting for the bus. It's all over my head. People ask me dangerous questions, like 'How're you doing?' What a question. How can I answer that? 'Fine, thanks.' But it's such a lie. I'm not fine at all. I'm filled with aches, I'm covered in bruises. So I stand there, a wallflower, a critic, a fellow passenger, trying to find the words to explain how I'm getting along, trying desperately to answer the most common and apparently innocuous question there is. I stand there, shaking with indecision, and my potential friend walks away, annoyed or bewildered, and looks for someone easier, more compatible.

I can't pretend to be all right when I'm not. It's a huge handicap, especially when making small talk. And the weather is almost as bad. 'Nice weather for ducks.' What? What are you talking about? Besides, I haven't noticed the weather, I've got other things on my mind, like sleep, like food, like naked flesh.

Roger is the master of small talk, just like Jay is the master of big talk. Roger knows the weather, he doesn't have to discuss it with me, he's got that one covered quite nicely on his own, thank you very much. And he knows not to ask me how I'm doing, he knows not to ask the question of death, and I love him for it. Roger may not appear to be the brightest man on the block, but he's sensitive to other people's moods and characteristics, he's sensitive to his friends.

Jay, meanwhile, can talk about anything, but he doesn't bother with small talk. He jumps right into any subject, the whole drugs, sex and rock 'n' roll story. He takes great pleasure in providing me with juicy details regarding his sex life (although I suspect, happily, that he saves the most succulent titbits for Roger). Then he'll tell me that I should get out more, or he'll recommend a particular actress, or particular drug combination.

'Amphetamines are no good for sex, dear Alasdair. It's all very well for theatrical purposes, a little upper, a little chemical nutrition, but speed turns your penis into a twiglet, and that's just not good enough. And Ecstasy? Do you really want to have delusions of love during intercourse? Of course not. No, cocaine is the only way to go. All pumped up and ready to go. Have you tried it? Here, it's on the house, I'm sure I owe you a small favour. Come on, old man, it's the real thing. Oh, Alasdair. Oh, *really*.'

Sometimes – as in this case – I'll have heard the spiel before. Jay can be entertaining, because he has a theory on everything, but he tends to forget what he's told you. So he can launch into some lecture on the state of the nation, and I rarely have the strength or inclination to tell him that I've heard it all before. So Jay will continue the rant, and I can settle back in my chair, comforted by the thought that I don't have to think of anything else to say.

Jay and Roger make a good team at Buddies. Good Cop Bad Cop, perhaps, to persuade the sceptical advertisers, or to win over the cynical critics, if you like. Of course Jay doesn't fully appreciate Roger's skills, and if Roger ever left, I think Jay would find himself in a lot of trouble. Jay has never been one for compromise, and I've seen him ruffle a lot of feathers. If it wasn't for Roger's ability to make friends with absolutely anyone, then Jay would find himself with a lot less business. Jay talks about his selling skills, but it's mostly down to Roger that anything businesslike ever gets done at Buddies.

I'm not going to claim that I have the best friends in the world. A little sad, perhaps, to still be hanging onto friends from my university life. But I'm hanging onto a lot of things these days, so there's no reason why my social life should be any different. I'll try and keep Roger and Jay, for the moment at least. I'll try and keep things the way they are. Change is a rare and frightening fish, and the very last thing I need on my plate right now.

JAY:
I'm really rather fond of Roger and Alasdair, if the truth be told. They're comparable to an old family pet, or your first car. The sheer sentimentality, the same quaint desire to hang on for a little while longer, ignoring their failing limbs and suffocating exhaust fumes.

It would be so easy for me to cast them off, to shed my platonic skin and acquire much more impressive comrades, but friends aren't just for Christmas. What would Roger and Alasdair do without me? I shudder to think what would become of them without my kind guidance. The producer, on the cusp of alcoholic obesity, floundering from one romantic delusion to another. The critic, who struggles to face his morning muesli, never mind the rest of the world. Lost, the pair of them, utterly doomed without me.

I have an excellent memory, and I have a vivid recollection of my first encounter with Roger Brown.

Early days at the university theatre, where I had already ensconced myself as a leading player, and a clutch of pseudo-thespians were discussing plans to revamp the theatre cafe. Amidst cries for a renewed alcohol licence, the new boy – round and flushed – stuck a chubby hand in the air.

Who was this big man on campus? He didn't look promising, he didn't look like *one of us*. But, ever the democrat, I beckoned him forth.

'Your name, good sir?'

'Roger Brown.'

'And what is your golden contribution to our little fray?'

'Sorry?'

The poor boy, pink and sweating, I could have squashed him there and then. But I know of the Christian virtues. I know all about charity.

'Your idea, Mr. Brown,' I said softly. 'What is it?'

And when Mr. Brown revealed his suggestion, I knew that I had to have him all to myself.

'Popcorn. Er . . . popcorn, for eating during the play. Because everyone likes popcorn, it would be just like the cinema.'

It was a terrible idea, of course, and was never implemented. The suggestion, in fact, was greeted with derision, and some quite vicious heckling.

But my colleagues, as always, were missing the point. Roger had the common touch. Unbowed by the traditions and norms of theatre, he wanted a play to be like a film. The same comforts, the same fun. Roger knew what every theatre-goer in Edinburgh secretly wanted, for a play to be as accessible as Hollywood, as straightforward as McDonalds. Roger knew, because Roger *is* the general public. So I took the vulgar young rascal under my wing, smoothed his rough edges, and Buddies revelled in innovative marketing and customer service that the old school could only dream about. I do appreciate Roger. He is so astoundingly average that I would be a fool not to employ him.

Alasdair has his positive side too, although it is not readily apparent. He has no life outside the theatre, and is a veritable font of artistic gossip. And, of course, he does write the nicest possible reviews for Buddies. What a friend, what a absolute *pal*. I put up with his miserable demeanour and brick wall silences with excellent humour. I do my best to let him in on some of the more basic secrets of threeplay, but what he really needs, obviously, is the love of a bad woman.

'Sex is about theatre, Alasdair. It's about showing your power, real or otherwise.' I try to maintain an air of noble honesty during these conversations, and as long as I avoid a direct visual hit on his complexion or adolescent posture, I am usually able to look him in the eye.

'You're a critic, Alasdair, use your strength. You can destroy a play with a few column inches, why should a woman be any different? Just do to her what you did to the Royal Lyceum last month and she'll be a rabbit in the headlights.'

Well, who knows? Anything can happen. Alasdair actually ending up in someone else's bed, however, may be stretching possibilities a little too far. But no one can deny how hard I try to help my friends.

Despite my youthful, bronzed appearance, I am wise beyond my years (any fool can see that), and I understand that it is my moral and social responsibility to keep these two gentlemen, who have granted me one or two clumsy favours over the years, on the right track. They are not men of the world. They do not truly comprehend the games that are played, that must be played, in order to succeed. But they are lucky, for they have me. I am the director, and I am more than happy to light the way.

14

Cheers

Yvonne Thompson is the striking older woman. Simon Wright is her younger, hunky husband.

But behind the seemingly happy couple lies a dark secret. For Simon, 29, has tried to run his wife over, torched her home and attempted to strangle her.

Incredibly, Yvonne, 44, won't testify against him, risking prison herself.

'He'll always be my Mr. Right,' says Yvonne, from Marchmont. She fears he'll kill her unless he gets help, but still cares for the only man she's ever loved.

– Evening News

ROGER:
I haven't told my mum and dad about Becky leaving. At first it was easy, because I actually thought that she was going to come back. In fact the first time we spoke on the 'phone I told them half the truth and said that the Beckster had gone home. For the week-end. And that's half-true, isn't it? Now the days have turned into weeks, however, and this stunt is getting a lot trickier to pull off. This is due to the fact that my parents actually like my girlfriend. A lot. They spend more time talking to her on the 'phone than to me (I've timed them, no lie); they always seem more interested in Becky's job than Buddies.

The Beckster didn't go to university. Sometimes I

think she was too smart for the whole higher education deal. She works for an employment agency, finding temporary and long-term jobs, finding temporary and long-term human beings. Accountants, legal secretaries, I.T., that kind of thing. It's a big agency, they've got offices everywhere, which is how Becky ended up in Edinburgh in the first place. An opportunity, a change of scene, a chance to see the talented Jocks in their native land, who would pass that up? So she left Hampstead for Scotland, finding Auld Reekie, finding a flat, finding me.

She makes good money and she gets good holiday time. The only problem is the people she has to speak to, every day of the week. People looking for work, they're like patients sitting in a doctor's waiting room. Flipping through old magazines, fingering scars, full of nervous twitches. They're tired, ill, they've definitely seen better days. But even worse, much worse than all the rest, these people insist on being on their best behaviour. When Becky works late sometimes I''ll sit in the shadows as these desperadoes flutter their eyelashes, flap their CVs, flash their smiles, a study in kinesics. Becky has to take them all on, onto the agency's files, no matter how bad they are, no matter how incompetent. It's company policy: quantity, not quality. Of course the truly bad ones never get jobs, but their names remain on the list anyway, looking impressive, waiting by the 'phone.

Chloe works at the same agency, a girl who drips with the promise of erotica. Legal eagles and computer nerds stride confidently into the office and are sent reeling by her legs and cleavage. Chloe is, as they say, a stunner. I find it strange that she and Becky are such good friends. I mean, they both tend to get what they want, but the Beckster is rather more subtle and a lot less vampirish in her planning and scheming. Perhaps I should ask Chloe how I can get Becky back, but to be honest she scares me a little. The most frightening event took place at the agency's Christmas party.

I was wading through the crisps and other nibbles when Chloe appeared from nowhere, her arms around my waist and her lips in my ear.

'Rebecca tells me you're a fabulous dancer.'

'I think she was kidding,' I replied, my mouth full of cocktail sausage.

'Well, there's only one way to find out,' she said, and so we bobbed and ducked to the Christmas party tape, ending up precariously close to the infamous office stationery cupboard.

'Rebecca is so lucky to have you, Roger. You're all man.'

I nodded, my ears tingling with embarrassment, and I tried not to spill any red while her hands went to some very un-platonic places.

I told the Beckster about this, when I'd had one too many of her father's Boxing Day cocktails, but she just laughed.

'Silly Tiger. Chloe's naturally flirtatious, she acts that way with everyone. Now come here, and I'll show you what sexual harassment is all about . . .'

Well, that's all very well, but I feel sorry for the temps. Chloe must be the last thing they want to have to deal with.

Now Mr and Mrs Sutton do speak to Mr and Mrs Brown occasionally; making deals over Christmas, engagement rings, frightening stuff like that. The odds, therefore, of my parents discovering Becky's departure for her homeland are getting shorter all the time. If they find out before I tell them then they will be understandably embarrassed, and understandably out for my blood.

But I know what you really want to know about my parents. You want to know if they're overweight. Is it genetic, is it upbringing, is it a reaction against dietary austerity. Oh I'm fat. I know what causes it: earning more calories than I spend. It's fish suppers, it's Tennant's, it's taxis. If cigarettes had calories I would be one dead whale by now, long since harpooned by evil Japanese fishermen sneaking into British waters. No, my parents aren't fat, and neither are any of my sisters. They waltz around the house, svelte and limber, while I stumble and bash, threatening to squash a sibling, threatening to crush a favourite pet.

I should own up, ask my family's advice on the Rebecca dilemma. Perhaps they'll have some words of wisdom, perhaps they'll give my lumbering behind a healthy kick. I need their input, especially that of my three wise sisters. They know how to sustain a relationship, they're so much more skilled than I am. My sisters like Becky as well, of course.

'She's so clever, Roger.'

'I know.'

'Your life would be an utter shambles without her, Roger.'

'Absolutely.'

'You wouldn't want to do anything to lose her, Roger.'

Oh, Christ.

Everyone likes Becky. So what could I tell them? The lie, the terrible, insane lie? I can't justify any of this mess, there'll be no sympathy from any corner. I have to sort this out on my own, and that's never good news.

*   *   *

I caught the eight o'clock service down to King's Cross. Not a good start to the day. Armed with only four cans of McEwans from the satanic buffet and a sack of John Menzies confectionery, I took my seat in carriage D, where the seats stank of Superkings and desperation. I endured five hours of monotonous chugging, five hours of smoking and sweating while an endless army of small children ran screaming through the train, saving their especially piercing cries for me.

'Mum said I could have half the money!'

'I'm the oldest, so I'm in charge!'

'But you're gonna buy crisps, and I want juice!'

'They don't have any juice, now shut up!'

'They do so, I saw it!'

Whack.

'Ow . . . *Mum!*'

The parents, of course, were oblivious of the carriage carnage, too busy . . . well too busy being parents, really, to find time to give their kids some deserving slaps and smacks.

I sat there, and even the Daily Record couldn't offer a real distraction. However, it wasn't the kids, not really. It was Becky. I had to be on form for this . . . this girlfriend retrieval exercise. But there was no form for Roger. I lacked any form at all.

The bad thing about being fat (no, you're mistaken, it's not the terrified arteries, it's not the suicidal heart) is that you don't feel 'fat' all the time. Of course you don't. When life is going well, it's just some extra baggage you're carrying around, no big deal. But sometimes, oh brother, something important comes up, and you really need to be not-fat at that point. Getting Becky back was one of those moments. It seemed very important, as I sat wobbling through Newcastle, to be slim when I knocked on Becky's door in Hampstead. Then I looked appraisingly down at my gut, and there was a second of mild surprise, when I thought hey, where on earth did *that* come from? You don't get fat overnight. But you *find out* you're fat overnight. And it hadn't mattered before. 'You fat bastard.' Yeah? I don't care, pal, sticks and stones. But it started to matter on the train, really began to be a specific concern, as we whistled closer to Kings Cross and I stayed fat.

I got off the train feeling bloated and confused, so no change there. Then I slobbered through Kings Cross and took the geriatric Northern Line to Hampstead. Have you noticed how little London changes? Same old nonsense, why do you put up with it, Londoners, what are you thinking of?

Becky's house hadn't changed either. Well, one of the cars in the driveway was a different colour, but nothing else. No, the same old story. Of course I wondered (of course I did! Do you think I'm a total idiot?) about Becky's parent's, and how their attitude toward me had developed during the weeks following the split. It certainly did not look favourable, as I scrunched up the gravel path.

I knocked, knocking inside, knocking everywhere, and Becky's father opened the front door.

'Roger.' His voice – deep, resonant and bored – told me that he had never really liked me. Despite the G & Ts, rounds of flatulent Sunday morning golf, and business anecdotes, he had only barely tolerated my presence in his household.

My voice, on the other hand, was full of tremor, full of fright, full of want. 'Mister Sutton. I've come to . . . ah, it's just . . . Becky?'

'Rebecca.'

'Yes.' I looked down, suddenly sure that my shoelaces were untied. Then I remembered I was wearing slip-ons.

Mr. Sutton sighed. 'Wait here, Roger.'

'Right,' I said. 'Thanks. I really am—'

But the door was already shut.

We took a walk into Golders Green for lunch. Mrs Sutton's car was sitting expectantly in the driveway, but I guess the Beckster fancied some fresh air. I didn't ask. My legs weren't impressed, but I was on my best behaviour, sauntering along with pace and vigour.

We passed the Heath.

'Remember football?' I said. 'Remember cricket?'

We'd had a lot of fun, Becky, her mates and I. Two summers, after the Edinburgh Festival, we'd come down to Hampstead to enjoy the last of the North London sun.

Becky glanced over at the trees and lawns with their familiar Saturday morning inhabitants, walking, sprawling, laughing, and said nothing.

'Remember Frisbee?' I asked.

Becky kept her proud nose pointed North, and quickened her pace.

'Remember picnics?' I said, bouncing after her.

No answer. There was a stiffening in her shoulders.

'Remember—'

'Of course I bloody remember!' she shouted, spinning round and stopping me in my tracks. 'Just stop it, will you? Just stop.'

She wasn't crying, but she was close. I knew her well enough, recognised her taut contours, squinting eyes, thin lips, to understand that tears were not too far away. So I stopped it.

After a few minutes of silent torture we reached Finchley Road, and opted, with a nod and a grimace, for Cheers Wine Bar, our customary hole. A spot of lunch? Yes, why not, I see indigestion is on the menu.

The same arcade machine was by the door, and under normal circumstances I would have got the drinks in and then strolled over for a quick Fatal Fury, or even a Soccer Brawl, but not today. And I didn't even touch the jukebox I was so focused. We brushed past the decrepit regulars and walked up the steps to the higher level with its glaring track lights and low, chocolate bar ceiling.

We sat down. Opposite me was a large gilt-framed mirror, so I could see the back of Becky's exquisitely shaped head, and my fat, hungover, flop of a face. Becky's view was taken up by a black and white poster of a couple kissing: the blond Adonis, with his exposed torso, had abdominals on his abdominals. I made the comparison for her, and a tributary of sweat trickled and tickled down my spine.

'Fat Cat misses you.'

'Oh, Jesus.'

'Really, he's malingering, maudlin, morose—'

'Roger!'

'Well, he does.'

I lit a crucial cigarette. 'Drink?'

'Orange juice.'

'And . . . ?'

'Ice.'

'Ah. Right.'

I fetched the drinks, choosing a calming lager for myself, considering spirits to be too risky at this stage in proceedings. My hands were relatively shake-free, and it was with no little pride that I placed the glasses down on the checkered plastic tablecloth, with minimal spillage.

'There you go.'

Becky didn't look up, poring over the six item menu instead.

'What do you fancy?' I enquired.

She tapped near the bottom of the page.

'Yeah, good idea. I'll have that as well, I think.' I waved at the barmaid and ordered two Scampi & Chips.

When the food arrived, the Beckster picked and plucked, while I pillaged and plundered. After I had finished, appetite barely satisfied, but not wanting to seem like a hog, I let rip with a magnificent belch that I felt sure would break the ice quite nicely.

Instead, Becky looked up from her cold chips with a pinched expression.

She sighed. 'What is it that you want, exactly?'

I looked at her, aghast. Why was the message not getting through? 'You. I want . . . isn't it obvious? I want you.'

Becky snorted. 'Are you out of your *mind*?'

Not quite the reaction I was hoping for. 'How d'you mean?'

'You know how I mean,' Becky said between her teeth.

'No I don't. What're you talking about?'

'Chloe!' Becky almost shouted, 'You fucked Chloe!'

I lowered my head to the table, feeling the Cheers locals gaze at me with tabloid amusement.

'Chloe?' I whispered, 'Come on, there's no way . . . I already explained in the letters I sent you, I didn't . . . I didn't do it with anyone, least of all her, she terrifies me.'

'I never read your letters.'

'What?'

'I threw them out.'

'Why?'

'Because . . . well, why the hell not? Besides, I know

117

that you've been seeing other people since I left, Roger, although why anyone else would put up with a fat lump like you I've no idea.'

Well, there's an opening. 'If I was slimmer, would you come back to Edinburgh? I know I could afford to shed a few pounds. How much would I need to lose?'

But Becky wasn't listening. 'Did you seriously think that I wouldn't find out about all your goings on just because I'd moved back home? You idiot, I've got friends in Edinburgh, people willing to tell me the truth, people who don't want to stab me in the back. I know all about you, Roger, so don't pretend you want to get back together when you're acting like a total slag!'

Becky pushed back her chair and started to put her coat on. I stood up and reached for my wallet.

'Becky, I swear to God, I didn't sleep with Chloe, or anyone else but you.'

'You . . . fucking . . . *liar*.' Becky opened her handbag and put a five pound note on the table. 'That should cover mine.'

I fumbled in my wallet. 'No, don't be silly, I'm paying.'

But the Beckster pushed past me and headed for the door. 'No thanks. I don't want anything from you.'

I threw my money down and tried to go after her, but my jacket got caught in my chair. I untangled myself and ran out into Finchley Road in time to see Becky get into a taxi by the cinema. I stood on the pavement, lit a cigarette with shaking hands, and watched the taxi as it disappeared around the corner, taking my love object with it.

*   *   *

118

I got back on the Northern Line at Golders Green station, where the tracks are in the open air. They change drivers here so I was treated to a further five minute wait. It gave me time to remember how the Beckster hadn't smiled once during lunch, not the merest flicker. It used to be easy, making her smile. But my Becky credit had run out, someone had cut my Becky Card into four pieces, returning my love on a tarnished silver platter. Who was bad-mouthing me here? Who was doing me this awful damage where I could least afford it? Was it Chloe? But I hardly even knew the girl, why would she lie to Becky about me? Where's the motivation in that?

Finally we got moving, trundling briskly along, and in due course the train was sucked with a great *whoosh* into the black hole of the London Underground.

15

Chanel

Then there is the Community, concerned with the social cost of an company's actions in terms of pollution etc. This was rarely accounted for in traditional financial analyses, but is now of growing concern. This is a matter of business ethics, and will be discussed in Section 137. Failure to pay adequate attention to these issues could result in strategic weakness.

– *Business Strategy in the Twenty First Century*

JAY:
Ladies and gentlemen, I was going to tell you about this before but I simply never got around to it. It's rather trivial, but my not mentioning it might imply I was deliberately avoiding the topic. So here it is, although the bare facts shouldn't be particularly enthralling. Just events really, they bare no scars. Here they are in any case; after all, I'm sure that any details regarding the Wellesley dynasty are bound to be of some titillation to the peasants.

When I was seven-years-old my mother left home and never came back. Why should I say more? But it's not nearly enough to quench the commoners' thirst. Their unwashed minds need unwashed

details. Ah, I know my audience. Let's be expansive.
Let's be vulgar.

The 1970s. What could be more vulgar than that?
Glitter and socialism, punk and pierced flesh. Re-
bellion, class war, a Winter of Discontent. Two dire
insults, when the working class steal from Shakespeare and then from Dickens, holding up their
plates of inferiority, asking for more, more, more.
After all we had done, letting their children out
of chimneys, giving them dentists and opticians,
they wanted even more. Organised into rabbles they
called trade unions, they stopped collecting the rubbish, they stepped out of the mines. And what
for? What else could they possibly need? A Labour
government, their just desserts, kneeling before the
union leaders, taking away jobs, swapping pay pack-
ets for soaring inflation. A lesson in economic policy
that even the peasants understood and in 1979 order
was finally restored.

In December of 1978, in the middle of all that
turmoil, I returned from Shepperton School for Boys
to the family home for Christmas. A fine school, lucky
to have me of course, but fine nonetheless. Standards
have sadly dropped since I attended Shepperton,
however. A cluster of socially and economically unfortunate developments in our fair land has resulted
in Shepperton opening its' heavy oak doors to girls
and even those on the Assisted Places Scheme.
Tragic, but never let it be said that I live in the past.
Besides, once the governors realise their error I'm
sure that things will soon return to their traditional
form.

I was blissfully happy at school, treasured by both
my peers and the teachers. Academically brilliant and
an unbeatable sportsman, I set a supreme example
for others to follow. I remained modest throughout

my school years, however, never one to blow my own trumpet. My golden combination of talent and humility meant that it was my report card that the teachers rushed to be first to shower with praise, it was my bed that the boys clustered around after lights-out.

'Wow, Wellesley, you must be the brainiest boy in the whole school!'

'Undoubtedly.'

Graced with a reply, no matter how short and dismissive, the bravest of my dormitory colleagues would creep over to me, to seek nuggets of advice to solve their own floundering academic progress.

'How do you do it, Wellesley? How do you get to be so clever?'

'It's all very simple, my dear friend. And I can offer you some exclusive and discreet tutoring, for the right price, of course.'

Yes, happy days, but I was also relieved when holidays came around, keen to return to the beloved homestead and cast off the pressures of school champion.

Seven-years-old, when the buds of my potential were immature but ready to blossom in magnificent fashion, my train rattled festively into the station and I emerged from the first-class carriage, weighed down with exceptionally well-chosen gifts. My father stood on the platform, a dusting of light snow on his hat and shoulders, and I struggled over to him. He offered his hand, I put down my cases, and we shook hands, father and son. Gentlemen. My father could have sent his driver to collect me but that would have been truly bad form.

He looked me up and down, looking for growth, for profit and loss.

'I trust the term went well, Jason?'

I nodded vigorously. 'It was perfect, Father, I'm winning at everything!'

'Good, good. Still, room for improvement, I'm sure. Now let's find the car before we freeze to death.'

I sat in the front seat of the forest green Jag, full of Christmas jitters, nervously self-contained, while my father drove in calm silence. Even back then, I admired his ability to stay cool under demanding circumstances. We arrived at the house in good time and I ran up the steps to the front door, expecting my mother to pull it open, smiling, smelling sweetly of Chanel, as she had always done before. Instead the door stayed shut, until my father caught up with me and turned his key in the lock. Pausing briefly to knock the snow from his shoes, he stepped across the threshold and went into the drawing room. I put my things down in the hall and followed him. The room was dark, lit only by the coal fire, cracking and spitting, trying to escape onto the polished wooden floor. My father was standing by the fireplace, his hat and coat lying over an armchair. I walked over and stood beside him, feeling the heat of the fire against my legs.

He spoke straightforwardly. Matter-of-factly, which was sensible of him.

'Now, Jason, I'm going to have a grown-up chat with you, so I don't want any sulking, or any other nonsense, understood?'

'Yes, Father,' I replied, excited by the elevation in my status.

He cleared his throat. 'There has been a disagreement – no, more like an adult discussion – and it has been decided that your mother should leave. It has been decided. She will not be coming back.'

I smiled uncertainly, chilled, despite the crackling fire. I looked away and saw our shadows dancing on the opposite wall. I thought to myself that these black versions of ourselves, they were so distorted, so bent out of shape, how could we be certain that they were really ours? Then I looked up at my father.

'May I be excused? I'm rather tired, and I need to unpack.'

He nodded. 'I shall call you when it's time for supper.'

I scurried upstairs to my bedroom, noting only then the lack of seasonal flowers in the hall, the absence of festive decorations anywhere in the house. I opened my cases, putting my unwashed clothes into the laundry basket, arranging my school-books methodically along the shelves. My parents' Christmas presents were cocooned securely in the centre of my case. I held them against my chest, feeling the start of an unknown illness, possibly just a stomach ache, then I put them under my bed, the usual hiding place, safe from over-curious mothers and fathers. Fathers. Father.

Quietly, already guiltily, I walked though to my parents' bedroom and turned on the main light. Looking around the room I thought at first that it was larger than before, but then I realised it just had fewer things in it. The doublebed, the bookcase that contained far more sophisticated texts than my own, these pieces of furniture remained. The dressing table, however, was gone, and there was only a single chair by the window. I crept over to the wardrobe and opened the door, finding suits and shirts, socks and ties. Only my father's clothes, spaced evenly throughout the wardrobe, as if hoping to conceal the absence of dresses and high-heeled shoes.

I closed the door and walked over to where my mother's dressing table used to stand. No more clutter of foundation and lipstick, jewellery and hairbrushes. As I stood there, I was sure I could still smell her perfume, just as I had when she kissed me goodnight. I was sure I could still smell my mother. A single concern, that I would never again see my mother put on her make-up – red on her lips, blush on her cheeks, the delicious ritual – gave me something, a peach-stone in my throat, making it hard to swallow. I gulped, deafening in the silence, and my eyes stung.

'Jason?'

My father's voice, crisp and authoritative from the dining room, broke the spell.

'Yes?'

'It's time for supper. Have you washed your hands?'

'I'm doing it now,' I replied.

I walked out of his bedroom, across the landing and into the bathroom. I washed my hands, checked my fingernails, and went downstairs to supper.

There were no hot rages, no wet bedclothes. I allowed myself a few cold tears, out of loyalty, out of loss. I kept the Christmas present I had bought for my mother: Chanel, as if she didn't have enough already. During weak moments, I would take it out of its box and spray some scent on my wrists, as I had seen her do. Sparingly, as she had done. Months later, when the bottle was finished, I didn't buy another one. By that time I had no further need for such childish comforts.

I was an only child. I am an only child. I am a broken family. Single parent, but my father had no difficulty in paying the mortgage, the school fees, the skiing holidays. Life went on, lighter, quieter, and my father remained single. He had no cause for secret girlfriends, hidden away in guestrooms; he had his son, which was fulfilment enough. Life went on, and my mother faded away. She yellowed at the edges, and it wasn't long before her face blurred in my mind, blurred to nothing.

With the benefit of adult hindsight, I'm glad she left. Like my father indicated at the time, she simply wasn't up to the job. I have none of her inferior genes, I truly am a chip off the old block. I am my father's son. That is all I need. You want me to be angry, you want me to be scarred. But there is nothing to heal, no nightmares to soothe away. I bear no grudge towards my mother, I have no memory of her. Photos were removed, relatives and friends informed, there was nothing more to say. My formative years, under her incompetent wing, they are a blank page. And I have no need to find her now, to search for those years. My lost time is efficiency, not a shield. I need space in my brain to remember important matters, such as bank details and telephone numbers.

If she were to come back and find me (and this is not something I often think about) perhaps we would go for coffee and discuss her maternal inadequacies.

'You don't know the whole story,' she might say. 'Let me explain, Jason, let me tell you what your father left out.'

But it would be too late for excuses, for exotic inventions.

'My name is Jay,' I might reply, gaining satisfaction from the look on her crumpled face. 'You don't deserve a son, you don't have one anymore. You'd better forget all about me.'

Then I would bid her farewell once more, back to a life more suitable for someone of her reduced standing. Perhaps she is a secretary, or even a teacher. As I said, I rarely think about it. These so-called broken families, demanding sympathy, reaching out for recompense; I don't know why they make such a fuss, I swear.

All is well at Buddies. The show opened without a hitch. Even a last-minute drop-out, an actress who shall never work in this town again, was solved by my astute drafting of Tara into her place. It isn't a large part, a line here, an exit there, more spear-holding, less speaking. An intensive bout of instruction ensured that Tara was up to scratch; competent, no more, no less.

'Do you really think I'll be all right?' she asks, after crashing about the stage and squeaking out her lines.

I smile encouragingly. I've given Tara so many encouraging smiles in recent days my face is starting to ache.

'A fabulous director doesn't make casting mistakes, Tara. He makes sure that every single performer makes the grade before opening night. Now do you think that I'm a fabulous director?'

'Oh, yes!' she cries. 'You're wonderful!'

'Well, then.' I hold her quivering hands in my own, passing on my strength. 'There's your answer.'

Of course now that she has experience of how utterly crushing theatre work can be, she will scurry back into her hole and I will not have to bother with the tedious chore of bumping her.

Roger came back from Hampstead, admitting defeat, tail between his legs. He is back in producer-mode, back where I need him. Sausage-fingers pressing telephone buttons, calling the press, calling the money. He does these things so adequately, I'm glad I took pity on him after graduation and gave him a job. Where would he be now if I hadn't taken him under my wing? Accountancy? Banking? I've saved him from his tedious fate, and he's paying me back, deal by deal, contract by contract. Roger solves the little problems, allowing me to provide the big picture.

Evening, half an hour before curtain. The cast gossip and stretch, slipping into their costumes, fitting into their roles. I listen with mild contempt to their rumours and statistics.

'We've sold out, they're turning people away, this thing could run and run!'

'No, it can't, it'll get canned before the Fringe, and you know it.'

'But I heard that we might tour it to Glasgow, they're desperate for stuff in August over there!'

'It's a Buddies show, it isn't going anywhere. Besides, I'm going to Corfu in August.'

Oh, dear. Corfu, indeed. Actors aren't artists, they're just double-glazing salesmen with make-up.

The lighting fellow, safe in the tech box, fiddles with the lighting, casting colours and shadows onto the stage. Roger and I sit in the front row, talking shop, the excited murmur of tonight's audience filtering through from the cafe, our audio backdrop. Oh yes. And Chloe's here as well. Her sense of timing is abysmal; in the early days of a Buddies run Roger only has theatre on his mind. As soon as Roger goes into the office I shall have some sharp words with her.

'I read *The Scotsman* review.' she says, a saccharin smile (about five hundred times sweeter than sugar but with no energy value) playing on her lips. 'You're lucky to have Alasdair on your side.'

'Alasdair is only on the side of artistic truth,' I say sharply. 'He is the most honest critic in Edinburgh.

Our social link is of no consequence when it comes to business.'

Chloe raises a theatrical eyebrow, perhaps she too is interested in auditioning for a future role. Then she turns her guns on poor Roger. 'So how's life after Rebecca?'

Roger shifts in his seat, no doubt looking for the ejector button. 'Okay. Well, you know.'

Now that's not really enough, is it? It won't do for Chloe to have her hopes dashed at this early stage. I put a fatherly hand on Roger's shoulder. 'Don't be modest, Mr. Brown. He's been a tower of strength, Chloe, he's shown the utmost powers of recuperation. I firmly believe, now that he's accepted that the runaway Rebecca has gone for good, he is fully on the way to romantic recovery.'

Looking optimistic and slightly confused at the same time, Chloe looks to Roger for confirmation.

'Well,' he says, 'I suppose I know that Becky isn't coming home. The trip down to Hampstead kind of didn't go the way I thought it would. You know I thought once she saw me, once we talked, that everything would be all right again. I guess I just thought we were fated to be together.'

'There's no such thing as fate,' I say, fishing around for Peter Stuyvesant, 'Sometimes events and people get in the way, but careful planning will ensure that we always get what we want.' I give Chloe a subtle wink. 'Destiny is what you make it, Roger, but your future is clearly a Rebecca-less one.'

Roger nods, round shoulders, long face, and Chloe charges on, a bull in a china shop. 'I don't suppose you've got anyone to take to the wedding next Saturday.'

'Not really,' says Roger.

'Well,' says Chloe, fit to burst, 'why don't we go

together? Weddings are far more fun when you're with someone, don't you think?'

Chloe's horns are going to cause serious damage if she isn't careful. Where's her pace, where's her sense of threeplay?

Roger shakes his head. 'I don't think—'

'You'll only be going as friends,' I say quickly, 'it can't possibly do any harm. I think it's a wonderful idea, well done, Chloe.'

She beams, innocence personified, and Roger shrugs. 'I guess I'll think about it,' he says, which means that it's a done deal.

So now all is right in the world. I want to run through the streets of Edinburgh, ringing my bell, declaring the city safe once more. Roger is back at Buddies for good, and Rebecca will soon be a distant memory. My trusty producer, young free and single; Chloe will soon get what she wants. Everything is coming together. But there will be no respite between now and the Edinburgh Festival. Now I have bigger rainbow trout to fry; Alasdair and his model. I shall make them twist and turn, I shall knock their heads together. And when the smoke clears, I shall take the miraculous Marianne as my deserved prize. Yes, ladies and gentlemen, there's no need to adjust your set. Everything is going to be just dandy.

16

Tokyo

ALASDAIR:

I'll tell you why I never get any. I'll explain why I never come close. It's my skin.

There's something wrong with my complexion. It lurches to and fro, from bad to worse, from awful to outrageous. It won't stand still, it fluctuates more often than the Scottish weather, and the forecast is always cloudy, dark skies on the epidermis horizon. All I want is some consistency, something to get used to.

I believed, before I got wise, that the skin served a natural purpose: a tough, flexible waterproof covering of the human body. Very naïve, I know. I'm smarter these days, my turn of the millennium wisdom tells me that my skin doesn't help me at all. Instead it holds me back, keeps other people away, keeps us apart. When you meet someone, the skin is the first thing you see, and it tells you so much about them. Dry, greasy, combination? Acne, moles, scars, blemishes? Does it shine with health, or is it dull and lifeless? Come on, how can I get into threeplay, how can I even begin, the odds are stacked against me as soon as we make eye contact. I would like to say, of course, that I can overcome this bias, that it's no skin off my nose, but that would be a lie. I'm not strong enough to turn the other cheek, far better not to face up to people at all.

I've tried everything, every product there is. Week after week I scan the shelves for a life-saver, hoping for a magic potion to make me human. I stand in the queue at Boots (they know my face there, the assistants chat and try to open me up) with yet another expensive mistake and I offer my Switch card with a cough and a blush. L'Oreal, Clarins, Almay, I know what I'd like to say.

'It's for my girlfriend. She didn't have time to go shopping. No, look, she gave me a list, see? No, seriously.'

But I couldn't pull it off, they'd never believe me. Why should they? Would you? Toners, cleansers, peels, replenishers, triple AHAs, my bathroom cabinet is worth more than my hi-fi. I should stop, get a handle on things, get a life, but how can I? When I'm so handicapped, so handcuffed, how can I get ahead?

Marianne helps. She's in the business, after all, of looking good. I drag her through Jenners, asking her opinion on the latest offerings, and she'll do her best not to dash my hopes all over the Clinique concession. Then we go for hot chocolate, and I try and think about something else. Of course, you might think that Marianne isn't the best choice of companion, given my unrealisable lust and her perfect face. But I like to look at her skin. I search out people with pure complexions, I can pretend I'm looking into a mirror. It's my fetish, if I have one: I can't begin to tell you how disappointing watching my first skin-flick was.

Like the blind, the deaf, the wheelchair-bound, I'm an expert on my disability, and Marianne feeds my addiction for tips and fads, straight from the horses' mouth, so to speak. She drops the information, random and exquisite, and I store it all for a day when I'll be clear enough to use it.

I could give Roger diet tips, for example. Going to a cocktail party? Load ice (it'll razz up your metabolism) and lemon (shrinks your stomach) in your drink and you won't eat as many nibbles. And a two-day diet: no salt, no bread, and garlic and papaya tablets before each meal: this breaks down fat, and acts as a natural diuretic.

Want to ensure your make-up lasts? Have a bath: the steam sets the foundation. Tired eyes? Put a cold spoon over the eye. Feeling flabby? Egg white is an inexpensive face-lift. And the best face-lift, the one that made sure I never looked at a supermodel the same way again: haemorrhoid cream. It's true, I swear to God. The cream shrinks your piles, which is skin, so it'll shrink your chin and the bags under your eyes too. This is what Marianne tells me. She says that all models know about this stuff. They're not all rich, she says, many of them have to economise just like everyone else. You don't need some expensive cellulite treatment; just use clay cat litter, it's the same thing. Lemon juice is a toner, almond oil is a moisturiser, fine oatmeal and oil is an exfoliator. Burnt toast and Colgate is a tooth whitener.

Find a model and ask them; they'll tell you the same thing, if you ask nicely enough. Think of fashion models, look in *Vogue*. They're all wearing food, they're all staying beautiful on the cheap. The wannabes, the high street desperadoes, they're the only people who actually buy the junk advertised as the next big thing. And me, of course. I still spend my money unwisely, despite knowing the truth. I'm still looking for the potion, the miracle breakthrough. I know it's stupid, but I have to keep the faith. You think I'm making too much of this. But don't you see, I'm just trying to save face. Besides, there's no way I'm putting Preparation H anywhere near my mouth.

*   *   *

'Do you think I should go?' asked Mari.

'No, you should stay in Edinburgh and be my constant companion for the next three months. Drink hot chocolate for ninety days and ninety nights. Of course you should go!'

We were sitting in the Merlin, as per usual, our hot chocolates topped with whipped cream and penetrated by a Cadbury's Chocolate Flake.

'Will ya miss me?' she asked, fluttering her eyelids like my little coquette.

'Like the deserts miss the rain. Like the desserts miss the rain, for that matter.'

'Clever Dick. You can write me letters. You write the best letters.'

'Consider me flattered' I said, flattered.

'So you think I should go?'

'Jesus, yes yes yes!'

'Well, you know I rely on your opinion.'

'Of course you do. And what do I get out of it in return? Not much! I tell you, this friendship is seriously off kilter.'

'Oh really,' said Mari, 'So apart from being seen with a beautiful model, what else would you like?'

(True, I do get a kick out of being seen with her. The shallow truth is that I prefer having attractive friends, I always feel that I'm having a better time. Social aesthetics are so important, don't you think?)

'Well, for my sensational friendship value I deserve at least a few small sexual favours.'

'Really? I wasn't aware of this rule. What do you want – a loyalty blow job?'

Loyalty Blow Job. Sounds good. Sounds like something banks should try. Better than record tokens, anyway.

'Be careful what you offer, Mari, I might just take you up on it.'

'That wasn't an offer. Besides, be careful what you ask for, you might just get it.'

'Was that a threat?' I asked.

'Just a friendly warning,' and she did something startling with her chocolate flake.

I looked around the bar, and couldn't decide whether no one was watching her or if everyone was trying very hard to look without appearing to.

She grinned at me from an odd angle, and I blushed at her squint face.

'I can play with you, Alasdair, can't I? That's what I like about you, my little mouse.'

'Rodent,' I countered.

'No,' cooed Mari, 'My nice little mousie. I could take you anywhere, my portable friend, my platonic Gameboy.'

'Hey, I'm at least a N64.'

'Come to think of it, your graphics are very impressive. You're my little CD-ROM, how about that?'

'No good.'

'How come?'

'I'm only compatible with your hardware.'

Mari barked a laugh which staggered violently around the bar. 'Holy shit! I'm out-gunned, out-punned, by an Edinburgh hack!'

'What would you do all day, Mari, if you didn't have me to abuse?'

'Oh darling Alasdair, if you didn't exist, I'd have to invent you.'

'That's reassuring.'

Mari laughed in polite appreciation of my sarcasm, and I forgave her for being such a silly bitch. I assumed this conversation was over, always the verbal optimist. You see, chatting with Marianne had a habit of turning into a serious wag about my problems with life, love and sex. Every time I would make a supreme effort to steer her away from discussing my inadequacies, but she seemed obsessed with sorting out my existence, or lack of it. This time, however, I thought the ordeal was over. She finished the abused remains of her flake and lauded praise over her hot chocolate.

'Hot chocolate. That's great. It's hot, and there's chocolate in it. What a great idea! These are the people who should be leading this country, people who invent things like hot chocolate.'

'And Marlboro Lights?'

'Yeah! Sure, I know lights are a rip off, but it means I can smoke more, I can actually smoke more often, and the action of smoking is half the pleasure. Jesus, I tell you every little thought I have, as soon as it jumps into my head. You should be a reporter!'

Mari contemplated her hot chocolate, and I guessed that she was thinking about Tokyo. She made plenty of money working in Europe, but Japan would be a fantastic break for her. I rather belatedly realised how excited and nervous she must be, and racked my brain for something wise and encouraging to say.

Mari had a very serious expression on her face, stirring her hot chocolate with unnecessary firmness, in my opinion. I tried to think of something sedate and calming to say.

Then there was a tenseness in her lips, it combined with the look in her eyes, she was set to start crying, a serious weep session. I searched frantically for, God, anything to say.

Then Marianne started to laugh. Was it hysteria? No, just something she found highly amusing. It was a tight laugh for once, more shake than noise, tears burst out of her eyes and rolled snail-like down silk cheeks, leaving black mascara trails. I groaned, knowing it was something to do with me.

'Sorry!' Mari gasped, 'I'm too awful, I know.' Then she was off again, shuddering with laughter. How funny could this possibly be?

'Come on, Marianne, share the joke with the rest of the class.'

'Right, sorry. God that hurts. It's just that, okay, I'm going to be serious now.' She took a few deep breaths in an effort to regain her composure. 'Actually it's not that funny.'

'Mari, for fuck's sake—'

'Okay, okay, someone, the other day, well, he said that I should . . . seduce you.'

Recovered, Mari looked at me with a mild smirk. I took whatever comfort I could from the fact that her make-up was wrecked.

Someone.

'It wasn't Jay, by any chance?'

'How did you guess?'

'A wild stab in the subconscious.'

'He called me up, out of the blue. Strangest thing. Said it would bring you out of your shell,' she said, adding detail to injury.

I looked at her, and played my part, determined not to let her see that her words had crushed me yet again. 'My shell's fine, thanks very much. All mod cons. I certainly have no intention of moving out.'

'Well, you could at least build an extension.'

'The council wouldn't let me. It's a listed shell.'

Mari tried again, as if the metaphor hadn't been stretched to absurdity already. 'Well, how about a new pair of curtains? John Lewis has some very nice material.'

'Look, Mari, I appreciate the concern, but I'm happy with way things are.'

She didn't look convinced.

'Seriously, I'm delighted with the status quo. Ecstatic.'

'Oh Alasdair . . .' Mari looked at me with affectionate concern.

'Oh Alasdair what?'

'Well, don't you think it would be good if you had a bit of a fling?'

Suddenly the option of shouting in her streaked face seemed like a fine idea. 'A fling? A *fling*?! Maybe I don't want to have a fucking fling!'

'Hey, I'm your friend, remember me? I'm just saying—'

'Anyway, what happened to your liking men who weren't sexually threatening?'

'I meant that I didn't like men coming on strong to me, I wasn't asking you to be a monk.'

'Thanks very much.' What a bitch. I felt the telltale jaw clench that meant I was close to ridiculous tears.

'Alasdair, I'm sorry. All I'm saying here is that you should get a little romance in your life. A little sexual frission, spice things up a little. You're a young guy, you should be out there breaking hearts instead of acting like you're married.'

I was trying to sulk, but the cow made me smile, saying that.

Encouraged, Mari mapped out my life for the next month. 'Okay, your mission, if you choose to accept it, is to achieve some sort of romantic attachment by the time I get back from Tokyo.'

'Fine, whatever.'

I would have agreed to anything in order to change the subject, but this was Mission Impossible, and we both knew it.

'It doesn't have to be the relationship of the century,' said Mari, warming to the topic, 'just something fun. These things *can* be fun, you know!'

'I know.'

We smiled at each other. Maybe she's not so bad.

'Get laid at least. It'll do wonders for your complexion. That reminds me, how do I look?'

Sweet revenge.

'Panda eyes,' I said as gently as I could.

'Shit!' Mari whined unhappily as she looked in her make-up mirror and surveyed the damage her tears of laughter had inflicted. I had limited sympathy.

'Serves you right for laughing at a cripple.'

'How d'you mean?'

'Didn't you know? I'm a sexual spastic.'

Mari dropped her mirror into her hot chocolate she laughed so hard.

And there it is. Jay was playing with me all along. I'm such an idiot. To believe that Mari would be interested in me, to believe that Jay was anything other than a manipulative asshole. Jay, the Grand Manipulator. There's a touch of Dostoyevsky, right there. Jay, if I can find a way to get you back for this, I promise you I will. I promise you, I'm really going to fuck you up.

Act II

GETTING BETTER

17

Marriage, And Other Dirty Tricks

Clearly the acceptability of strategies to the key
players should be a key consideration during the
formulation and evaluation of new strategies.

Often the most difficult stakeholders are those
in segment H. Although these stakeholders
might be relatively passive, stakeholder groups
tend to emerge and influence strategy as a result
of specific events. It is therefore very important
that the likely reaction of stakeholders towards
future strategies is given the utmost consideration. Damaging situations can arise if their level
of interest is underestimated and they rise to
frustrate the developing of a new strategy.
– *Business Strategy in the Twenty First Century*

JAY:
The social event of the year? The summer? The day?
Well, who knows what place this particular episode
will have in Edinburgh's cultural history texts. But if
you ask me, this is just another Scottish wedding, full
of accents, nervous flatulence, and an insufferable
ceilidh. The happy couple deserve no introduction;
they're not important, they really have no bearing on
my grand designs. I was certainly relieved during
the overly-Christian service, however, to see that the

bride was no shining beauty. Always such a shame, don't you think, to see a pretty girl snatched up in such tedious fashion by a conservative fool, only to be burped back up, weighed down by baggage, during the inevitable divorce proceedings.

Weddings always make me cry. Such a waste of money, such a waste of flesh. I sit on the lavatory, weeping hot tears, mourning the loss of what might have been. Then I wash my face and join the wedding party, sniffing out fresh, untainted blood.

'No sign of Becky, then?' Alasdair asks. His wedding etiquette suddenly comes under close scrutiny.

Roger gives a little twitch, and his chins ripple like a pink waterbed. 'There's still time,' he says. He turns to me. 'There's still time, isn't there Jay?'

I smile benevolently across the table. 'There's *always* time, Mr. Brown, but I fear the charming Rebecca may have chosen not to attend this particular event on the social calendar.' I bend towards him, taking advantage of Tara's momentary absence from the table. 'If you'd only taken my advice and invited Chloe, then you wouldn't be sitting there like the last chocolate in the box.'

Veronica, sitting beside Alasdair but scoping the hall for potential one-night scrambles, gives a less than attractive snort of laughter.

'Come here with Chloe when Becky thinks we've slept together?' whispers Roger. 'Are you nuts? Besides, why would she want to?'

I lower my voice, cutting the venomous Veronica out of our tete-a-tete. 'I've told you before Roger. Chloe likes her men on the large side and you more than fit the bill. Now she's here somewhere, so why don't you two get together for some light relief? It'd be a great pre-Fringe stress reliever and Rebecca would be none the wiser.'

'She bloody would! She's got spies everywhere. Besides, I don't want to do anything with Chloe, she's not my type.'

I groan with just the right degree of pique. 'Type? This isn't about brand names, Roger, this isn't about variations on a theme. You have to try different things.' I take a sip from the limp, inexcusable wine that I've paid for with a Kenwood bread-maker. 'Besides, after being with Rebecca for so long, how could you possibly know what you want in a woman? Your senses are dulled, your reactions are blunted. Just take my advice and give Chloe a try, it's just the spark of fresh vitality you need. Who knows, you might discover that Rebecca isn't worth chasing after all? Of course . . .' and I sit back in my chair, 'if you're not interested in the well-meaning advice of an old friend, then I won't bore you with another word.'

Roger leans across the table, risking a cheap sauce stain on his Marks and Spencer shirt. 'No, it's not like that! You know I appreciate everything you're doing, Jay. I'd be lost without you.'

I nod, still wounded to the core, of course. Perhaps events will turn my way after all.

'Well, I'm not one to take offence. Say, why did you order the chicken when beef was surely the correct option?'

'You talking about me, lover?' Tara marks her entrance with a hand on my shoulder, then she sits down beside me and does battle with a predictably stale bread roll, knife against concrete.

'Only indirectly, my sweet.' Alasdair looks at me with a definite smirk, and I make up my mind to utterly humiliate him in some fashion before the day is out.

*   *   *

Chloe didn't sit at our table. I asked her not to, so she didn't. That is how life works, when the remote control is in my sure grasp. Chloe and I, we had an important matter to discuss in private. We find each other between meal and dance, a pre-arranged corner, clandestine.

'What a delightful dress, my dear. You look positively ravishing this afternoon.'

Chloe plucks at her cotton mistake, pleased for a moment, then looks me in the eye. 'So are we all set, then?'

Ah yes. Direct and to the point, Chloe doesn't mess about, which is why I'm able to tolerate her presence.

'Well, I've done my best, but you can't expect me to do all the work. I've set the stage, the rest is up to you.'

'What's that supposed to mean?' Chloe says. She pouts, and what a pout! I can see how it might work, on a man weaker than myself. Roger, for instance.

I lay gentle hands on her waist. 'It means that I've talked to him, and he's very much aware that you're hoping for a meeting of minds, so to speak.'

Chloe looks up at me, wrinkling her nose in distaste. 'It's not his mind I'm after, Jay.'

I laugh, patting her firm behind with discreet fingers. 'Don't worry. The seed has most definitely been planted, I'm sure you'll find him to be receptive. He just needs a little push in the right direction and you're just the girl to do it.'

'Damn right,' says Chloe, putting her arms around me. 'I'm the cat's fucking pyjamas.'

'You know it amazes me that you were such good friends with Becky, you're chalk and cheese, you really are.'

'Amen to that.'

We look at each other, almost nose to nose, almost

out of focus, and I think that I might kiss her, just out of interest, just for effect.

'Jay?' Tara's voice, her diabolical timing for the second time today, and I whip around to see her walking towards me, a grinning Alasdair by her side. Someone really ought to do something about that fellow. My partner in crime coughs and examines her nail polish, leaving me to do the introductions.

'Hello, love. Have you met Chloe, a very good, very old friend of mine?'

'I've seen her around, yes,' says Tara, vague suspicion shadowing her features. Then she brightens. 'Hey, I've been telling Alasdair about our plans for Buddies and the Fringe. He was very impressed, weren't you Alasdair?'

'Oh yes,' says Alasdair, 'it all sounds very . . . ambitious.'

'Now Tara my dear, it's not good form informing the press of our plans before everything is finalised.'

'We were just *talking*,' she whines, and Alasdair nods his agreement.

'You're secret's safe with me,' he says, making Tara beam once more.

'There, you see? I didn't do anything wrong.'

'I'll leave you to it,' says Alasdair, leaving me with what is, for once, an inscrutable expression.

'Wait for me!' Chloe scampers after him, on the hunt for Mr. Brown. I watch her go, and surmise that Roger doesn't stand a chance. Not fair at all, really, not one bit.

Tara stands as tall as she's able; hands on hips, face jutting out at me. 'You weren't being naughty with that girl, were you?'

'Define naughty. No, of course not. We were just talking, like you and Alasdair. Why, don't you trust me?'

'I've heard about your track record, Jay, and I wouldn't put anything past you, especially at a wedding.'

I smile at her, the silly bitch. 'Don't panic, love. Chloe has eyes for only one man, and it certainly isn't me. Now let's go and have a dance.'

'Oh.' Tara stands at ease, the wind taken out of her tantrum sails. She's disappointed, visibly annoyed, at not getting a row out of this. 'Well, you were gone at least half an hour, is that how couples treat each other where you come from?'

'More like ten minutes. Besides, you had Superhack to keep you entertained, and Chloe needed some advice. We're old friends, for goodness sake. So will you dance with me?'

Tara scowls, determined to quarrel; someone should tell her how uncomplimentary that looks. 'Honestly, Jay, didn't your mother teach you any manners? You really . . .'

And she says something else – I see her scarlet lips moving up, down and around, a suffocating old trout – but I can't hear her. The world is bleached, as I use all my powers of restraint to keep from hitting her. And not a slap; a real crack across the face, broken bones, to stop her talking for ever. To stop her mentioning my mother. I grab her by the arm.

'Come on.'

'Ow! Where are we going?'

'Out. Wherever you want, I'm sick of this damn wedding, let's go.'

'Jay, you're hurting me! What about the dance? And where's your jacket?'

I let go of her arm and keep walking, down the hallway and into the lounge, out the front door and towards the taxi rank. Tara can follow me if she wants, no one's stopping her.

148

18

Chloe

A suspected road rage incident is being treated as attempted murder after an assault in the city centre left a man fighting for his life. The victim, 24, stopped his red car in St Andrews Square on Wednesday evening to remonstrate with a black man in a blue car. He was hit twice on the head with an unidentified weapon.

Police stress the motive may not have been a driving dispute.

– *Evening News*

ROGER:

I 'phoned Becky to ask her if she was coming to the wedding. I spoke to Mr. Sutton, father and guardian, and said that it was very important that I speak to his daughter. He let me speak to her, with a sigh and a caution. We'd received the invitation months ago, addressed to Becky, but everything was different then. No, she said, sounding distracted, sounding very far away. No, she wasn't coming up for the wedding. I put the 'phone down and ran through my flat, throwing out rubbers, disposing of lubricants, massage oils. My place is monkified, and with a twist of a key I made sure that Becky's was too, sneaking into her flat and removing all traces of contraception and STD protection.

Weddings. There's a lot of them around these days, it must be my age. Friends from university, they're dropping like flies, ha ha. And Scottish weddings, with their guarantee of bad weather and frightening celidhs. It's the one thing we have in common, Jay, Alasdair and me, apart from theatre; our mutual hatred of Scottish dancing. Jay finds it most uncouth, all that sweating and shouting, and I just can't do any of it, treading on vulnerable feet and losing my North and South. Now Alasdair, you might think, he's Scottish, he has to like them, but no. A strict wallflower at the common garden-variety disco, he's hardly like to strut his stuff at something as raucous as a ceilidh.

The actual service was a little too religious for my taste. I know they're supposed to mention God at some point, I know the drill all right, but these guys were out of control. The minister, he was one manic preacher.

'I'm so happy to see all of you here today, to help this young couple as they start on their journey through life, and I'm sure you wish them every happiness. But our loving support and guidance does not stop today. We must help them, as we help each other, through the rough spots that occur in any marriage. In today's society, with its moral disintegration and loss of virtue, we must be extra vigilant in our reinforcement of Biblical teachings.'

I think he was proposing a Holy Neighbourhood Watch. And hand gestures? Oh yes, he was creating his own wind tunnel up there. A fervent sermon, to say the least; he could give even the unconventional vegetarian a run for her money. The basic premise was that all divorcees burned in hell at the Devil's leisure, and I saw more than one frightened expression on the faces of the congregation.

'Can you feel the heat? For temptation is all around us! I implore you all, do your utmost to keep this loving couple out of Satan's clutches!'

Great voice projection though, I'll give him that.

A lot of the wedding guests were in on the act too. A lot of gratuitous 'Amens', a lot of mad staring eyes. And during the hymns, I kid you not, they would get so excited they would raise their arms in the air, grinning like maniacs, singing like the possessed. I ask you, is this normal? I glanced over at Jay to gauge his reaction, but he was stone-faced; clearly his mind was on other matters. Lucky for Jay; at least he won't have nightmares.

But don't get me wrong. I like weddings, overall. I'd like one of my own, to be honest. If Becky came back today (she won't, of course, I asked her) then I'd definitely propose. Not right away, I mean I'd let her get her feet in the door, see Fat Cat, have a cup of tea. But soon. This is what I thought about when the bride and groom were exchanging vows.

Down on one knee in the sitting room, with Fat Cat there for moral support.

'Becky, I think . . . well, you see, perhaps if you're not too busy, and I mean, as I love you and every-thing, maybe you'd like to marry me?'

Yes, something like that, nice and slick.

And she'd laugh, and cry, and get down on the floor with me.

'Oh, Tiger, I've been waiting so long for you to ask me! This is the happiest day of my life!'

And then, of course, she would say yes.

This is what I thought about, and this fantasy has enough material to last me for weeks.

When we got to the meal, a presumed safe-haven from bibles and lessons, a frightening-looking man with unfeasible eyebrows and a beard that could slice bread was called upon to say Grace, and that lasted for days.

'Before we begin to enjoy this veritable feast, it is of course important to say a few words of thanks . . .'

Tick, tick, tick.

'And now I would like talk about God.'

Oh, dear. I felt myself wasting away as he droned on and on, and by the time he had finished I was amazed there was anything left of me.

'And finally I hope you'll join me in a short prayer.'

Well that goes without saying, I suppose, but it still came as an almost mortal blow, and it was only through supreme will power that I avoided diving into the soup tureen.

The food was great, though. I chose chicken instead of beef. It wasn't about mad cows, I'm sure it's far too late in the day to do anything about that. A more radical move, really – I'm trying to make real changes in my life. I'm trying to . . . no, I won't talk about that now, just in case things don't work out. I don't want to end up with egg on my face.

We all sat at the same table, the only person missing was Becky. And Tara was the new addition, ignorant to most of the in-jokes but catching up fast. I sat opposite Jay, who was a rather limited footsie partner, and in-between Alasdair and Veronica (I haven't fucked her either, by the way, so I guess that makes two of us). Tara demanded Jay's attention as soon as we sat down, so I ploughed through the chicken, which was delightful apart from a dubious sauce even I couldn't stomach, then set about the red with a passion.

After the first bottle, with Tara's chattering finally dulled, I felt a hand on my knee.

'I like a man who can hold his drink,' said

Veronica, with what I suppose was meant to be a demure smile. Oh Jesus.

'Oh,' I said, 'actually I'm terrible with alcohol, one sniff of the barmaid's apron and all that. I tell you, by the end of the next bottle I'll be in serious trouble. I'd stay well back if I were you, I wouldn't want to get any puke on your outfit when the inevitable happens.'

The hand was removed from my knee with impressive speed, and I turned to Alasdair. 'So Marianne couldn't make it then?'

'She's working in London this weekend, then she's back for a rest before the Tokyo trip.'

'Right.'

'What's this about Tokyo?' Jay turned away from Tara in mid-sentence, and she went off to sulk in the toilets.

'Mari's going there for a month, she's got a contract.'

'I see. I was under the impression the Japanese only wanted blondes.'

Alasdair shrugged. 'I don't know. Maybe she'll dye her hair.'

'Maybe,' said Jay, rubbing his chin. 'So when does she leave?'

'A week on Sunday,' said Alasdair. 'Why the sudden interest?'

'But she'll be in Edinburgh next Saturday, yes?'

'Yeah, I suppose so. Why all the questions?'

But for Jay the conversation was over, and he produced a pack of Peter Stuyvesants from his trouser pocket. 'Post-meal, pre-indigestion cigarette, Roger?'

I shifted nervously in my seat. 'Ah, well, I'd like to, but you see, I've kind of quit.'

Jay's reaction was as I expected. 'What? You're

kidding! I mean bloody hell, Roger, you are kidding, aren't you?'

'Well, no, actually.'

'When? When did you quit?'

'Thursday. I just thought—'

'You bloody traitor! I don't believe this, what are you thinking of? Have you gone mad? Who am I supposed to smoke with now?'

'I'll have one, if you like,' said Veronica hopefully.

'Christ,' said Jay, 'this is a nightmare, an absolute nightmare. Well, it won't last, you'll see.' He thrust the cigarettes back into his pocket. 'You'll be back in the club before Monday, trust me, I . . . Christ! I don't believe this!'

I was about to leave when it happened. There was going to be a disco before the ceilidh, some bizarre compromise that satisfied nobody, but there was no one to dance with. I walked through the lounge, heading for the exit. I looked at the wedding guests that I knew, and I thought, these are our friends, Becky, you should be here with me. People asked after her, embarrassed or intrigued, and I bluffed my way through. Because if you asked me, how is Rebecca these days, what could I answer? I don't know how she's doing. I don't know because she won't tell me. She's cut me out of her life because of something that never happened.

'Hi!' Chloe ran up beside me, out of breath. 'Roger, I was hoping I'd catch you.'

She was wearing a dress that was so . . . well, I just wonder how she got into it in the first place. 'Consider me caught.'

'Wonderful! Let's dance.' She took my hand and started back in the direction of the hall, but I stayed where I was, making her jerk like a dog on its leash. 'What's wrong?'

'What do you think, Chloe? Becky thinking we slept together is the reason she and I split up, so us dancing doesn't exactly fill me with happy thoughts.'

'So I heard,' said Chloe, poker-faced.

'But who told her?'

'God knows. Maybe no one did. Maybe she dreamt it, she was acting pretty weird before she left. I reckon you're better off without her, she's totally lost the plot.'

I looked at her, confused. 'Hey, I thought you were supposed to be Becky's friend.'

'Well, yeah,' Chloe said quickly, 'of course I am, but she left, and she's not coming back, so let's stop talking about her, it's . . . uh, a painful subject for me.'

Chloe took my hand and tried to get moving for the second time, and I let her pull me along toward the dancefloor.

'Well, she may be gone for now,' I said, 'but I haven't given up hope. I'll do absolutely anything to get her back.' And this time it was Chloe's turn to stop in her tracks.

'I thought you weren't interested in Becky anymore.'

'Are you kidding? I'd—'

'Jay said you were up for it, he said you and I could get together. He said we could have a meeting of minds!' Her face, it looked so much better before, when it wasn't so red, when it wasn't so crumpled. We stood there outside the doors to the hall, and as wedding guests milled past, I knew this looked bad.

'Us?' I said. 'You mean you and me?'

'Yes,' Chloe said between clenched teeth.

'But why?'

She let out a choked laugh. 'Why? You stupid

bastard, because I want you, that's why. I want you more than Becky ever did. I'm better than she is, can't you see that? I'd appreciate you, Roger, I'd look after you, Oh God!'

And I know I was pretty stupid not to see this one coming.

My voice was so flat, it was a pancake. '*You* told Becky we slept together, didn't you?'

'Yes!' She rubbed at her eyes. 'You've no idea the trouble I took over this, all that shit . . . I can't believe you don't want me after all this – fuck!'

'Don't cry, Chloe, it's the last thing I need, okay?'

She looked at me, on the brink, then gulped and sniffed. 'But Jay said you'd be up for it. He said you wanted me.'

'Look,' I said, 'Jay's been looking out for me, and he probably thought he was doing us both a favour, but this time he got it wrong. He's been a great friend to both me and Becky, but he's made a mistake here.'

Chloe gave me a strange look. 'Oh Roger, you don't know the half of it. Jay's been—'

'Now I want you to call Becky when you get home, put her straight, got it?'

'But Roger, it was Jay's—'

'For fuck's sake Chloe!' I shouted, shaking her, 'Just fucking call Rebecca, I'm dying here!'

She looked down at the ground, then back at me, and her face had hardened. 'Fine,' she said in a cold voice. 'I'll call her.'

I breathed out. 'Thank you. I'm sorry about that, about shaking you.'

'I have to get my coat.' And with that Chloe walked stiffly toward the cloakrooms, and I walked stiffly outside into the sunshine.

This should sort things out with Becky, don't you think? She can come back, and everything will get back to what it was like before, at home, at Buddies, everywhere. That's all I want, and it's not very much to ask for, but nothing seems to ever be that simple anymore.

19

Taking Things Personally

JAY:
Tara clings to me like a wet shower curtain.

She talks to me of theatre, of getting on, getting ahead. She goes down on me with a cluck and a gobble, and talks of important female roles. This I do not need. This I did not order. Waiter, take this dish back to the kitchen; she is tepid, she is giving me indigestion.

Her demands on my time are becoming most tiresome.

'Where are you going, love?'

'Just Buddies business, Tara.'

'But I bought some things for dinner. I thought we could have a night in, watch a video.'

She reaches up and runs her fingers through my hair, upsetting its shape, ruining my good mood.

'Can't you do your work-thing tomorrow, honey?'

I remove her pincers from my scalp. 'Sorry, Tara, time is money. You wouldn't want me to let things slip, would you?'

She grins, reaches down and unzips my flies. Then she proceeds to do something I had taught her during a free moment last week.

'Christ,' I whisper. 'Go on, then.'

*   *   *

I finally slip away from Tara's choke-hold at around eight o' clock. I make my way down Nicolson Street and then The Bridges, for once not taking for granted the eclectic mix of monuments and bingo halls as I approach Princes Street and the East End. It's a warm evening and the city is pulsing with life, from teenagers pretending to be more drunk than they actually are, to middle-aged couples pretending they still love each other.

Yes, perhaps you're right. I'm not as chipper as I might be, verging on the morose. Problems with Roger, Chloe blowing her threeplay. Not that it really mattered whether Chloe succeeded in her little game, but if they end up go together everything would be so much neater. It's all Tara's fault, of course. She's depleting my magnificent life-force with her tedious ambition. And who does she think she's kidding? Doesn't she know who she's dealing with? Tara's playing a dangerous game, and there'll be tears before bedtime. Quite why I didn't bump her weeks ago is beyond me.

But enough about her. Tonight, a far brighter jewel sparkles before me. Marianne, and all her exotic riches, packing away in her tidy Leith flat. She's going to Tokyo tomorrow so I have to move fast. I'm not really in the mood, to be honest with you, but I can hardly leave this piece of threeplay half-done, that would be most crass. Ah, the role of the Director. I must motivate my star players, but I must also motivate myself, despite my momentary malaise. This is about the hunter and the hunted, the sweet taste of victory, a glorious score. And I have to keep my world, our world, in order. I must keep on spreading myself amongst them, I must keep them in their places.

Marianne lives in Constitution Street, which is

close to Leith Docks. As I reach this notoriously shabby part of Edinburgh, I keep my head down to avoid eye contact with the seemingly endless layer of soulless life-forms that pass for the Leith population. I hate their accents, their clothes, their cigarette brands. Class War surges through me as I evaluate their lives; disaster at school, marry too young, watch satellite television for fifty years, then die because, well, let's face it, what else is there left for them to do?

I look at them out of the corner of my eye, swimming in ignorance and hopelessness, and I barely suppress the urge to scream, why don't you just kill yourselves now? Why choose the long term option of street and prescription drugs, cheap food and poor personal hygiene? What are you waiting for? You're definitely not having a good time. Ah, poverty, perversity, filth and ignorance, it fills me with violence. They had better stay away, this turgid underclass. I'm not a violent person; you poofs, you bums, you vagabonds, you violators, stay away, and you'll be fine. Give me grief, and there'll be trouble. Give me grief, and I'll do you some damage.

But I say nothing; just put a piece of Doublemint in my mouth and keep on walking. And after all, as I've already pointed out, what would be the good of showing the peasants their awful life? Hold a mirror up to their miserable existence and they won't thank you for it. Of course they won't. Ignorance is not only bliss, it's essential to the stability of British society. So I pass them in silence, tolerating their presence on my planet, for they are here for a reason. Sent here to provide a shabby backdrop for me to shine against. The frayed and the hesitant, the sleek and the bold, the odd fish and the callow youths. They need me, worship me, weave back and forth, side to side, hoping, ever hoping, for a hank of golden hair, a drop of mercurial perspiration.

'Knock knock?' A charming smile, and I even brought wine. Sounds simple enough, but a charming smile is something you're born with, it can't be taught, and as for wine selection, well, that rather goes without saying, does it not?

'Jason. What're you doing here?'

Ah yes. The crucial element of surprise. 'St Nicolas de Bourgeil, my dear. Lively and fruity, you won't be disappointed.' I proffer the bottle and Marianne takes it to her bosom, gamely retreating into the flat as I pad masterfully into her hallway. 'So where do you keep your glasses?' I follow my nose into her cramped but homely kitchen.

Marianne scurries in after me, no doubt delirious with joy that it is Jay, renowned purveyor of fine wines and sensational sexual technique, as opposed to Alasdair, with his customary bottle of Lucozade and limp libido.

'This is very nice, Jason, but I'm leaving on a job tomorrow and I have to get ready.'

'Friends and lovers call me Jay, and as we've been stuck in a lift together, I think we're half-way to something intimate already, don't you?' I deftly unhinge her corkscrew from the mass of metal implements in her drawer and get to work on the Cabernet Franc.

'Really, Jason, I'm not finished packing, and—'

'There we go! Now let us retire to the *salle de sejour* and let that rascal breathe for a while, hmm? And would you care for a Peter Stuyvesant? I'm severely in your cigarette debt, as I recall. You would? Excellent!'

We sit in the living room, Marianne and I, a

large and overflowing suitcase wedged unhappily between us on the sofa.

'Yes,' I say, waving my hand over her case, 'Alasdair mentioned your impending trip. Indeed . . .' and here I adopt a martyred look that has stood me well in the past, 'he's talked of nothing else.'

The delightful Marianne smiles her perfect smile. 'He's the best friend a girl could have.'

'Yes, a loyal beast is our Alasdair.' I stroke my chin in rehearsed contemplation. 'So he hasn't made a play for you then?'

She laughs, chronic and throaty, full of blackened lung, a smoker's laugh. 'Of course not! Don't be silly, I told you on the 'phone, we're just good friends.'

'Amazing.'

'Why? Why can't Alasdair and I be friends? You know, I told him about your seduction idea. He was utterly unimpressed.'

'You think?' I pass a filthy black ashtray to her, and our hands brush together, sexual static crackling along our fingertips.

'Yes. Why does there have to be anything else to it?'

'Ah.' I sigh with the tortured air of someone cursed with secret knowledge. 'So naïve.'

Marianne stubs out her cigarette, then reaches for a second. I zippo into action, and she inhales, pauses with closed eyes, then exhales through her nose.

'What the fuck are you talking about, Jason?'

Oh come on, catch up, stay with me, you don't think I'm just going to come out and tell her, do you? Ah, silly, won't you ever learn, won't you ever get the hang of the threeplay?

I raise a sensational eyebrow at her dubious language and lay a hand inside her suitcase. 'So tell me. What does a go-getter model-type girl like your-self put in her case these days?'

'You really want to know?' Mari asks, caught be-tween a huff and a hard place.

'Of course. These are the little details that keep one up at night.'

'Whatever the client tells me to.'

'Ah.' I say no more, and let the silence draw her out.

'You'd make a terrible reporter,' says Marianne, 'you ask the wrong questions.'

'And?'

'What do I take as carry on luggage? That's the key, that's the character that separates the profes-sionals from the wannabes.' Marianne extinguishes the under-used Peter Stuyvesant with such grace, such *habileté*, that I feel momentarily unworthy of smoking in her presence.

'Well,' I say, 'consider it asked.'

She smiles, sphinx satisfaction in her face as she examines her fingers. Fingers which, ah, I just wish I had the remote control.

'I keep a black box,' she says, revelling in her own joke. 'I call it my in-flight record. It has all the essentials: Lauder's Time Zone Eyes, Guinot Hydro-zone, Givenchy Number Seven. A long flight, what else is there to do? I get on the plane, wash my face, then coat it with a very heavy moisturiser, say, Estée Lauder Triple Creme Hydrating Mask. When we're close to landing I sponge my face all over with a good toner, then put on my day moisturiser, mixed with a little self-tanner. It gives you a little bit of a glow, you know?'

I nod, enjoying her voice. A Scottish accent that doesn't make you reach for ear plugs, it's a rare treasure.

'Sure.'

'Then it's just mascara and lipstick. The Givenchy is wonderful for travelling, 'cause it's perfect no matter what my skin tone.' Then she looks at me and laughs. 'Perhaps you'd make a good reporter after all.'

'Perhaps.' I pass her another cigarette and light one for myself. 'You certainly know your stuff. Have you ever tried to give Alasdair the benefit of your knowledge?' I gaze at her dimpling cheeks as she inhales.

'We've tried everything: triple AHAs, even acid peels. It looks as though he's been cursed with an indelibly Scottish complexion.'

'Damnation indeed. But I'm sure he's very grateful for all your efforts.'

'Alasdair's my best friend,' Marianne says without a hint of a blush. 'We do all sorts for each other.'

And time for the kill.

'Alasdair made an interesting confession to me that time we were in Jenner's Cafe.'

'Hmm?' Marianne looks mildy interested, mildy amused, but I'm about to kick in the pace. I'm about to change the scenery.

I open my mouth, and the telephone rings. A black mark against my usually immaculate timing. I lean back with a thin smile and Marianne slides off the sofa and goes through to her bedroom. I prick up my ears, but there is no need.

'Hi!' she cries, 'what a coincidence, Jason's here too!'

Ah, it must be Alasdair. Perhaps his spider sense has warned that I'm about to squash him under my heel. With no desire to hear their last comfortable conversation, I go over to the CD player and insert the least offensive of Marianne's three CDs.

Something approximating music plays, and I think of Tara with renewed optimism. I'll bump her. Bump her for good. She's getting too close, too keen, she's having dreams that are never going to happen. I'll be gentle, of course, you know me. But it would be better for all concerned if Tara didn't hang around Buddies anymore, after her bit-part in the current show ends. Yes, it's decided, and it fills me with strength. A night with Marianne, and then new victims next week during auditions for our Fringe show. The possibilities, the shapes and curves, they're almost the most exciting part.

Soaked in confident anticipation, I turn down the music and I hear Mari as she dishes out a slice of dietary opinion to Alasdair.

'I've got an acid test for food; if you can hold it under running water and it remains intact, it's okay. Apples, broccoli, you get the idea. Chocolate cake fails, of course . . . yeah, that too, unfortunately.'

It can't be Alasdair after all. He knows his food; his E numbers, his allergies, he's a living chemical reaction. Amused at this turn of events, the mixing of threeplays, I switch off the CD player and stroll delicately through to Marianne's bedroom just as she hangs up the telephone. I stand in the doorway, muscular and dynamic, casting one hell of a shadow if the truth be told.

'Roger,' says Marianne.

'I guessed,' I say.

Marianne holds the 'phone on her lap. 'He's gone on a diet. He was calling for advice.'

I walk over, sit down on the bed and clear my throat. 'Roger sins against food, and gets his just desserts. His salvation, like everyone else on this planet, lies in attaining the ideal body. Fat is profane. To be fat is ugly, weak and slovenly, to have lost

165

control. Achieving the proper weight isn't just a personal responsibility, it's a moral obligation.'

'Well,' says Marianne, obviously impressed, 'you take this health business very seriously.'

'Business is right,' I reply. 'It's no good for Buddies to have an obese producer. No one takes fat people seriously, no one gives them money, and why should we, they're only going to spend it on strudel and ice cream anyway.'

Marianne shakes her head. 'I think you're exaggerating. Anyway, I'm sure that Roger will slim down soon enough.'

'If only I shared your confidence, but alas, Marianne, I fear I know Roger only too well. A man with an excessive and addictive nature, his calorie cornucopia is heading to a culinary coronary, without a doubt.'

She snorts, putting the telephone back on the table beside the bed. 'Did you just make that up, or have you been waiting all day to say it?'

'Ever thought of the theatre, Marianne?' I ask. 'Ever thought of the stage?'

She turns her head and looks at me. 'Is that why you came to visit? To give me an audition?'

'Perhaps.'

'No thanks.'

I sigh. 'Such a waste. You have such presence, you'd blow them away.'

'I bet you say that to all the girls.'

I put a finger under her chin. 'No man can resist you, Marianne. They'd come from all over just to gaze at your beauty.'

Marianne takes hold of my finger and presses it against her lips for a moment of delight. 'Love you too, sweetie, but I think you're overestimating my appeal.'

'Come now, Marianne. Even the lacklustre Alasdair is in lust with you, that's proof in itself.'

'We're just friends, Jason, I told you that already.'

'Alasdair wants you for more than afternoon tea, he just doesn't have the spine to ask.' And with that, I let my hands off their leash. 'Face facts, Marianne, no man could be satisfied with being friends with you. Always that urge, sitting between—'

'Jason, what're you doing?'

'Sitting between you, waiting for its moment to erupt. Just accept what you are, sweeheart, a walking—'

'Please get your hands—'

'—wet dream. And just like everyone else, all I really, really, want—'

'Jason!'

The slap is hard and fast, I almost lose a contact lens.

I touch my face. It feels red, sunburnt. 'Excuse me?'

'Go.'

'What do you—'

'Go! Bloody hell, Jason, just go. Get out.'

I stand up, and the ground spins a little before retaining its usual stance beneath my feet. 'You hit me.'

Marianne snorts. 'Well, I doubt it's the first time a woman's given you a slap.'

I take a step, a stumble backwards, feeling for the door. 'Well . . . yes. I mean, actually . . . yes it is.' Christ! Where did my voice go?

Marianne stands up and gives me a look, the kind women don't give me, never ever please don't do that you don't realise the power you have.

'First time for everything,' Marianne says, hands on model hips, eyes burning through me. 'And you know why, don't you Jason?'

'Please. I'm going. Look, I'm going home.'

'Because you don't have anything I want. All those girls, I've heard Alasdair and Roger's stories about you, maybe they're even true. But they were all actresses, Jason, just reading their lines.'

'Look, you see?' I hold onto the wall with blunt fingernails, stepping into the hallway and down to the front door. 'I'm going home.'

I'm a whisper, a croaking trickle, as I fumble with the latch.

Marianne follows me to the door. 'Did you really think you could just come round and fuck me? Don't you get it? These girls, all they want is Buddies, dickhead. All they want is theatre.'

Finally the door opens and I burst out into the stairwell, jumping down the stairs and into the violent street.

I run, I've never run so far, all the way to Tara's flat, gasping and choking, I press the buzzer and dive into her; we have working class sex, fast, angry, desperate, trousers around my ankles. I come, crying, jagging, holding onto her for dear life.

20

The Sugar Bowl

It was supposed to be the most romantic day of the year, but Tracy Hunter was miserable. At twenty stone, she felt too fat to enjoy an intimate Valentine's dinner with her boyfriend Angus. The stares of other diners would ruin it.

'I looked in the mirror and a great big lump of flab stared back at me,' says Tracy, 28, from Polwarth. 'What's romantic about that?' So instead of going out, she stayed in and sulked.

The following day Tracy resolved to beat the bulge and join a slimming club – she had twelve months to make the next Valentine's Day an extra-special occasion. 'I knew that if I didn't want to feel like a freak, I had to diet,' she says. – *Evening News*

ROGER:
I look different. Can you tell? I mean, I know we – *cigarette* – haven't known each other very long, but there's something contrary, don't you think? Something – cigarette – more defined about my features. Perhaps, yes, it's even possible that there's less of me than before, in the physical sense at least. But my presence, don't pretend you didn't – *cigarette* – notice how much more confident, more assured, I appear. Yes, it's obvious isn't it? I've lost – *cigarette* – weight.

Oh yeah. And I quit smoking too.

D.I.E.T.

Used to spell disaster in my book, but I've learned my lesson. This excess baggage, it's weighing me down, making me crawl, drawl, scrawl, lose time. I remember what Becky said, calling me a lump, and I know that my best chance of getting her back lies in losing the sausage rolls, Mars bars et calorific cetera. Besides, I read all about it in the *Evening News*; fat just isn't sexy.

I woke up one morning, full of fervour, and ran into the kitchen, determined to throw out all unhealthy foodstuffs. And do you know? Can you possibly imagine? *There wasn't any food in my kitchen.* Nothing. At least nothing you could eat by itself. I looked in the cupboards, bare as a children's folk story, save for the case of Whiskas tins. I looked in the fridge, and above the beer and vodka shelf, lo and behold, the condiments collection. Ketchup, brown sauce, salad cream, mustard, mayo (hold the mayo!), a seemingly infinite display of caked and crusted bottles and jars.

Yes, the truth is, your Honour, that I never went to Tesco on Sunday, never shuffled over to Scotmid between Buddies shifts. The truth – oh here it is – I never bought any food. The Concorde Fish Bar, Fernando's, the snack section of Victoria Wine; carry outs, take outs, phone outs, what was I thinking of?

It's easy to say theatre; theatre does that to you. Strange hours, even producers work strange hours, no time to shop, no time to cook. Cold, dark, windy, hungry Edinburgh; let's get a pizza tonight, let's do brunch at Negociants tomorrow. You know something, when I was a student, I wasn't fat. I wasn't thin, but I wasn't a lump. I couldn't afford to spend what I've been spending in the three years since

Buddies started. When I think about it, when I really stop and think, theatre has done me considerable damage.

So welcome to the new Roger. I'm going to Tesco and I'm counting the fat grams. I plan my meals for the week and I avoid the carry out on the way home from Buddies. Is this hard? Of course it is. Anyone who has never tried to lose weight, you have no idea, you have no clue how bad a pork pie craving can get. But I'm sticking to the diet. You know why.

Cigarettes. Now here's the fucking hard part.

I haven't had a cigarette since getting back from Hampstead. Four weeks, twenty eight days, that's eleven hundred and twenty cigarettes I haven't smoked. Cigarette? No thanks, I quit. No seriously, I don't. Look, get those Marlboros out of my face, mother-fucker! Very hard, this quitting smoking business. I shouldn't even be telling you about it; the more I say, the more I want one. I never tried to stop smoking before. Not once in seven years. Not because I didn't think I could, but because I never wanted to. My life used to be – *cigarette* – punctuated by cigarettes. Not any more.

I've cut down on my drinking, too, which is to help with the not-smoking. I don't have a drink until five in the afternoon. Of course it's amazing how much you can drink between 5pm and last orders; I'm impressed, I really am. And Jay's been upping his drinking quota recently, always good to see. He's got girl problems too. In fact the only person who is actually having a nice time with the opposite sex at the moment is Alasdair, which is pretty ironic, don't you think?

It's funny, but until last Wednesday I don't think I'd ever done something with Alasdair that didn't involve Jay or theatre. On Tuesday, feeling very cigarette-needful and drink-desirous, I called him, hoping for a sobering influence. And guess what? It worked. And guess what else? Alasdair's quite a witty guy when Jay isn't around with his acidic vibe. Yeah, stranger and stranger. So Alasdair invited me along to a book launch at James Thins, Scotland's largest book store – a book of poetry no less. How much more sober and smoke-free can you get? The perfect solution, and no mistake. I hung up feeling fresh, invigorated and spiritually sound.

A gorgeous summer evening, and I followed Alasdair through the door of James Thins, feeling that despite my efforts at self-improvement, there were better things to do on a Wednesday night in August. But at least, unlike Buddies, no one would be smoking. All day and all night, that theatre is a shuffling ash tray, killing me softly. And drink. Ah! Sober all day, feeling more and more sober. I had no idea sobriety could hurt so much. Fortunately, once inside the bookshop my expert eyes picked out a figure with medicine. With wobbly cough and shaky hand I made our presence known, and a woman, an angel, rustled up to us with a tray of glasses.

'Red or white?'

'Red. Jesus. Of course red. I mean what . . . *red*. Alasdair?'

'Orange juice, please.'

What is this thing with orange juice these days? Why this sudden desire for sobriety? Where are you going, society? Don't you think you're taking things a bit too seriously?

We strolled upstairs – past the top ten hardcovers, past classical CD and cassettes, even past gimmick-laden jelly beans that screamed my name – to the area where the launch was due to take place. There we found an impressive block of shelves, all devoted to poetry. Who would have thought there were so many poetry books?

'Look,' said Alasdair, 'your favourite section.'

I looked. 'Wow,' I said. 'I never knew Thins had a theatre section.'

Alasdair gave me a suspicious glance, then realised I wasn't joking. 'Don't you need books for Buddies?'

'Oh, sure, I've got three. *Marketing for Small Businesses, Accounting,* and *Business Strategy in the Twenty First Century*, except that one's really Jay's. Hey, I've got the *Excel* handbook, that makes four!'

'I don't think that really counts as a book.'

'How about the *London A to Z*?'

'Sorry. A bit . . .'

'Desperate?'

He smiled. 'Yeah.'

'Oh well,' I said. 'Maybe I'll buy one tonight. Hey, where'd my red go?'

'I think you drank it.'

'Right,' I said. 'Back in a minute.'

I jogged back downstairs and found the angel. I took two glasses this time, not taking any chances. The red, no doubt, was cheap and bland, but my taste buds, reckless and carefree after their release from cigarette jail, rejoiced in the swirling flavours. I sloshed, gulped, bobbed and smacked, then wrestled my way back upstairs.

There were more people now, far too many for an event like this, I thought. And then it got busier. A final throng squeezed into the room, easily fifty poetry patrons.

'Hey, Alasdair, the average Edinburgh Fringe audience is seven, so what's going on here? What's the attraction? Al . . . ?'

173

But Alasdair's attention was elsewhere. I followed his distracted gaze, and discovered a short girlish stray, with cropped blonde hair and impossibly thin limbs. She looked less like she lived and more like she simply existed, desperately subsisting in a cruel world called Earth. She wore, well, rags at first glance, but a closer inspection revealed ripped denim and tattered cotton. The only expensive-looking item was her sunglasses, perching precariously on her snub nose. And here was me thinking that Alasdair had been chasing after Marianne all this time, when in reality he preferred famine victims.

I tapped Alasdair on the shoulder. 'She needs some Kibbles, man. She needs some bar snacks. Should I get her some of the jelly beans?'

Alasdair turned to me, his gaze finally broken. 'What are you talking about, Roger?'

'The skeleton girl. She doesn't look well enough to attend a book launch. She needs a pot noodle, not poetry.'

Alasdair laughed. 'But that's Erika Cameron.'

'Who?'

'The poet. It's her book they're promoting.'

'No kidding. I hope she sells a few, she definitely needs a few trips to Scotmid.'

'Very funny. Look, they're starting.'

We looked over as a bulky man who could have fitted Erika into his pocket tapped into a microphone. The audience smoothed itself into a crescent with a murmur, and the man began to speak.

'I'm sure most of you here need no introduction to Erika Cameron's work. And anyone who isn't familiar with her poems is in for a . . . vibrant surprise.' Laughter wriggled around the room. 'Erika will be signing copies of her new collection "The Sugar Bowl" later on this evening, but right now she's going to read some of her work for you. What's first, Erika?'

She murmured something, picking at a loose thread on her shirt.

'Of course,' said the bulk. 'Stung.'

Erika stepped gingerly forward, and the man lowered the microphone. Then he merged into the audience, and everyone grew quiet.

I wasn't optimistic, as I watched Erika shoe-gaze. She looked distinctly on edge, positively unwell. I glanced at Alasdair, and he looked worried as well.

Then Erika Cameron took off her shades, and her bright eyes caught the attention of every person in the room. She blew gently into the mike and I could feel the power behind that breath. Her body relaxed but her posture improved. The slouch had disappeared, and finally she looked as if she belonged in front of an audience. This was theatre, I thought.

Then she began to speak.

> 'It's nice to be a WASP
> I have middle-class stripes
> It's a good buzz (Man)
> Can you dig it?
> I can
> Because I'm a WASP
> And Proud'

I gave Alasdair a subtle nudge. 'What's she talking about?'

'It's a joke,' whispered Alasdair. 'Sshhh.'

'Right. Sorry.' But I was lost. And her voice. Powerful, despite her build (where did it come from, that presence?), but with little variation in pitch, almost monotone. What was she about?

'I have a Catholic friend
Catholic first, friend second, stung last
My sting is poisonous
Boy it hurts like social security
I'm a straight WASP
No curves on me Bud
I'm kinda furry, rather wurry, cutesy apple pie'

I had to nudge again, as a rather worrying thought
had just popped into my head. 'Hey.'
    '*What?*' Alasdair seemed a little annoyed.
    'It doesn't rhyme. Isn't it supposed to rhyme?'
    'Are you taking the piss?'
    'Well isn't it?'

'I had a WASPish nightmare:
I was a working class nigger bender
Bouncing cheque return to sender
Pillow biting Salman baiter
Trainee artiste Itai waiter
Lottery number anticipator
Melrose Place imaginator'

'Hey,' I whispered with relief, 'that rhymed!'
Alasdair smiled, and I could tell he was relieved
too. Things were definitely looking up.

'Then I woke up (what a buzz!)
But I'm a sensitive WASP
Had a wet day-dream about the cute bee in the
    honey nut cheerios commercial
Good golly gosh inter-species sexual fantasies
Turn me on!
Hey
(I'm no bigot)
I just want to fuck a poor person

They need to be stung so they have something
interesting to complain about.'

Erika gave the barest hint of a smile, and the poem
was over. A ripple of bookshop applause curved
through the room.

I turned to Alasdair. 'So what happens now?'

'Couple more poems, book signing, more wine.
Usual stuff. Good turnout, eh?'

'Absolutely. I never knew poetry was such a big
deal.'

Alasdair shook his head. 'It's not,' he said, 'but
Erika is.'

'Erika? How come?'

'You really are stuck in the mud at Buddies. She's
doing the Assembly Rooms during the Festival. Reading her stuff, but with a band, plenty of gimmicks. It's
going to be big.'

'Assembly Rooms,' I said, suitably impressed.
'What time?'

'Midnight.'

'Oh, the death slot.'

'Not for Erika,' said Alasdair, 'she's going to blow
them away.'

'You really think so?'

'Well, I'm going to give her a killer review for a
start,' he said with a grin.

I looked around for the saviour. 'It all sounded a
bit right-wing to me,' I said. 'Sounded like something
Jay would come out with, to be honest with you.'

Alasdair sighed. 'Come on,' he said, 'let's find your
red.'

One hour, not nearly enough wine, three poems and
a book signing later, I was scouring the theatre
shelves for something to dent my Switch card with,

leaving the ever sober, ever working Alasdair to discuss God knows what with Erika Cameron. The bookshop was still crowded; much milling around, much purchasing, the shop had the delicate odour of exhausted wallet. Finally I found a heavy volume on *"A Midsummer Night's Dream"*, which Buddies is doing in the Fringe, and staggered back to find Alasdair.

When I saw them together in the corner with Erika – vision shaded once more – looking as though she was about to rape him there and then, I barked a laugh of sheer disbelief.

Alasdair looked my way and smiled. 'Hi, Roger, did you actually buy a book?'

'Yeah! I found a—'

'I have to call Steve,' said Erika, and shimmered grandly past me.

'Steve's her agent,' said Alasdair.

But I didn't really care who Steve was. 'Points on the board, Al! Who would've thought it? Shall I leave you two rascals to it?'

He shook his head. 'No, it's all right, it's just work. Just for the review. She has to be nice, for promotion, right?'

'Hey,' I said, 'I'm a producer, remember? I know being nice and I know *being nice*. Your poet's definitely on the second one.'

Alasdair just smiled. 'I don't think so, Roger. That sort of thing doesn't happen to me.'

I put my hand on his shoulder. 'It just did, and your ship most definitely just came in. See you later.'

Who would've thought it eh? Alasdair scores in the big league. Alasdair, with a soon to be famous poet. A poet! That old devil, that old *rogue*. Alasdair. Who would've thought it?

*　　*　　*

But hey, friend, comrade, playmate, don't think I don't still cry at seemingly random moments. Don't think I don't still lie awake in bed, torn and desolate. I thought that Chloe's 'phone call would sort things out with the Beckster, I thought that she would come home. But no. Becky has stuff to consider before she makes any big decisions. Hey, buddy, pal; Rebecca has issues. She asked me, during the latest claustrophic telephone confrontation, she asked me how Chloe knew to tell her she was the Other Woman on the very night that I made my false confession. How did Chloe do that, if neither Becky nor I had told her? That's a very good question and I don't know the answer. Perhaps Chloe's right, perhaps the Beckster has gone off the deep end, because she *must* have spoken to Chloe before she made her play. There's no other possible explanation. I don't care about that, though. I just want Becky back. I'll make her better, I'll make her see the light.

So this is all for her, the new-improved Roger. All to add weight, if you'll excuse the metaphor, to the Roger argument. It's hard, with the Edinburgh Festival approaching; much work, much perspiration. But I'll do what I have to. I'll prove to her that I'm good and wholesome. Of course her little informer, the misleading supergrass, doesn't helping matters. What if Chloe is still following me around, raking non-existent muck?

Oh, I'll do what I can. Kick the fat, kick the fags, kick some drinking. Sounds extreme I know, sounds like there won't be much of the old Roger left. Do you think I might be getting a little carried away? Do you think, oh man, surely not, that I might be getting a little like the Unconventional Vegetarian?

179

Jay seemed upset by my change in lifestyle. He said that such dramatic change wasn't good for a person, especially someone like me. Now what do you suppose he meant by that?

21

Tinted Sex

A most enjoyable evening at the Festival Theatre, from a young company that has taken Edinburgh by storm. With minimal budget and sparse staging, they have managed to transform Britain's largest stage into an intimate box of delights.

Perhaps the performances are not the most polished this venue has seen, but this is more than made up for with pace and exuberance. A production that deserves to run and run, surely theatre doesn't get much better than this.

– The Scotsman

ALASDAIR:

Sorry I've been so quiet lately, but when I tell you what's happened you'll be impressed, I think. Because things are definitely looking up.

I have a new life. Brand new, hot off the press, it still has that new car smell. With new clouds, trees and birds, I look out of the window in the morning and watch the shiny happy people walk past. My old life? You've heard about it, experienced it with me. I rustled quietly along, inconspicuous and somnolent. Sometimes a person would notice me, notice my life, but I would give them a gentle pat, a silky stroke, explain their mistake, and they would move on, eyes clouded once more.

But no more of that. Now I scream through the day, making myself heard. I'm a new man, hear me roar. It's taken me some time, of course, to get used to my new body. I spent the first few days feeling as though all my clothes were the wrong size. But it wasn't about muscle or fat. I stumbled to *The Scotsman* and slipped behind my desk, hoping that no one would notice that I had shed my old skin, notice how I had let it go.

Me and Erika. This came from nowhere. I've had two weeks to get over the utter shock of it all, but I'm still shaking, my vision's still blurred. What happened to threeplay? When did it happen, did I miss it? Me and Erika, we're going out. Me and Erika, we're sleeping together. Me and Erika, we're an *item*. But seriously, what happened to the preliminaries, what happened to flirting, what happened to waiting for the telephone to ring? All I know is, one minute I'm listening to her read at James Thins, the next minute we're in my room sitting on my bed and she says, 'So, are you going to kiss me then, or what?'

This made a big impact on Veronica. Don't get me wrong, she hasn't tried to fuck me yet. Some things are just never going to happen. But she looks at me differently these days, and I sense our horrendous late night sessions – with Veronica weeping out her sexual tragedies and trumpeting her grand schemes – are now defunct. Now Veronica has realised that I am a man, I am a bastard. *I'm one of them.*

The morning after the night before, Veronica sat at the kitchen table with wide eyes and distracted fingers, her jaw hitting the ground when Erika kissed me goodbye and hit the road (or the publicity trail, to be precise). I sat down opposite her with my first cup of coffee in three years and almost wished I smoked. She gazed at me, baffled, an un-believer, taking in every inch of my appearance, checking for something she might have missed the first time. I sipped my coffee, savouring, and Veronica pushed her toast around her plate, lost for words. I could imagine her brain sending frantic messages: *does not compute, system error, please shut down and try again.*

I felt bad about upsetting the flat dynamics. Okay, I didn't feel bad at all. But I felt a little sorry for my flatmate, this was a pretty big shock for her to handle. I sat, sipped, and sent her sympathy vibes over the milk carton. Finally, as I was about to get up and head for the bathroom, she reached over and grabbed my hand. She opened her mouth, closed it again, then finally said:

'You and her.'

'Erika.'

'You and her. Last night.'

'Yeah.'

'And her?'

'Yeah.'

She gave my hand a violent squeeze, then stood up and looked down at me, shaking her head. 'Wow.'

My sentiments exactly. Wow.

Erika has blonde hair which was clearly made in heaven because that's what it smells like. Yes, cringe if you want, but the comparison had to be made. Christ, if she could patent that scent, she'd be set for life. I say that her hair is blonde, but straw is a more exact description. And straw-coloured hair sounds great, because it is. If everyone had straw-coloured hair the world would be a far brighter place. She has good feet as well, very important in my opinion. You might think that they're not a critical part of your partner's anatomy, dangling inoffensively on the end of their legs, but you know they're there all the same, and sooner or later they have to be reckoned with. And if the feet are bad, let's just say it's not a problem that can be solved overnight. I can say these things now, ha! and no one can say, what do you know T.U.? Two weeks, that's what I know. Please God, I don't believe in you, I know you're not there, but please, don't let me fuck this one up.

Erika wears sunglasses for an extraordinary amount of time. Extraordinary for someone living in Edinburgh, at any rate. Is this curiously endearing affectation brought on by a sensitivity to sunlight? No sir, Erika just likes the dark, that's all. A tinted world. Tinted sex, sometimes as well, which might sound a little sinister, but I don't mind. In fact I find it rather exotic. Even better, Erika isn't an actress. For despite Jay's advice on thespian partners, impotence has never been the problem, and besides, I'm a terrible actor.

I didn't chase after Erika, didn't obey Mari and Jay's orders to go after anything in a skirt. Instead she chased me. And I mean chase, because I'm rather myopic when it comes to sexual advances. When she complimented me on my *Scotsman* articles I took it as, well, just a compliment. When she started to put her arms around me, to nuzzle and snuggle, I assumed that she was a generally touchy-feely kind of girl. Then, after the poetry reading, declaring a sudden (and, it turns out, a very rare) attack of hunger, she slipped out of her flat poet shoes in L'Auberge, a French restaurant of some repute, and placed her left foot firmly in my crotch.

'How's the *creme brûlée*,' I gasped.

'Nice,' she replied. 'But it's not nearly enough.'

'Oh. Well, I think we'll get some mints with our coffee.'

She grinned. 'There's something you'd better

understand about me from the very beginning, Alasdair. I don't drink coffee.'

Then she caught a passing waiter by the wrist and said, 'Bill. Right now. *Please.*'

Our post-dinner sex woke up my appetite and I became very hungry for her. In the days that followed I was unsure as to whether my passion for Erika was simply my way of returning the compliment. After all, it's only natural to want to be nice to someone when they're nice to you. I also worried that I might simply be going through the motions (or emotions) just to please Marianne on her return from Japan. But fortunately Erika's conquest meant that she was able to reveal her true self, nice bits and nasty bits, and I've found that I like all of them. Of course I'm looking forward to telling Mari about her all the same, I'm looking forward to changing the subject once and for all.

And Jay? I restrained myself. There's no contract out on him, no DEAD OR ALIVE posters, no bounty. I opted instead for a more subtle approach, I'm sure he'll appreciate it.

22

Ditch The Bitch

Lastly, it's always a pleasure to welcome a new talent onto the Edinburgh theatre scene, and I'm happy to draw special attention to Tara White's dazzling performance in Buddies' latest production. Despite her limited stage-time, Tara's magnetic presence and wonderful characterisation saved an otherwise ordinary play from mediocrity.

No doubt we can expect much more of Buddies' rising star in their Edinburgh Fringe production in August.
– *The Scotsman*

JAY:
Sleep.

You can't go wrong with it, I swear. No hidden agenda, no false promises, sleep delivers every time. Apart from the horrific nightmares, you really can't complain.

But today I'm lying in bed at nine o'clock, and (here's the rub) I feel rotten: rotten in the stomach and in the throat. Heavy, leaden, out of tune. I lie in Tara's bed. I've been spending far too much time at her place but I need the warm squalor while I lick my wounds. I lie in Tara's bed, while the Klingon rattles and shakes around the kitchen, rearranging the dirt.

So this is how it feels when you crash and burn. I'd always wondered, hauntingly in the back of my mind, how it felt. To be rejected, laughed out of the party, thrown onto the street. You poor bastards, I never knew, I had no idea. Really and truly, if I'd had the slightest inkling, I never would have laughed. I would have put my arm around your shoulder, patted, consoled.

'You *are* getting up, today, aren't you?' Tara stands in the doorway, washing up bubbles adorning her hands.

'Of course I am.'

'When?'

'Soon.'

'When's soon?'

'Jesus!'

Tara bounds over and jumps onto the bed, a smirk on her face that I would gladly take off with a carving knife.

'I'm hitting Tesco,' she says, 'We need Daz.'

'We?' I sit up, vague and crumpled.

Tara strokes my face, sensing my creases. 'Half the dirty clothes here are yours, Jay. You've been a messy boy this week.' She sniffs, proletarian and insufferable. 'Can I borrow your Cashline card?'

'Inside jacket pocket.'

'Angel.' She grins, then gets up and reaches into the wardrobe. 'Okay. Now I want you out of that bed by the time I get back, yeah? I want to wash the sheets.'

'Whatever.'

Tara skips back over to me and puts a hand to my cheek. 'You know it's weird the way you've been sweating these past few nights. That bed just stinks.' She kisses, perfunctory, casual. She's lost any trace of self-consciousness she once had. Then she's off, skipping away with my money and violence. I open my mouth and use my new voice, only to hear it crackle and splinter with uncertainty.

'Persil, Tara.'

She pauses at the door. 'Huh?'

'Not Daz. Get Persil. My mother . . . I mean Daz is so . . . Christ, just get Persil, okay?'

'I'll see what they've got.'

She leaves, slamming the door on her way out.

I lie in Tara's bed. And you think, perhaps, judging from my condition, that Marianne only happened last night. No. Marianne happened three weeks ago. And life's been getting worse and worse. Look out the window, can't you see? Everything's going to hell.

Ah, I have to get a grip on my situation. We're holding auditions for the Fringe show next week and I need to be a prime mover for that. *A Midsummer Night's Dream*, and all that sweet Shakespearean comedy. Can you imagine the form, the sheer confidence, required for this?

Five hundred theatre companies take part in the Edinburgh Festival Fringe each year, and about fifty offer Shakespeare to the tired tourists and truculent locals. Normally Buddies does something very different, very contemporary, and very hip. But this year, ah, I thought, oozing conviction, let's beat those tired hacks at their own game. Let's kick the hell out of Shakespeare.

Roger and I decided on *The Dream* back in March, in time to get our listing in the Fringe Programme. Roger, predictably, was happy to do something conventional. We celebrated; with verve, esprit, and the Buddies Amex, accompanied by the then unproblematic Rebecca and, ah, I forget who I was courting at the time. But a good evening was had by all, I can promise you that.

Ah, spring. Everything looks better in the spring. Everything looks manageable. Then came Roger's disintegration, and ladies and gentlemen, don't blame me, I was only playing. I didn't expect him to actually go with the pretend affair routine. He asked me for advice, remember? I didn't push it down his fat throat.

And when he threatens to rumble down to Hampstead to sort things out 'for as long as it takes' and then, against all advice, *actually goes*, what was I to do? Unlike Roger, I put the theatre first. Business before pleasure, if you like. Buddies before friends, if you insist. I did what I had to, Roger would understand, if he knew. I really had no idea he actually loved the girl. Did you? Was it that obvious? Well there's nothing I can do about it now, the damage is done.

I swing my legs over and sit on the edge of the bed. A brief carpet spin and I'm ready to put my feet on the floor. I step gingerly over the mess of clothes and Tara accoutrements, then make my stiff way to the bathroom. I turn on the shower and slip into the heat, letting the steam build and soothe as I remember the crash and burn of last month.

Marianne. Sweet, irresistible Marianne. A wolf in designer clothing, she drew me in with her duplicitous flirting, only to reject me in the final Act. Ah, boys, girls, you can't go around treating people like that; they will grow hard and callous.

Mixed signals? I don't think so! Marianne knew exactly what she was doing. That's her bloodsport, I'm sure that Alasdair is an expert on her game-play. How I fell, I've never fallen so far. I feel so crumpled, so much less than I was.

What do you think? I know, I've never asked your advice before, but you know where all the pieces lie, perhaps you can see a move that I've missed. The path has always seemed so clear before, but now, all is disarray, all is carnage.

Oh, of course. People recover from these little rejections of the heart. They get up the next day, iron shirts, go to work, smoke cigarettes, and then one day try it all over again. But I'm not like other people, everyone knows that. This rebuttal from Marianne has caught me flatfooted. I'm a bull in a china shop, and I'm going to have to pay for what I've broken.

There's only one thing I can do. I must build up my girl-confidence. Take it to the heights of before, when I cruised victorious and supreme. I must lay myself open to the jewels that come to Buddies this week, grease myself up and slide among them. I must remove all baggage and fly free as a bird. I must ditch the bitch.

Soon I am fully spruced, altogether more human than I've been looking in recent days. A slight pallor, perhaps. A pinched quality to the face, certainly. I look ordinary, average; I probably look a little like you. But as I throw on the least dirty clothes I can find, I feel confident of success, confident that I am on the road to recovery, a road which will lead to delightful debauchery. I play with Tara's battered cover-stick, masking a face whipped but not beaten, and I'm combing a final disoriented hair into place when I hear the first shout.

It's faint, barely noticeable, a muffled yell coming from Montague Street. I move from the bathroom through to the kitchen, to catch a glimpse of the *mêlée* though the smeared window. As I stand there, Tara looks up at me; grinning, delirious, waving a copy of

The Scotsman in the air. She shouts at me but I can't make out the words. I open the window.

'—fucking star!'

'What are you raving about?'

'I'm gonna be a fucking star!'

Actresses, you see. Even the bad ones are psychotic. They're so much harder to bump when they're like this, but hey, today's the day. A thought, toxic and blinding, flips through me, regarding the newspaper Tara's clutching. Then I discard it, confident once more.

'Come on up!' I close the window and turn around, waiting for Tara to make her mad way up the stairs to her mad flat, mad kitchen and very ex-lover. I listen to her feet clip-clopping closer and closer. I look around the room, wondering what she will throw, because they all want to throw something when you bump them. The dishes are back in their cupboards, but the cutlery waits ominously beside the sink; draining, drying, ready for action. Tara fumbles her key into the lock and I steel myself for the tears, the shouts, the theatre. It's not all fun, my life. Surprising, I know, but sometimes my life is jolly hard work.

She opens the door and smiles, and yes, ladies and gentlemen, she looks quite mad.

'Look!' she cries, holding up *The Scotsman*, 'There's a review of last night's performance, and they loved me!'

I keep my stance, back against the window, resplendent in my shining dignity, while the turbulent Tara looks set to turn cartwheels.

'Don't be silly. They reviewed the show three weeks ago, and besides, they would have called. No critic is about to pay for a theatre ticket.'

'Ha!' Tara skips across the kitchen floor towards

me and I flinch back against the window. Where did all this fear come from? What did Marianne do to me? Tara makes the final jump to land in front of me and thrusts the newspaper into my warm hands.

I look at the review, the second review, the unmentioned review that Alasdair has written. And I see the name Tara Whyte; once, twice, oh Christ, it's all about her. The whole damn thing. What is Alasdair playing at, doesn't he know the damage he's causing, what could he possibly have against me? I ask the questions that matter, and they ride the brain-train, not getting off, just keeping their feet on the accelerator, while Tara shudders with excitement behind the newspaper. I fold *The Scotsman* up and place it on the windowsill.

'Tara, I'm afraid we're the victims of a practical—'

'Let me be Helena!'

'—joke. Pardon me?'

'In *The Dream*. Let me be Helena. I know I can do it, I know I'm ready, and the review proves it. You were right all along, Jay, I'm going to blow them away!'

With pale face and shining eyes, Tara puts her arms around my waist and her crazed lips to mine. I submit to a final kiss, then peel myself away and walk around her, standing beside the sink, between Tara and the knives and forks.

'I don't think you're quite ready for Helena, not yet. In fact I was going to suggest that you took a break from acting after this show ends. It's not a good idea to over-expose yourself early in your career. We don't want our little star to burn herself out, now do we?'

Tara's mouth drops open in a remarkably comic fashion, I've clearly been miscasting her all this time, and then she actually shows some backbone.

'No way! I'm not missing the Fringe, Jay! Come on,

you read the review, they're *expecting* me to be in *The Dream*! They're expecting something big!'

And I could find a way to calm the hysterics, couldn't I? As director, I can control any situation, no matter how volatile, how flammable. But I'm tired these days, I'm sick of the floundering fools and talentless tarts. I don't want to play this game anymore, I just want to go home.

'The review's a joke, Tara. They're having some fun with us, that's all.'

'But Alasdair wrote it. *Alasdair*. You said he was the most honest critic you'd ever read. "Tough love" you said.' She talks in a voice hardly louder than a whisper, ready to crumble.

'Sorry, love.' I move forward and prepare for the bumping speech. I get ready to ditch the bitch. 'You know, you must be tired. All those performances, I know how it can get on top of you. A holiday, that's what you need, a break from Buddies. You're stressed, worn out, and as for me, I'm draining your energy, I can feel it. Yes, why don't you take a break from old Jay, as well?'

But as I get within firing range Tara suddenly springs away from me and points an accusing finger.

'Are you insane? I've been working up to this for months. Do you think you're just going to snatch it all away from me?'

'All I said was take a break.'

'I heard you! I think I'm hearing you for the first time. Oh yeah, I know you.' Tara walks slowly over to the window and turns back with a look in her eyes I've never seen before. 'What, you think you can just throw me away? I get it. You've been stringing me along all this time, offering me titbits, when you never took me seriously at all.'

'That's not true at all.'

'Shut up!'

'It's not true, Tara.'

'Bullshit! You strung me along, but now you've fucked up, because everyone knows I've got talent, I'm going to be a star, and I don't . . . need . . . you!'

Tara punctuates the words with a finger pointed firmly in my direction.

My old self. The old Jay would have been out of here ten minutes ago, a spring in his step and a twinkle in his eye.

My new self. Who am I? Do you know people like me? Have you seen them in the street? What do they look like? Are they resplendent? Are they *clean*?

'I've worked so hard for you, Tara,' I say, 'and this is the thanks I get. I'm only concerned for your health.'

'Your only concern is where your next lay is coming from. But I'm not playing your sick games anymore, Jay. Give me Helena or we're through.'

What's happening? *I'm* supposed to be bumping *her*. Ladies, why do you all want to hurt me like this? What have you seen, what has changed?

I look at Tara with wide eyes. 'Are you seriously telling me that you'll ditch me if I don't cast you in *The Dream*?'

'As Helena. Yeah.'

I walk to the door and turn to face her as she stands against the window, black as tar, the bright sun dazzling my eyes.

'Well guess what?'

'What?'

'You can go fuck yourself.'

23

Damage

ALASDAIR:
Seven more days, and Erika's still here. She's still here with me. And the novelty is far from wearing off. At night, when we're together, on the couch, in bed, on the kitchen floor, I can't help thinking that any minute she'll come to her senses and run a mile. She'll look at me, rub her eyes, look at me again, and then run puking to the bathroom. Three weeks. The longest relationship of my life. Call Guinness, it's a new world record for the sexually incompetent, it's a personal best for Alasdair. Whatever happens from today, it's a definite improvement on my girlfriend statistics.

This morning we were walking down South Clerk Street and I played a little game. I tried to make eye contact with every man I saw. I walked with Erika, and I tried to make them see that I was not alone, I was with my girlfriend, the poet, and I was having a hell of a good time. But they weren't interested, these men, these scoundrels; they swept back and forth, uncaring and ignorant. It was upsetting, this lack of impact. Before Erika I felt too exposed, it seemed that everyone was looking at me and my skin. I needed a shield, a magic cloak, to defend myself from their silent mockery, their sneering glances. Now, I *want* people to look, I want them to see what I have.

'Why do you want to go in here?' I grumbled.

'It's full of poetry.'

'It's full of crap.'

'Come on, Alasdair, you've got a lot to learn about the human condition.'

This must be true. As Erika pulled me into Ali's Cave, no one stopped to stare at my new-found wealth, my sheer credibility. People are so un-observant, to miss the changes in my appearance, my confident swagger. They clearly have other things on their mind. As for me, I notice everything. These men and woman, I'd never been the slightest bit curious about them before. I'd classified them into threaten-ing and safe, drunk and sober, poor and poorer. But now! Christ, in a discount store nightmare, with the lowest of the low, I look at them all and think, are you happy, are you sad? That guy, do you love him? That girl, did you hit her or hug her last night, when she burnt the dinner? What did you have for break-fast? Can you afford to buy that?

'What about this?' she asked.

'That's the ugliest thing I've ever seen.'

'But it tells a story, don't you think?'

'A horror story.'

'Alasdair, you're not even trying.'

But I was trying. I was just further behind than she could have possibly imagined. I ran like the wind, desperate to catch up with the human race. I've been wasting my time, going over the same neuroses hour after hour, year after year. But Erika has opened my eyes to the city in which I grew up. It's full of history. It's full of life. So many questions. They're not dots on the horizon anymore; I brush against them, smell-ing their skin and bones, comparing the scent with my own. We're alike, I discover. We have things in common. Big things, like sex and death. I want to ask them if they're satisfied with their lot. I want to ask them if they're as happy as I am.

It's okay. I know what you're thinking. You're looking at each other, nodding with tired eyes. You think that I've gotten carried away with my poet and her poetry, that I'm heading for a crushing disappointment when Erika tires of me and leaves for someone new. Or when I discover that Erika's not as perfect as I believed her to be. And yes, perhaps I am a little overwhelmed, perhaps I have blinkered myself against potential disasters. But I haven't lost twenty five years of pessimism overnight. I know that events could turn away from me at any time. It's just that now, I feel strong enough to take it. I appreciate that Erika isn't perfect (although I've yet to find a fault). I appreciate that three weeks isn't a long time. Of course we don't know each other very well (although I've told her an awful lot). But don't tell me your doubts. Don't tell me your bad experiences. Just let me be, for a while, at least. Just let me enjoy the moment.

The doorbell rang at around noon, interrupting a spectacular daydream involving Erika and black velvet. Unhappy with my reality crash landing, I stomped into the hall and made a great deal out of unlocking the door.

'Mari!'

She was back in Edinburgh three days early, but I forgave her change of plans with the minimum of effort.

'Hi, Alasdair.'

She gave me a smile unworthy of our twenty seven days apart, but I put it down to jet lag and gave her a hug. It was good to have her in my arms, and perhaps it was my happiness that blinded me.

Because looking back, she was thinner. Looking back, she felt tighter, somehow, as I held her. There was no give. I wish I could go back to that moment and suck out her pain, make her better. But there's no way.

Mari disengaged herself from my limpet grip and blinked at me. 'You look different,' she said. 'Vibrant.'

'Well, I've been having a vibrant time' I replied, desperate for her to ask me why I just exuded sexual energy, why I consisted of pure unadulterated *fuck-icity*.

'Can I have a cup of tea, Alasdair?' she asked quietly.

Rats. Well, I'd manage to steer the conversation my way soon, and I figured on the perfect venue.

'Let's go to the Merlin!'

'I'm a bit tired, actually.'

'Tired shmired! I'm choking for a hot chocolate! C'mon, lets go go go!' And I grabbed my jacket and her hand, and ran down the stairs into the street with both of them. 'Taxi!'

It rained that day, thick grey clouds darkened the sky. A true test for Erika's tinted vision, I found myself praying that she managed to avoid being hit by a no. 23 bus.

'So did you bring back lots of free samples?'

'Hmm?'

'You know, all that make-up they used during the shoots, did you get to bring the rest back with you?'

The look Mari gave me was as cool as her neglected hot chocolate. 'Alasdair, sweetie, the make-up artists use whatever

they have on them for whatever effect they want to create.'

'But what about in those magazines of yours,

where under the photo it says which stuff was used for what. The list's always enormous, do they have to carry all that gear around all the time?'

'Look,' she said, 'they don't really use all that make-up. They just say they do so the magazine can please the cosmetics companies who placed big advertisements that month. The bigger the ad, the longer the list.'

'Oh, I said. 'That's rather deceitful, I'm glad I'm not a poor girl rushing to Jenners to buy all the gear that isn't even used.'

'I work in a deceitful business, just like you, Alasdair.'

Charming.

We sat opposite each other, toying with our lights. Before, Mari would be up front with what was bothering her, but this time she was shut tight, preferring to take her black mood out on me. It wasn't just that she was quiet. I also got a really bad vibe off her, a feeling that I'd done something to really upset her, only I'd no idea what I could have done wrong. I should have asked her what happened.

Then she fetched up a sigh so deep I could feel the air vibrate. 'I just want a place to hide,' she said quietly.

Well, at least she was talking to me.

'Why?'

'Why d'you think? Jesus, when something's so crystal fucking clear, how could you possibly not get it?'

Marianne looked at me, but I'm not sure she was actually seeing me.

'Sorry,' I said.

The worst thing is when you're expecting something to be so great, and then it all goes down the toilet. This was definitely what was happening right then. Into the bowl, round the U-bend and out to the Dead Sea. I said nothing, and we continued to sit and play. If I was a better person I would've handled the situation with a greater degree of skill. Unfortunately my parents brought me up like they were human beings. Pity, because I really needed a pair of super heroes if I wasn't going to screw up. My screw up fantasy. A fantasy happening right then, play by play, blow by blow. I never even saw it coming.

Marianne looked at her hands, then covered her face. 'I don't have a friend in the whole fucking world. '

'Hey . . .'

I touched her hands but she slapped me away.

'Talk to me. What happened in Tokyo?'

'I can't.'

Her voice, muffled, choked. I'd rather she screamed than sound like that.

'I thought you could tell me anything. You said you told me everything.'

She took her hands away from her face, and looked at me with scorn. 'Oh Alasdair, no one tells someone everything.'

'Since when?' I asked.

'Since forever! Do you think married couples share every secret? Every shitty little fear?'

I was losing her, if I ever had her in the first place. It was clear to me, this loss. Tangible, I could feel it happening.

'I told you everything about me.'

The words came out sulkily, I didn't mean them to. I didn't mean to sound so immature.

'I don't think that's quite true now, is it?' Mari replied with a thin smile.

I looked away, hating the situation, almost hating Mari. I looked out the window, I saw the people of

200

Morningside carrying their Safeway bags home. How upset was I? Off the scale, that's how.

'You're treating me like shit, Marianne, I don't deserve this.'

She muttered something.

'What?'

'You're a man,' she said. 'You wouldn't understand.'

I wasn't a man before. I was a friend. I was her best friend. 'I guess not. Sorry for being so male.'

I got up and walk away from our table. Walking towards the door, I waited for Marianne to call my name. I waited to hear it, so I could go back and hold her. Silence. At the door I turned around, but she wasn't even looking in my direction. She didn't see me leave.

24

The List

ROGER:

A busy day at Buddies today, a real back-breaker, not helped by Jay's attitude. He appeared, prickly and wide-eyed, at one o'clock, two hours late but with no explanation. I didn't push, always the sensitive producer, and gently guided him through to the auditorium, where the stalls buzzed with nervous actors, all swapping wild rumours, all trying to give nothing away. Jay look at them coldly, not a welcoming look, not a gracious director. He stepped up onto the stage and sat on the bed, only to jump off it as if stung, then stood centre-stage, taking them in, examining every thespian pore.

Jay didn't look good. He seemed, as he might say, precariously unkempt, on the verge of scruffiness. Wrinkled, sallow. If I get up close, I thought, there might even be body odour. The way Jay is, the standards he has, I decided that something very bad must have happened to leave him in such poor condition. I stepped onto the stage and walked up to him. There was no stale sweat; in fact he smelt of deodorant and aftershave, but the scent was too strong, as if he was trying to mark something.

'All right?' I asked quietly.

He looked at me, narrowing his eyes. 'What do you mean?'

'You know,' I said. 'Just . . . all right. Are you all right?'

'Of course I am. What sort of cretinous question is that?' He took a ragged Peter Stuyvesant from his jacket pocket. 'Smoke?'

'No thanks.'

'Hmmm? Oh yes, that's right, you've joined the other side, haven't you.' He lit the cigarette and inhaled deeply. This resulted in furious activity from the stalls, where the actors and actresses wrestled and twisted for their own cigarettes.

Jay stepped forward and clicked his fingers. 'Hey! I'll thank you to remember that this is a non-smoking auditorium. Besides, you all have work to do this afternoon, and you'll be far better off listening and considering, rather than worrying about your own nicotine fix.'

The actors and actresses, those who knew Jay, those who didn't, they all quietened down, they all put their cancer away and paid attention. When we were at university, trying out different things, Jay was never a flexible actor. He did one thing – himself. He did it very well, of course, but even Jay admitted that he was never going to amount to much on the stage. He always had presence, however. When Mr. Wellesley was up there you would pay attention; whether he was good, bad or indifferent, you weren't about to fall asleep. So all eyes were on him as he stood there, hands clasped behind his back, looking down at the hopeful and the hopeless.

'Well, this is where I usually thank you all for coming, but really, why should I? All you've managed to do is get out of bed and stumble down here, and where's the valour in that?'

Jay paused, taking a drag from his cigarette, then flicking it recklessly toward the wings. I walked over to pick it up, grateful that no one had tried to answer his question.

'You're auditioning for roles in *A Midsummer Night's Dream*. We need ten men, eight women, and one Puck. Anyone who's looked at the script, well done. Anyone who's prepared a speech or dialogue for this afternoon, forget it. Mr. Brown, the producer, has been kind enough to find a play that hopefully none of you have ever heard of, and we're going to be using that.'

This was, of course, news to me. Strange things happening. Strange things going on in the director's head. I shuffled, I tensed, I waited for the punchline.

Then Jay started to recite the List. 'Anyone who can't read Shakespeare, leave now. Anyone who can't dance, leave now. Anyone who has a problem with their own bodies, is having trouble sleeping, or is on medication, leave now.'

A half-snigger from the middle of Row F, but one sharp look from Jay put an end to that. The problem was, the List is *supposed* to be funny, it's supposed to relax everyone. Light relief, before the game of selection and rejection begins. It's been a tradition, the List, started from Buddies' very first set of auditions. We dreamed it up, Jay and me, late at night in Negociants, getting more and more ridiculous, more and more extreme as time went on. The last item on the List, 'anyone without talent, leave now,' was the key moment. Jay would pause, then say, 'Anyone who doesn't want to be a star, leave now.' And of course they all laughed, every time, and they all stayed, and they all did their best. They all wanted to be stars, which was fair enough. They also all thought they were talented, which usually proved to be ironic (while it's true that no one will audition for an acting job if they don't think they have talent, it's surprising how many grossly untalented people believe that they can act). So yes, the list is a joke, good clean fun, albeit with a barely hidden slight on the hopeless wannabes who dare walk through Buddies' doors.

This time, however, for whatever reason, Jay was taking it deadly seriously. Worst of all, he had seen fit to add a few new items to the List.

'Illiterates, idiots, the dazed and confused, junkies and tarts, leave now.' The audience shoe-gazed, unwilling to commit to either laughter or heckling. Jay stepped off the stage and stood before the first row. 'Bastards, bitches, whores, back-stabbers, two-faced manipulators, leave now.' He coughed, then turned around and nodded to me. 'They're all yours.' He pulled another Peter Stuyvesant out of his pocket, put it in his mouth, then walked out of the auditorium.

I smiled weakly; staying on my feet, waiting for Jay to come back in. I breathed in, heard the side door slam shut, then breathed out. 'Well,' I said. 'Let's get started, shall we?'

And the auditions themselves? They went averagely, I suppose. I called them in and sent them away. They came alone, in pairs, in threes, and they did their best, presumably. I had never conducted auditions by myself, since starting at Buddies, anyway. I could have done with another pair of eyes, a second set of ears. If the stage manager had been around I would have asked him to sit in. Hell, I even would have welcomed the lighting guy. But they were off, scot-free, not due in until tonight. It wasn't their responsibility, this hiring of temperamental talent.

Yes, they went okay. The first auditions only separate the no-hopers from the competent anyway, with a few likely candidates thrown in.

They read, they spoke, they hammed, they under-played, then once in a while someone with ability would come in and take me by surprise. Perhaps I should say that I was distracted by Jay's bizarre manoeuvre. But to be honest I couldn't afford to let that happen. Get the job done, I told myself. Wait until the recalls, when Jay's back on form, and every-thing will be all right. Everything will be just fine. So I watched and wrote, choking for a cigarette, begging for a drink. It's the drugs that get me, not the human beings.

The auditions ended, finally, inevitably. They handed me their completed forms, then they went away; off to get drunk, off to get laid, off to wait tables, off to count money. If they were bad, I promised to 'phone them. If they did well, I invited them to the recall. They left, electrified, and I shuffled photocopies, not drinking, not smoking. Then I went home to spend some quality time with Fat Cat. I 'phoned Jay, after much pacing up and down, but there was no answer. I called Tara, but she claimed that she hadn't seen him. Desperate for small talk, I asked her if she was coming to the next days' auditions. Tara laughed, a strange bark, then told me to ask Jay, which was just too strange, because I'd already told her that I couldn't contact him. Other people seem to have a lot on their minds these days. Other people aren't making sense.

25

Fire

JAY:
Bad things are happening. More bad things on the
way. Should I tell you about them? Do I need your
sympathy, finally, after all the glory? Perhaps. Go on.
Feel sorry for me. Forget about the other two; they're
fine, they're flourishing. I'm the one who's going
downhill. I'm the one without brakes. I'm the one
heading for disaster.

Afternoon and evening followed the Tara debacle.
Time always carries on, no matter how traumatic the
event. Time must be awfully strong, to keep going no
matter what. One of these days, I think that Time will
have had enough. One of these days, as Roger would
say, I believe that Time will finally crack up.

I spent the afternoon. I can't remember what I did,
but now it's two o'clock in the morning, so I definitely spent it in some respect. It wasn't good, but I
can't put my finger on what went astray. There were
auditions, but it somehow didn't seem judicious to
stay. That's surely what delegation is all about. It was
the evening that was memorable. It was the evening
that changed my mind. As for tonight's performance,
the show runs itself, more or less, so I stayed in the
flat, unplugged the telephone, stripped down to
my boxers, opened a Pichon Lalande, and read *A
Midsummer Night's Dream*. I thought of a thousand

actresses I would have play Helena. Tara didn't make the list.

Helena has the most lines in *The Dream*, did you know that? You might have though that it was Puck, or Lysander. But no. It's Helena who suffers from the verbal diarrhoea. It's a wonderful role in a wonderful play. To give it to Tara would be an affront to Shakespeare and a killer blow to Buddies' Fringe. And I decided (of course I did!) not to give it to her. A simple decision. I don't need her. There are plenty of Taras in this world, I can take my pick.

So I can't explain why at eleven o'clock I finished the wine and started on Roger's Macallan. I truly can't explain that at all. But it helped. My decision grew stronger with every swallow. Tara didn't stand a chance. I resolved to stroll into Buddies in the morning, take charge, smooth Roger's undoubtedly furrowed brow. I felt dynamic, resilient. I felt like my old self.

And that's when the doorbell rang.

It has to be Tara, I thought, as I padded to the door, bottle in hand. She must have raced over from Buddies. She must have seen the error of her ways. Smiling, feeling the world come back into focus, I opened the door.

I opened my mouth, and then closed it again, discovering that I had nothing to say. It was Chloe. An angry wasp; threeplay was all around me, coming back to haunt me, preparing to sting.

'What's wrong with you?' she said. 'You really do look like shit.'

'Long day,' I said, I croaked. 'What do you want?'

'I told Becky about the lie,' she said, ignoring my question. No one, these days, seems to pay the slightest attention to anything I say.

'I know,' I said, I crackled. 'Roger informed me. It

208

won't make any difference, Becky's staying put.'

Chloe pouted, peevish, petulant. 'She doesn't know that it was your idea, I didn't tell her that.'

I smiled, lips splitting, cheeks ripping. 'Congratulations.'

'But I will now. I can't keep this up, Jay. It's Roger, he's never going to . . . I feel sorry for him, he's supposed to be your best friend.'

Standing in the doorway, standing in my underwear, I should have told Chloe that giving Rebecca the truth wouldn't do anyone any good. That things were fine the was they were. That I would deny everything. Looking at her, I should have promised her the earth. But then I realised – I had already done that.

'I'm too tired for this, Chloe. Do what you want, I really don't care anymore.' Christ, my voice again. For a brief moment I was terrified; I felt as though I were bleeding inside.

Chloe seemed equally perturbed. 'I'm amazed, I thought you were so much stronger.' She looked at her watch, shook her head, then turned and walked back to the stairwell.

'Wait!' I cried, suddenly conscious, suddenly wanting more. 'I know you, from before, I know you!' I ran barefoot onto the landing. 'Don't go, I need your help, I think you might be able to help me . . .'

But Chloe didn't stop, just hurried down the stairs, and as I heard my door click shut behind me, she called out, 'I thought you were stronger!' And then she was gone. That girl left me weaker than before, I think she may have taken what was left of my backbone, even if she didn't mean to. I looked down the spiralling stairwell and thought of Marianne, Tara, Chloe and the doubtless others who were bent on doing me damage. And I felt lonelier at that instant that I had ever felt in my whole adult life. Smaller. Uglier.

I walked back and tried the door. It was locked, of course. I stood on the landing in my boxer shorts. I thought to myself, fool that I am, that this was as bad as things could get. Then the building let out a piercing scream, and the fire alarm sent me scrambling into the busy Edinburgh night.

Finally, Tara answers, indolent and vapid.

'Huh?'

'You can have it.'

A pause, history turns over in its grave.

'Who is this?'

'You can have the . . . it's Jay. You've got the part. You can be Helena.'

An intake of breath, sharp white noise, I can almost feel Tara's hand as it tightens around the telephone receiver. Then she coughs, suddenly nervous, as unfamiliar to success as I am to failure. 'You won't be sorry Jay, really. Roger called, he wasn't sure where you were. Are you in a 'phone box? Oh Jay, I know I can do this, I'll work so hard you—'

'Come'.

'What?'

'Just come around to the flat'.

There's silence, long enough for her to look at the Aladdin's Cave clock on the wall. 'It's very late, Jay'.

'Come. Just come over, you've still got my Cashline card, take a damn taxi. And bring your set of keys.'

'Yeah.' Another pause. What is Tara thinking about? I've never been in this particular nightmare before, I really couldn't say. But my inability to get out of this hole, it makes me feel desperate, makes me feel crazed.

'Christ, Tara, come on, I'm boiling over here!'

'Okay,' she says quickly, 'I'm coming, I'm coming.'

Tara hangs up, and I'm left with the dead line. I get out of the 'phone box and walk back to the door of my building. I hold the second ten pence piece, the second coin that I begged but didn't need, it grows hot in my fist. I sit on the step, bubbling and curdling, mind in manic replay while my soul wings its way from St Leonard's to Morningside in the Devil's black cab.

26

Lights

Music, dance and masks come together in an
original if rather fraught attempt at bringing fuck
fuck fuck fuck fuckshitcunt Marianne whatthe-
fuckisup christwhy does this have to happen
now forfuckssake
C:\SCT\ARTS\REVIEW\AM\MYTH

ALASDAIR:
I tried doing some work at The Scotsman but I
couldn't concentrate so I came home and moped.
I could mope for Britain, really make a name for
myself in any international mopathon. I can see the
headlines now. Hell, I'll write them myself, I've al-
ways fancied doing the sport pages. The telephone
went at eight o'clock that evening, ringing in the
darkness of my bedroom.
  'Hey.'
  'Hey.'
  A minute's silence. Paying our respects. I broke it
first. 'Where are you?'
  'In bed.'
  'Me too.'
  'Sorry about before.'
  'Me too.'
  Silence. I could hear Mari breathing, but I didn't

appreciate it at the time. I put the duvet over my head and curled up with the telephone, trying to get closer to her in the warm blackness. My bed smelt of Erika, but I pushed her out of my mind.

I spoke softly into the receiver, trying to kiss her better. 'Do you want to talk about it?'

'I don't know where to start.'

Mari gave a little laugh, a little snort, that would have tickled my ear had she been beside me.

'You said you wanted to hide,' I said.

'I'm being watched,' Mari replied, 'night and day, there's no respite. I'm on display, and there's no getting away. And I need to get away, you don't know how bad I need to get away.'

I listened to Marianne, and I knew she was in the dark as well. 'Who's watching you?'

'So many people. Mostly men, ogling me, ogling what they think is me. Ogling what they want me to be.'

'Marianne, you've been working solid for a month in a foreign country, you're bound to feel a little whacked. You need a holiday. Let's go somewhere, a weekend away, we can leave on Friday. Somewhere isolated, no one will see you. You can recover.'

'Too late. My picture's in so many magazines. Someone could be looking at me right now. I can feel the voodoo pain as someone turns to my page, as they twist the paper knife.'

I had to sort this out, I had to stop the flood. 'Mari, listen to me. You've been a model for as long as I've known you. When people look at your picture, or look at you in person, they're admiring you, ad-. miring what you're wearing. There's nothing malicious in it, Mari. Don't you remember, you told me how you felt when you got your first job, when you saw yourself on the page. Don't you remember how wonderful it was?'

'I don't want it anymore,' she said. 'I can feel the attack, Alasdair, it's so real, and it's getting worse all the time.'

'I don't understand.'

'No, I guess not. But that's not your fault.'

'Well, help me! Help me understand, Mari.'

She started a sigh, but it got caught in her throat and she coughed it out. 'It's rape. A mental rape. They take everything I have, every good thought, every memory, and now there's nothing left. I can feel their eyes on me, forcing themselves into me. I want to scream out to them – are you screwing? Are you screwing, and you don't even know my name!'

I pushed the duvet back and switched on the bedside lamp. The light was blinding for a second, but I forced myself to look at it. I needed the brightness, it's a camera flash that never dims.

'Mari, I'll come round to yours. Do you want me to come round?'

'No. No, it's all right. I need to get some sleep, I'm totally jet-lagged, completely jet-*fucked*, actually. I'm sorry, I'm just being silly, don't take any notice of me. A holiday sounds nice, just what I need. You're the best friend a girl could have, Alasdair.'

I felt her smile, and it had never seemed so sweet. And I let myself believe that everything's going to be all right. Let myself believe, because I couldn't face the flip side. I should have gone round to her flat, should have refused to take no for an answer, should have swept her out of the darkness and back into the light.

'Okay,' I said, quite as a mouse, a good little rodent. 'So I'll see you tomorrow.'

'Tomorrow. Good bye, Alasdair.'

'Mari?'

'Yeah?'

'What about the lights?'

'Hmm?'

'The lights, the little things, you said they kept you going.'

There was a second of barren silence before she broke my heart.

'I can't see them anymore.'

Something happened inside of me at eleven 'o' clock that evening. I was still in bed, with the light on, writing a piece of shit, a nothing. And I started to cry. Really bad crying, messy, you know? Coming out of my eyes and my nose and my mouth. I was hitching and gulping, and I didn't know why, but I didn't seem to need a reason. I sat up in bed, spilling myself onto the paper. The dark stain of grief. The black smear of an awful mistake.

27

Jumping Off The Bridge

An Edinburgh fashion model fell to her death last night, from Commercial Street Bridge in Leith.

Musselburgh-born Marianne Falconer, 29, was said to have been suffering from a severe depression, and one eye-witness felt that it was definitely suicide.

'She didn't fall. She jumped. I saw her jumping off the Bridge, it was obvious what she wanted to do.'

– *Evening News*

ROGER:

I'm almost twenty-six years old. Things must have happened to me in that time. You don't get this far without having a few bad days. I'm still here, however, and I intend to stay here for as long as I can. I don't think of suicide; perhaps, as Jay argues, I'm not imaginative enough to contemplate such a theatrical device.

Or maybe there is no drama, no detailed trauma. Is it sensational? Is it harrowing? I'm sure the *Evening News* readers won't have any trouble sleeping to-night. She has turned into column inches. She's detached, decaying, she's lost the ability to shock. Perhaps someone will mention the story over dinner, over drinks, over the bathroom routine. I can hear the tut-tutting from here. Her death is mundane, she is over and done with, they won't think about her tomorrow. I wish I could join the masses. I wish I could forget I ever knew her.

I had scraped into the University of Edinburgh. No unconditional offers for me; I greased my brain and slipped under the door, an academic commando armed with a telescopic biro. 'A' Levels weren't easy for me, I don't think I've ever had an easy exam, but those 'A' Levels were especially painful. I sat at the kitchen table, sisters and parents buzzing around the house, and told myself that it would all be worth it. I pictured myself amongst the Jocks, living it up, living away from home. Doing my own thing. Doing everything. Doing Angela, whenever I damn well pleased.

My girlfriend also set her designs on Edinburgh. We had everything planned out perfectly, in the eighteen-year-old sense, at least. Many hot and glowing moments of hilarity, lips together, swapping legs, breathing our dreams into each other. The smell of her Tic Tacs, the feel of her brown suede jacket, the sight of her maddening Star Wars figures. I thought that these things were coming to Scotland with me, along with her contact lens solutions. I sat at my kitchen table, revising for freedom, for sex, for puppy love.

But my girlfriend – who also had sisters, parents, a house – didn't think it was worth it in the end. By the time 'A' Levels came into view, Angela had things on her mind other than breath fresheners, other than saline, other than Luke Skywalker.

Something broke in her, I think. Something important, something inside. A stoic girl, quiet and funny, she became loud and complaining, wet with tears, running hot and cold, the changes coming faster every day.

'How can you stand it, Roger?' she said more than once.

'How can I stand what?'

She sniffed. Even when she wasn't crying her face seemed wet.

'All this deceit, all these lies.'

I held her hand, held on tight.

'I'm not lying to you,' I whispered. 'I'd never do anything bad to you, Angela, you must believe that.'

She looked straight through me. 'I don't believe anything, these days. It's a lot easier to act as if none of this is real.'

'Why?' I cried, desperate. 'I don't see what's gone so wrong, I don't see what's different from before!'

She closed her eyes and smiled. 'Could you make me a cup of tea, Roger? I'm feeling awfully thirsty all of a sudden.'

Angela talked to me about things she didn't understand, about things I didn't know existed. She was brittle plastic, she was thin glass. We made a list of words that had upset her, between sex and loathing, between Maths and Biology. Big things; media, nature, people, famine. Then little things; colour, sound, Princess Leia, skin. The list didn't do any good. The things that upset her, they became our vocabulary, they became past, present and future. There was nothing I could do to stop her screaming, her crying.

There's no support when you're eighteen, falling out of the nest. You're in the middle of that long phase where you don't want your parents to know anything about you, where your teachers are already thinking about the fresh crop of mediocrity. We had each other, Angela and me, and we weren't nearly enough. I tried silence, I tried noise, I tried touch, I tried space. Nothing slowed the flow of tears, nothing stopped the breaking of her glass. I moved my fingers across her, an experiment in fear, and she was no longer smooth, as she had been when I had fallen in lust with her suede jacket and popular culture eccentricities. My hands dragged and bled. She was cracked, invaded by a virus that didn't know when she'd had enough, that didn't know when to stop.

On the day of my first exam, our first exam, I walked to school alone, leaving her in her infected house. I had rung the doorbell, not sure if I wanted her to answer, and when the door stayed shut I didn't question her decision. I stayed at school during lunch, staying away from the gates, avoiding the telephones. Morning and afternoon, while we chewed on pens, while we scratched our young heads, Angela's chair stayed empty. The invigilators circled around the blank space, nodding heads, ticking boxes. Her space, quiet at last. I was on autopilot, with two sets of questions to answer, and I thought of myself, because I didn't understand my girlfriend. I wrote, spiders across the page, and I asked, if anything happens today, will it be my fault? The exam ended, as they all do eventually, and I had to walk through the chattering children, I had to leave them behind.

When I got to her house one of her sisters answered the door. The TV was on, blaring out greed and intoxication, and the sister's face said nothing. I walked up the stairs and pushed open the bedroom door. Angela was standing in her bedroom, not looking out the window, just staring at the glass. She had been crying, surrounded by the smell of burning plastic. Unwilling, I moved closer, touched her, held her, and she was soft, putty. Powerless, I could have done anything. She wasn't dead, still breathing and buzzing, and I thought at the time that if she had died, I would have known what to do. If she had killed herself it would have been a lot easier, it would have been black and white. I stroked her face, learning how to hate her.

She smiled. 'I couldn't go to school today.'

'That's okay,' I said softly. 'We'll work it out.'

'I've been here in my room, and I had the strangest dream. Would you like to hear about it?'

I sniffed at the air, and looked over at her bedside table.

'Why did you set fire to Princess Leia, Angela?'

She frowned, then smiled again. 'There was this lovely spot in the countryside, it was wonderfully clean. And there were razor blades, and they were clean too, not rusty or anything. It was so quiet. Just me sitting in a golden silence, amongst autumn leaves and a fiery dying sun.'

'Angela.'

I put my arms around her and kissed her face.

'We should go there sometime,' she whispered. 'Then everything would be all right.'

We moved in parallel that summer, not mending, not breaking. Saying our goodbyes as I put my cases in the car, I told her to take care, and she told me to take her suede jacket. I didn't, though. She needed it more, she had always looked cold that summer. I zipped her up and patted her away, fighting for breath, desperate for clean air. I got into the car and my father drove off, North and the future, and Angela diminished in the mirror, hands bunched in her jacket pockets, until she was a speck, until she was nothing, until we turned the corner.

We didn't keep in touch. Now I'm here, and

I wonder if Angela's still there. At home, in the country, on the planet. Perhaps you think it strange that I don't know, but I couldn't see her again. I didn't want my words to upset her anymore, I didn't want to see what could happen to ordinary people. I didn't want to feel her madness, I thought that it might be contagious.

We're no good. We don't take youth seriously, we think they're invincible. Children, teenagers, the young don't die. How could they? That would be unthinkable, too awful. But they do. Taken out before they have a chance to live. Snuffed out, the young leave such a mess. Leaving us behind to put them in boxes, below ground, out of sight.

The resilience of the human spirit. But it doesn't always apply, we don't all get the same share. Look around, please, take a good look. Your friend, your lover, your daughter, they can vanish in an instant. Individuals make their own decisions, good or bad, live or die. But their decisions reflect on us, we affect each other every day. Every person you come into contact with, you're changing their future. Fate is a myth, nothing is predetermined.

So next time you're in a position to throw an insult, a piece of mockery, next time you're feeling poisonous, just remember, we are responsible for each other, and there really is no limit to the damage you can do.

I first met Marianne at a party held by a mutual friend, a freelance photographer, who stays in the New Town. That night I saw what I considered to be the most beautiful girl in the world, sitting quietly on a bean bag in the living room, a can of Tenant's Lager in one hand, an unlit Marlboro Light in the other. A voice from God told me she was waiting, had been waiting all her life, for me to come along and light that cigarette for her. I fought my way through the drunken throng and sat down opposite her. Cross-legged, we looked as if we were about to begin some kind of ritual, which, of course, we were.

I struck a match and held it out to her. 'I offer you fire,' I said with all the gravity I could muster at two o'clock in the morning.

The woman looked at me, *glared* at me. 'Are you trying to chat me up?'

I blew out the match. 'Well, I was talking to your cigarette, but I'll chat you up if you really want me to.'

She smiled. 'What an adorable little ice-breaker you are,' she said softly, looking at me properly this time.

'Not so little, I hope, but thanks. Actually, I'm a professional ice-breaker. Ships hire me to stay on board just in case they hit a glacier.' Another match, and the woman either snorted or sniffed (I forget which, but it was a positive sound in any case) and dipped her cigarette into my flame.

'Fire and ice, you truly are a man of extremes,' she said dryly, far too dryly for that time of night. I decided to revert to a more conventional mode of conversation.

'So now that you know what I do for a living, why don't you tell me your profession?'

'Guess'

'Ah, there's a problem there, because if I really say what I think you do, then you'll think I'm trying to chat you up again.'

I guessed right, of course. Marianne could have only been a model. But I also guessed that she was okay, happy, whatever you have to be to stay alive.

So I guessed wrong. I took one look at her and made a thousand assumptions.

I see myself and Becky now. I've become my age, at last. Events change us, events change our mind. I haven't stopped thinking about Becky since she left, but she was always in my mind-frame, it was always about me. Now I think about her, and now I think about her pain. I dealt her a grievous blow, helped along by Chloe, but dealt by me all the same. I played with her, I wasn't thinking about the damage I was causing. Here I am. I'm a big boy now, I want to make things right, I want to make her happy. It's still in my power, I think, to make her laugh, to bring her into the light. I treated her so badly, but I'll never do it again. I'll make her number one. If she comes back, I'll put her above everything, I'll put her on top of the world.

I tell these things to Fat Cat, and he purrs, unbelieving. I scratch his ears and tell him I've changed. He sits on my lap, weight on weight, doubting my pledges. But at least he stays. I'll tell Becky, if I get the chance. I'll tell her I've grown up.

28

Education

At the outset of this odd treat, the audience is warned that when an actor shouts 'fire!' halfway through, it is not really a fire – just time for the interval.

Representation tries to challenge reality in this stylised drama about love and relationships at the turn of the millennium, blending relationship angst, theatrical allusion, anxious lyricism and bickering.

It might not make it, but there is no doubting the sincerity of the attempt . . .
– *The Scotsman*

ALASDAIR:

After Robert promised me that the older boys would flush my head down the toilet, I developed a morbid fear of starting school. My parents, however, felt that primary education was an essential part of growing up and used a cunning trick of deception to ensure my attendance. It involved wild promises of the fun I would have once I joined my fellow classmates in the state tutelage system.

One such inflated claim was multiplication tables, which after my parents had finished describing sounded like an elaborate carnival of joy.

'When are we doing the times tables, Miss Ogylvie?'

I spent my first year pestering my class teacher for

a sneak preview of these fantastic tables.

'Are you finished with the paper glue, Alasdair?'

'Yes, but when are we doing the tables?'

She sighed. 'Put the glue away, Alasdair, you can worry about the tables later.'

Miss Ogylvie was no doubt curious as to my fascination for mental arithmetic. One year later so was I. No Blake's Seven until I'd done my tables. No camping in the back garden with my oh-so-right brother until I'd done my tables. I must have been the bitterest six-year-old in town.

My point, oh yes there is one, is that events rarely turn out the way you predict, and my reunion with Mari on her return from Tokyo crushed all my expectations. But like school, I learnt my lesson from this experience, because in most situations I now fear the worst possible outcome. I fear the absolute worst, not so I won't be disappointed, but so I won't be destroyed.

29

Blame

JAY:
Pack your bags, ladies and gentlemen, we're going on a guilt trip.

Act III

GETTING EVEN

30

Unconventional Human Beings

A pregnant woman had her front door smashed in by police officers last night – because of a leaky tap.

Mum-of-three Lynne Ewart was woken when a policeman shone a torch in her eyes and told her to get out of bed. She found two officers, accompanied by a plumber and a joiner, had entered her flat.

Terrified kids Sarah, 8, James, 5, and Victoria, 3, huddled together while the door was fixed.

But Lynne, 33, who is seven months pregnant, said: `I didn't hear any banging on the door.

'The first I knew there was a problem when this bright light was shone in my face. I was terrified. I've never been in trouble before and had no idea what was happening.'

Lynne, of Livingston, phoned her security guard husband, Derek, 34, who rushed home from work.

He said: 'The police said there had been flooding in a flat below us caused by a tap in our home. By the time I got home the woman downstairs said the problem had been sorted.

'I think the police over-reacted and they didn't even offer us an apology.'

– *Evening News*

ROGER:
What I want, I think, at the end of all this, is for someone to explain to me what is true and what is

false, what is good and what is bad, what is black and what is white. Much is happening, and I should feel happy, but I should also feel sad. Who can help me clarify things? Who's going to sort it all out? One thing's for sure: I'm going to stop reading the *Evening News*.

The night before Marianne's funeral I 'phoned Alasdair; figured it was my turn to help out, but all I got was his answerphone. Now this might sound weird, but when I was leaving my message I thought about the mad night when I called the Lonely Hearts number. I thought about the morning after, when I couldn't remember, I had no clue, who I'd called, what I'd said. But time has made me smarter, time has taught me lessons. And now, as I approach another birthday, I knew what to say to Alasdair, I understood the message I had to leave. Such clarity of thought and speech, when it mattered. Don't you think I'm looking older? This life; it's not getting any more fun, but I think I'm getting a little better at it. I think I'm actually growing up.

The first rehearsals for *The Dream*, but Buddies was not a happy place to be. Jay was acting very badly, although not as badly as Tara, ha ha. He pushed that girl into a huge part that even I knew was a mistake. It was his call; despite what he says, I've always let him cast the shows. But God, Tara was looking distinctly shaky. The funny thing was, she had such confidence, such total self-belief, from the day Jay gave her Helena. She strutted across Buddies' stage, causing despondency and disarray with her sheer lack of talent, but always enjoying herself.

As I watched from the centre of the stalls, too baffled to be truly horrified, my paper and pen stayed largely untouched. I watched the actors grind through the read-through, and it became clear that any number of rehearsals would not fix this particular mess. Soon I will lose my hold on the production; audiences will steal my place as the judge of Buddies' efforts. I glanced back at Jay, who lurked at the back of the auditorium, intently smoking cigarette after cigarette, and I wondered what he was thinking. I wondered what game he was playing. We're in the grey area at Buddies, I can see that. They're playing their game, Jay and Tara, and our Fringe is going down the toilet.

So I left, feeling much alcohol-desire and nicotine-urge (when does the urge go, incidentally? It's been weeks, it's been so long since I quit, when does it stop hurting?) and placed myself in the vicinity of Negociants, for a very large glass of red. Something spicy, I decided, something that would make my gums hurt. Warm enough to sit outside with the locals, with the drunks, the homeless, but I needed to be inside, to be out of sight. I swung through the doors, and it was wonderfully busy. So much noise; I could lose myself here, I thought.

A waitress eased her way through the crush and gave me a harassed smile. They know me here, the staff. I've been coming to Negociants for six years, and there's a new place open beside it – Iguana, with its superior patisserie – but hey, I'm a loyal dog.

'I just want some red,' I said. 'I've had dinner.'

'You lost weight?' the waitress asked, looking me up and down. I'm worth that these days, you see, a looking up and down.

'Yeah.'

'Where's your director?' she asked.

'Trying to work miracles.'

She laughed, which was nice, and I took her all in, eyes tits legs, despite Becky, despite Marianne, because you can't help it sometimes, can you? Then I got shoved from the side, pushing me and my thoughts away. Sorry pal, yeah, cheers mate, aye, cheers. And it's gone.

'You mind sharing?'

Of course I minded. 'No problem.'

She led me towards the back and pointed to a stray chair, vacant and out of place. A table for two, and when I sat down the woman opposite looked up. We exchanged faces, and I couldn't just turn away as if I hadn't seen her. Locked together, neither could she. We shared half a smile each, both embarrassed, but neither about to leave.

'Well, Roger,' said Elizabeth, 'how's life in the theatre?'

And it wasn't so bad. Actually, it was probably what I needed.

The Unconventional Vegetarian was drinking as well; no food, just red, so I got a bottle. It was my turn, wasn't it?

And?

'I've never been here before. It's nice. I, er, remembered you mentioning it, yes, nice.'

'I come here a lot. Close to Buddies. Well, close enough. The burritos are addictive, but you get used to a place, you know?'

'Sure.'

The conversation staggered along; bruised, rotten, we weren't saying what we meant. We didn't want to do that. It wasn't so much discomfort, more displacement. We'd only had the one date, but it certainly hadn't been boring. We had history, Elizabeth and me, even if it was only one night. There was a kind of intimacy, definitely something between us. We sure were having a moment.

I looked at her. She made me desperate to crack a joke. She made me desperate for a cigarette.

'So how's . . . life?'

She sniffed. 'It comes and goes. Better than before, if that's what you're asking.'

'Yeah. That's kind of what I meant.'

A pause. Time moved on, I'm sure, but you never would have known it. I gritted my teeth. 'Elizabeth, about that night.'

'You don't have to apologise.'

'It's just that I kind of came to your place under false pretences.'

She took a sip of the spicy red. 'How so?'

'I'm not much of a vegetarian. Not really a vegetarian at all, really. I'm sorry, it's difficult to explain.'

'But you're very good at explaining things on the telephone.'

'Sorry?'

'The message you left for me. It was very eloquent.'

I blushed. 'To be honest, Elizabeth, I can't remember what I said. It was a bit of a wild night, and I was kind of drunk.'

She looked up in surprise. 'You sounded very sober in your message. And your accent, it was positively regal.'

'How d'you mean?'

'I can't remember exactly. But it was distinctly upper class, you sounded very sure of yourself, I was swept off my feet. Do you always sound that way when you're drunk?'

An idea occurred to me, but it was so impossible that I pushed it away and decided to never think it again.

'No,' I said, 'I never sound like that.' I reached for my cigarettes, and then remembered that I didn't have any. 'Elizabeth.'

'Yes?' She sounded light-hearted, but she knew what we had to talk about.

'I'm sorry about what happened. It was wrong of me to come round like that, pretend to be something I'm not. I didn't mean to . . .'

'Hurt me?'

'Yeah.'

She smiled, and I felt young and foolish all over again. 'We both did silly things that night, Roger, don't beat yourself up about it. These things happen, you know.'

'Right.'

These things happen. But not to me. Not ever. Not before. I don't want these steps into the grey, where's no one is to blame, where everyone is guilty. I thought of Marianne, and I could have told Elizabeth that I wasn't up to this, I had a funeral to go to, I was in mourning. But that would've been a device, a sneaky get-out clause. I couldn't use Marianne like that. You shouldn't abuse the dead.

'You don't really want to talk about this, do you?' Elizabeth said.

'It's just that I'm not very good at it. I mean, we probably should talk about it. I think that's what people do, in situations like this.'

She laughed; amused, friendly. 'But who wants to be conventional, Roger?'

I smiled back at her. 'Not us.'

Silence, almost comfortable, we looked at each other, then around at the other people, going through their motions, then back at each other.

'You mentioned a woman. What was her name?'

'Rebecca. Becky.'

'Your girlfriend?'

I sighed. 'Was. Might be. Who knows? I'm still hoping.'

'Well, you'll be glad to hear that I don't chase after lonely hearts on the rebound anymore.' She smiled, adding light to proceedings. She can do that now; she can mock herself, make herself human. She's still unconventional, but she's not just a vegetarian. And it's my turn to ask a question.

'How's all that green stuff?'

'Still going, Roger, still fighting the fight. But you taught me a lesson, with what you said to me. You were right. Now I'm letting people in, I'm letting them help.'

'I'm glad,' I said, 'but I don't think I've ever taught anyone anything before.'

'Yes, you have, Roger, it's just that no one has ever admitted it until now.' She poured the last of the red into our glasses. 'So how's your theatre? You must be very busy these days.'

'It's pretty wild at the moment. You should come and see our Fringe show when it opens. I'll get you a couple of freebies.'

'Thank you, that would be nice.'

'Hey, why don't you come along now, you can watch a rehearsal. I mean, sitting in on a read-through might not be your kind of thing, but people seem to like watching actors before they get it right.'

Elizabeth shrugged. 'Won't they mind?'

'Elizabeth, I'm happy to say, they don't have any choice in the matter.'

'Such abuse of power,' she said with a sly grin. 'You really are intoxicating, Roger.'

'That's settled then.' I stood up. 'I just have to pay a visit, then we're out of here, okay?'

'Sure.'

I paused. 'Elizabeth?'

'Yes?'

'You taught me a few things as well.'

She nodded. 'I know, Roger. I can tell.'

I slid between the other tables and jogged down the stairs, then through the basement crowd and into the Boys, past the red crew cut and freckles. Feeling shy, feeling a little gay, I stood in one of the corrugated iron stalls, having a lager-free piss. It wasn't quite the same, but there was something there, at least. A shake, a zip, a push-button flush and I stood in front of the mirror, looking at my face, looking into my eyes. Alasdair once told me that Negociants was the only bar in Edinburgh where the toilets had flattering lighting. But surely there's a market here? Surely someone with kind lights and forgiving mirrors could make an absolute killing. We're at our most vulnerable, standing, post-piss, drunk or sober, laid or not. Why doesn't someone come to Edinburgh and help us out? There's money to be made, vanities to save.

I washed my hands. I looked at my face. It's changing, it's going somewhere else. One less chin, slightly more cheekbone. Hair, nose, ears, they're still in the right place, still saying the same thing, but my eyes, my mouth, they're moved on, they're having a whole different conversation. I smiled, an experiment. I grinned, flashed my teeth, ear to ear. My skin wrinkled and folded where it hadn't before. It used to bounce, a trampoline. Some of this is lost weight, but some of it is lost time, a waste of birthdays and anniversaries. It's a warning to us all, this lack of buoyancy. Our skin knows what we do our best to deny. It knows that time is always running out.

And how did Marianne feel, the last time she looked in a mirror? What was her face saying, could she understand the language? Did she see sags, bags, the beginning of the end? People don't feel sorry for ageing models. They mock, or sneer, their jealous fantasies at last being realised. Crows feet, turkey neck; age dehumanises us, or so we're told. How did Marianne feel? Was that what did it, approaching thirty? I can't believe it. She was too strong to think such things, but I had also thought she was too strong to jump off bridges. Hell, I shouldn't hypothesise, I shouldn't make up idle stories when I don't know the basic plot.

Becky must feel older as well, but at least her clock is still ticking. I imagine her getting older; thirty, forty, fifty and beyond. The thought of seeing her age and wrinkle doesn't upset me. It's the thought of not seeing her, of missing it all, that grips my heart and twists it into knots.

We walked out of Negociants and started to make our way down to George Square and along to Buddies. It was warm. Edinburgh felt Mediterranean, a city in short-sleeves. I sniffed the air, and it felt old but friendly, superior but benevolent. A homeless guy, someone I had seen many times before in the same spot, called out as we passed him.

'You young lovers got any spare change?'

I stopped and turned around, embarrassed. 'We're just friends. Really, there's nothing going on.'

Elizabeth laughed. 'He doesn't care, Roger, he wants some money.'

'Oh. Right. Got it.' I reached into my trouser pocket and gave the guy a pound coin.

'Cheers!' he said. Then he winked. 'Off for a romantic stroll, then?'

I blushed, feeling the heat. 'It's not like that! Seriously.'

Elizabeth took my hand. 'Bloody hell, Roger, he's just teasing. Come on.'

We walked, past McEwan Hall where I had graduated, and made my mother cry with relief. We walked, alongside the University Library, which my father once described as a giant car park. I thought of the homeless guy, I thought of the homeless.

'So does saving the world include saving that guy back there?'

Elizabeth nodded. 'Absolutely. We're all responsible for his situation, Roger, we all have to try and make it right. It's a waste of talent, a waste of youth.'

'I saw a guy begging on Princes Street the other day,' I said, 'and he had this great big Alsatian with him. I've always thought what a great marketing ploy that was; no one can resists dogs, it's foolproof.'

'It's unfortunate,' said Elizabeth, 'but there are a lot of people who think that the homeless are automatically guilty of something. If he looks after the dog then I don't think it's such a cheap trick.'

'That's just it,' I said. 'A woman came up to the guy and his dog, she was middle aged, middle class, weighed down to the ground by Marks and Spencer plastic bags, you know? Anyway she takes a tin of dog food out, opens it, and then doles it out in front of the Alsatian, ignoring the homeless guy the whole time.'

Elizabeth didn't laugh. 'And what was your gut reaction?'

I smiled in spite of myself. 'I thought it was a pretty cool move, to be honest.'

'We're a rather mixed up race, aren't we.'

Was she attacking me, herself, everyone? I wasn't sure. 'I guess so. I don't know what to do about all these problems, I'm sure that if I was in charge I'd make an awful mess of things.'

We left George Square and walked into the Meadows. It wasn't busy, but soon the area would be full of Festival-goers. Still holding my hand, Elizabeth looked at me curiously. 'You know for a producer you seem strangely lacking in confidence at times.'

'Theatre is different,' I said. 'Me and Jay, we really do the business together. We're a great team, he makes me feel invincible. At least, he used to.' I looked up into the night sky, and thought of how Buddies had been only a few weeks before. Turkish Delight. It's amazing, to me, how quickly things can fall apart.

'So this Jay, he owns the place then, eh?' Elizabeth asked.

'He likes to pretend he does,' I said, 'but it was his father who actually signed on the dotted line. Just as well, Jay isn't exactly a financial wizard. I do my best to keep things in the black. God, I remember . . .' – I smiled at the memory – 'Wellesley Senior standing on the Buddies stage for the first time. I mean the place was a wreck, we didn't even have any seats, he looked me in the eye and said "Now, ah . . . Roger, yes, I believe that Jason deserves a chance with this . . . place, but please, just please make sure he doesn't do anything too bloody stupid." '

'And have you succeeded?'

'Not recently. We're not really getting along like we used to.'

'Poor Roger,' said Elizabeth. 'I'm sure you two will work things out. I can't imagine you fighting with anyone for too long.'

'Yeah, you're probably right. It's just a blip.'

We smiled at each other. This wasn't black and

white at all, the way I was feeling, but it didn't matter as much as before. I could salvage *The Dream*, I decided, sort out Tara, calm the other cast members. I walked with Elizabeth, strolling into the grey, and it didn't seem frightening at all.

31

Crumple Zone

JAY:
Everything is better now. Tara is safely under my
wing, docile and subservient. She knows her place; in
the shadows, in the wings, out of sight. Buddies, after
the storm, is well-oiled, in top gear, ready to make
money. I receive the directors of inferior companies,
begging for time and space. I listen to their schemes,
take their deposits, make arrangements. The sight
of money has made me well again, gold has been
my elixir. The Festival is coming, keeping me busy;
there's no time to consider past mistakes.

Soon we shall be in the thick of things, and my
father will arrive for his annual visit. We will shake
hands, gentlemen, and he will examine the premises,
watch the production, then shower me with deserved praise. We will have lunch, opulent and
divine, and we will discuss business. Father and son,
very civilised. Then he will leave, back to England,
back to make money. We are family, he and I. We are
a blood line. He will not be disappointed.

No, do you see? Even my lies have lost their sting.
Why do I bother even trying to convince you, ladies
and gentlemen of the jury, when Roger and Alasdair
are there to prove me wrong, to shine light on my
falsehoods. When Marianne is still warm, unburied,
haunting my nights with her hazel eyes and accusing

tongue. Sleep is no longer a refreshing dip into the black. It is crass, stereotypical. I have become ordinary, I have become accused.

Ah. You know me well enough by now, I'm sure, to realise that I'm an educated fellow. So you'll understand if I call your attention once again to Schubert's Fourth. There's a moment, after much initial lamenting, much lulling, when exactly two minutes into the first movement, the theatre really begins. Go on, spoil yourself. Give it a listen. You'll know why they called it the Tragic Symphony, I swear.

Oh, and yes, I know that everyone says that Schubert's Fourth in C Minor is considered to be inferior to Beethoven's Fifth. But what everyone forgets, what everyone fails to realise, is that Schubert was only nineteen years old when he composed it. What were you doing when you were nineteen? Sitting your driving test? So give Schubert a break, we all make mistakes in our frail youth.

I arrive bright and early at Buddies, preparing to wipe the slate clean with the second set of auditions. Helena might be lost, but there is more to *The Dream* than one smitten woman. There is more, and I can mend what has been broken. I sit behind my desk, in control and in demand. The telephone rings unrelenting; people wanting my time, people wanting to give me money. I blow smoke into the receiver, making appointments, making profit. Everything is as it should be. Only Roger is missing, late for once, no doubt hungover. It is only a matter of time before he cracks under the Festival strain and returns to his true form: full of cigarettes and alcohol.

He arrives at eleven o'clock, confirming my predictions with his pale face and albino-pink eyes. He squeezes his way into the office and sits on the edge of the Tatty Sofa. I lean back in my chair and give Peter a gentle shake. 'Cigarette, *peut-être*?'

'Fuck off.'

'I see. Very civil, I must say. And you aren't setting a very good example to our potential cast members, looking like that. Did you forget where your bathroom was this morning?'

My producer looks at me, and I can only guess at the thoughts grinding away behind his bloodshot eyes.

'I was working late last night, Jay, which is more than I can say for you. What the fuck did you think you were doing, disappearing like that?'

I smile, the mysterious director. 'All part of theatre, my dear Roger. Just wanted to keep everyone on their toes, yourself included. I'm sure you did a sterling job without me, it's about time you took part in the creative process.'

He sits back, confused but placated. 'Well, warn me next time, okay?'

'Absolutely. Next time you'll be the first to know.' I offer my honest smile, and light a cigarette.

So today we return to our accustomed roles. Roger searches the Rolodex for hidden treasure, caressing its letters and digits for gold and jewels. And the telephone continues to behave itself, wailing for attention, shrill and insatiable. I, meanwhile, take the actors and actresses under my expansive wing. I show them the ropes, and wait to see whether they end up hanging themselves with it.

A *Midsummer Night's Dream* is fantasy, a break from tedious theatrical realism, an escape from the kitchen sinks of the politically correct. It is a stylised sport, *The Dream*, and these hopeful thespians have to realise this. When the mischievous Puck, in the first line of his epilogue, 'If we shadows have offended,' refers not merely to the fairies but also to all the actors that have taken part, we realise that Shakespeare is making it clear to us that we have been watching a magic lantern show. Appearance, not reality, is the operative factor.

But do actors understand this? Ah, the modern performer, he is so earnest, so desperately sincere. I don't want these bit-part reformers with their ignorant suffering. I want to be fooled into fantasy; I want manipulations and machinations. They must show me their ability to deceive, if they are to join Buddies in its Fringe onslaught.

I explain and expound, I give them themes and specifics. Of course it is a typical crop this afternoon; few understand what is expected of them. But I am in excellent form. I hit peaks and don't come down, while the actors bare their souls, fawning, obsequious. Some of them might be good enough. Some of them might make the grade. I put them through their paces and they put their pride away, locking it up for the afternoon. I make them laugh, I make them cry. I tell them to hate me, to love me, to give me everything. I command them. I am in complete control. Anything is possible.

Before we really get down to business, before we start to look at words on a page, Roger shuffles into the auditorium and asks me to come into the office for a moment. He fails to notice the magic I'm working, he's upsetting the spell. I follow him out, grinding and prickly.

'You know the rules, Roger, this had better be of the utmost importance.'

'Alasdair called.'

I snort, amazed at the critic's impertinence. 'To

apologise for his incendiary review, I trust. The trouble that foul cretin has caused with his meddling. I tell you, old T.U. can beg and grovel, but he's not stepping into this theatre ever again. He causes far too much damage.' I give Roger my stern look, then notice that his left leg is shaking. 'Well?'

'Marianne,' he says quietly. 'She killed herself. Marianne's dead.'

Words, a sentence, they travel through space and slap my face. Blood rushes, disoriented, going to all the wrong places, I feel the heat rush away from my cheeks and into my heart. It pumps, it is on fire. Marianne is dead. The words leave me speechless. I turn and walk back into the auditorium.

I am the director. Does this mean nothing, all of a sudden? Why are people insisting on being unpredictable, why are they hellbent on upsetting my plans? I look into myself, and for the first time the future is far from set. I'm losing ground, I'm losing my grip. You know my tenacity, I will not be denied. But this is a dark time, where so much seems to be falling apart around me. For the first time, the first time ever, I can take nothing for granted.

32

Success

ALASDAIR:

I am in Marianne's flat. I am standing in her living room. I am not crying.

A few seconds ago I was standing outside her front door. It was not locked. I must have turned the handle, I must have crossed the threshold. I do not remember these things but they must be true because now I am standing in Marianne's living room.

It is morning. This is the best time to be here: in bright sunshine, before ghosts creep in. No, stop that. There are no such thing as ghosts.

There are no dirty coffee cups. There is no dust. She cleaned up before she left. She polished. I can smell Windex. I can smell Mr. Sheen. The living room has the brisk scent of sanity; nothing untoward can have happened here.

Marianne has left me nothing – there was no note, but she never was much for writing letters – so although I will not admit it to myself, I am here to take something. I am here to steal from the dead.

There are her magazines. The *Vogues*, the *Tatlers*, the rags. They must be thrown away. Not recycled. Dumped, burnt; they are tainted, they are filled with deceit. I turn, walk over to the music system. The three CDs are safe in their cases, cocooned against contamination. They are not for taking; I have heard them all before, too many times. They were the background, she never was much for listening to music. She preferred the quiet, she preferred the golden silence.

I am not crying. I am solid steel, shining in the sun. I will not leak, I will not rust. Metal, I walk through to her bedroom. Her bed is made. Her clothes sleep in ordered drawers, in an organised wardrobe. I won't touch her clothing. I will make myself forget. Her portfolio sits on the bedside table, accused. It is tidy. She did not slice the photographs. They remain in place; not torn, not ripped. They no longer remind me of her. They are not for taking.

I am a solid wall; brick by brick, I will not crumble. My face is dry. Granite, I walk through to her kitchen. The surfaces shine, the sink sparkles. I can smell scouring pads, I can smell Jif. There is metal on the kitchen table. A corkscrew, a set of keys. I put the corkscrew away, safe with the other utensils. I put the keys in my jacket pocket. Everything is in its place. There is no madness here.

I am stainless, I am polished silverware. I walk through to her bathroom. Her toiletries lie behind mirrored sliding cabinet doors. They are hidden, but I can hear them whispering, I can feel their promises. The bathroom is filled with madness. I look at myself in the mirror. I am still the same, there has been no radical transformation. I am untouched, I am clinical. I turn away from the mirror and kneel down, moving away the bath mat and pulling up the floor boards. The ends of the wood are rough, with splinters, but I am safe, I do not bleed. I am invincible. I look down into the black, I am not afraid. I reach into the gap, and it is cold. She turned off the hot water before she left. I should be staggered by the sense of orderliness, but I feel nothing.

I am not searching for clues, I will not find anything down in the gap under the bath. I let my fingers walk along the bottom, and it is dry, smooth. Then they brush against something; small, plastic. It is nothing. I pull it out. A travel alarm clock, to wake her up. To wake her up when she was sleeping under the bath. It is nothing. I replace the boards and mat, then go into her bedroom and put the clock on top of her portfolio. Everything in its place. I am not covering tracks. I am not providing alibis. There is nothing amiss.

I walk back through her living room and into the hall. Marianne's tennis racquet is standing on its head, lackadaisical. I pick it up. It is light, it will not weigh me down. Worn handle, scuffed head, it has seen better days. I carry it out of the flat and close the door. Keys in the lock, a metallic click. All items are checked off the list, and Marianne has left me with nothing.

Roger was there, of course. He came up to me at the graveside and I was glad to have my friends, her friends, close by.

'Are you all right?' he asked gently.

'Still alive,' I replied.

He put a hand on my shoulder. 'I'm right here, Alasdair. Okay?'

I tried a grin, but it came out all wrong. More like a grimace, a shudder.

'I'm right here,' he repeated.

'Okay,' I replied.

'Good,' he said. His eyes said more. His eyes said everything.

Rebecca was there too. I think that they're getting back together. Perhaps, maybe, possibly. You never can tell. But Roger and Rebecca look natural together, did I ever tell you that? They look as though they belong together. I hope it all works out for them.

You bitch, how could you turn me away like that? How could you turn out the lights?

When I was five-years-old my grandfather died. My mother was too upset to tell her sons, so my father told us, only he used the wrong words. Said that Granddad had 'passed away'. Like I knew what that meant. The next day my brother said that Granddad was dead, and I didn't believe him. Ran to my mother, asked her to make him stop saying that. Can you imagine?

I want to ask the same question at Marianne's funeral. I want to ask someone, someone who looks like they're on top of things, is she really dead? Seriously? You know I find that very difficult to believe, I really do. But there's no one to ask. No one's up to answering my question.

I think of Marianne playing tennis. She never played well and she had no poise on the court. She stumbled from point to point; my ungraceful, disgraceful model, laughing and loving the game. She wasn't particularly interested in winning, but I let her win anyway, just to see her smile. I can't help the question in my mind, why would someone so beautiful kill herself? I can't help asking the question, and its shallowness exposes me, betrays my crass mediocrity. She's left me alone, and Erika can't fill the gap that's been so brutally exposed. That's not her fault. We don't have history, Erika and I, we don't go way back. She can stand beside me, she can hold my hand, but she can't pull me out of this chasm.

That was Marianne's last public appearance, jumping off her bridge. As we bury her, I can note the bitter irony that people really did ogle that night, look at her broken death and decide who she was, decide who they wanted her to be. Other people are here, standing by as they lower the coffin, but they are blurred, they are inconsequential. Jay is here, without Tara, and I don't think I've ever seen Jay by himself before. He looks pale, torn, he looks like he cares. But it's just a mask, just another piece of theatre. He doesn't give a damn, why should he?

I'm the one on trial here, I'm the one to blame. I know that I should have saved her. I was her best friend, I should have seen what was coming. I should have been her insomniac, should have discovered the theft, gone to her bridge and found her, shaken her, slapped her, saved her. When Mari's parents walk up to me I feel I should get down on my knees and beg forgiveness for my failure.

We're in Musselburgh today, a small town close to Edinburgh. The deceased's mother is shattered by grief but her soft accent does not waver. I clench myself, to stop myself crying in front of her. It's the least I can do. I notice how good she looks in black and narrowly avoid throwing the compliment her way. Funny the things you think about at times like these. Erika gives my hand a squeeze as we walk away and I wonder what she could possibly see in me.

33

Tiger

ROGER:

It was a lovely service. No. Of course not. It was shit, it was fucking awful. It was a funeral.

Funerals are not like weddings, even though the venue is the same. They are softer, with blurred edges. People can't stop talking about us when we die, but we lose our definition all the same. The minister spoke; he had known Marianne when she was young. This is a small town, the Falconers are known, many people attended the service. The minister spoke, and the people sang.

'In times of tragedy, it is tempting to ask why, why did this happen. How could it happen? But now is not the time to ask questions. We must work together to help Marianne's family and friends in their loss. We must give them the strength to grieve, then heal. We must help them, in the aftermath of this terrible, terrible accident.'

God had no problem letting Marianne in, despite what the rule-book says. It was a terrible accident, everyone is agreed. And this is no lie: every suicide is an accident. No one can really mean to do it, can they?

I walked up to Alasdair at the graveside, and once again I knew what to say.

'Alasdair, man, whatever you need, I'm right here

for you. Whatever you need, I'm right here, okay?'

He had this strange look on his face, and I think he might have burst into tears, or just started screaming. But I squeezed his shoulder, looked him in the eye.

'I'm right here, Al.'

He nodded, straightened up, and I knew he would get through it.

I'm getting so damn good at these things. I'd make a good friend, don't you think? Maybe we should get together sometime, if you're not too busy. Do you need a shoulder, do you need an open hand, a listening ear? I'm here for you; boy, girl, man, woman, let me tell you: I'm here for you all. Let me in, before we all run out of time. Let me in, and don't let this happen again.

Our friends are dying. They die in flight, in motion. The young, they rush towards death. They hit concrete, viruses, oncoming traffic. There is rarely any warning, it is always unexpected. Our friends are supposed to get married, they are supposed to start families. Dying like this, they are breaking rules written in stone. We go to their funerals and we feel cheated; they have stolen something precious from us. When we get old, our friends will desert us in greater numbers. Our bodies will let us down, the vital organs will give in to gravity. Look inside an elderly body; it is yellow, dry, used up. The old die quietly; even a heart attack lacks drama, it shows itself only in their eyes, the colour of their skin. We shall get used to their funerals. There will be tea and sandwiches, gin and old jokes. Our black suit will lie in the wardrobe, passing in and out of fashion, only the waist will be adjusted. Our friends are dying, and in time, years from now, we shall get used to it.

Poor Marianne. My sisters say a woman is like a tea bag: it's only when she's in hot water that you realise how strong she is. That's what my sisters say. Poor Marianne, how did things get so bad? What was wrong with your friends, what was wrong with us, to make you feel so hopeless? I shall never understand this, I shall never understand suicide. There must always be something else, some other solution. Is it my lack of imagination that leaves me blind to the horrors that Marianne must have seen? How can things get so bad? We think we know people, we think we know our friends.

I spoke to her on the telephone the night before she left for Tokyo. She was full of life then, she made me laugh. We talked about food, about diet.

'I'm looking for the golden rules,' I said. 'I'm looking for the secrets of the thin trade.'

'Roger, sweetheart, I think you might want to give fish suppers a miss from now on. I think you might want to give Fernando's a very wide berth.'

She laughed with that great rolling chuckle she has. Had. Perhaps she was highly amused by the thought of me actually losing weight. But she was helpful, full of neat little tricks concerning cake, broccoli, and Special K. She sounded so up, so happy.

But perhaps she was desperate even then, perhaps I am easily fooled. Was it Tokyo? Was it Edinburgh? There was no note, no explanation in black and white. Welcome to the grey; it stings your eyes, it leaves you blind. Jay was there, the night I 'phoned. Perhaps he saw a clue, perhaps he felt something in the space she inhabited. I should ask him, but I know I won't. I can't talk about this, I don't understand enough to even begin.

Hunched, Alasdair spoke to Marianne's parents. Erika stood by, without sunglasses, holding his hand. I'm impressed that she's still around, in the middle of her hype-drive. But yes, she's still here with Alasdair, trying to help him through something she had no part in, helping him mourn someone she never met. It isn't good for them to go through such a trauma so early in their relationship. They haven't set the guide-lines yet, they're having to make up the standards as they go along. Too fast, they will make mistakes. But Erika is still here, there was no flash in the pan. I am glad.

Marianne's parents did not look like the mother and father of a fashion model. Their skin was ashen, they had not slept. But there were no hysterics, no clawing at their eyes. They were civilised, they were going through the motions. Their daughter was lowered into the ground, and they showed their strength. I couldn't imagine what they were going through, I had no clue.

I looked away, diminished, and saw Jay talking to a woman I didn't know. She was attractive, perhaps she is a model too. Perhaps she best understands what had rushed through Marianne's mind. I did not ask her. Instead I stood and watched, as Jay talked his talk. I didn't need to lip-read, I knew what he was saying.

'My dear, I hate to talk business on such a dark, dark day, but I couldn't help noticing your fabulous features. I'm a theatre director, you see, and I was wondering, have you ever considered a spell upon the stage? Perhaps, not today of course, but perhaps you would care to join me for dinner, so we can discuss your . . . prospects.'

The same old lines, the same old promises, toned down for a sombre occasion, but underneath they were identical. Jay talked, then the woman had a look of sudden distaste, as if she had been half-way through a meal and had just realised that the food was off and the wine was corked. She grimaced, then walked away, leaving Jay alone. He looked different by himself, he had lost a few inches. He looked as if he needed a friend, but I didn't want to talk to him. I turned and started to walk back to the church, needing to be by myself.

Becky. She was sitting on a bench, looking at her hands. She wore a T-shirt and jeans, she didn't have any bags with her. I drew my own conclusions. I padded up to her, bare feet on grass, a jungle cat.

'Hi.'

She looked up, gave me a strained smile. 'Hello, Tiger. Why don't you take a seat?'

'Yeah.' I sat down beside her, closer than I had been for months. I couldn't tell how much space there really was between us. She looked tired; peaky, her mother would say. Still beautiful though, still what I wanted.

She looked at me, smiling that strange smile again. 'You look different. You've lost weight?'

It wasn't a question. She could tell, our bodies know each other so well.

'I went on a diet,' I said, suddenly feeling foolish.

'Fernando's must be heart-broken. Why'd you do that?'

'For you. Sounds pretty stupid now.'

'It wasn't about weight, Tiger.'

I shrugged. 'I had to do something.' I looked at her. 'I was treading water without you.'

'Tiger.' Becky reached for my hand, but I stood up and moved away. My throat felt thick. I fought it off; crying would have been disastrous.

'Are you here for the day or what? You've missed the service.'

'Yes, it was a bit of a rush. I wasn't really dressed for it anyway.' She stood up and walked over to me; one, two, three steps, very close. 'Alasdair called, to

255

tell me about the funeral. I was sorry to hear about Marianne, I know you were keen on her.'

I said nothing. I know now that silence is less incriminating. There will be no more words out of turn. This had to be our official breaking-up conversation, our just good friends chat. Becky was here on business, to clean up the mess. I wished I had a pack of cigarettes, just to spite her.

'I wasn't going to come,' she said, 'but Chloe called last night.'

I sighed. 'What shit is she spreading this time?'

'Tiger.' Becky took my hands in her own, and this time I let her. 'It was Jay.'

I looked at her, confused misery. 'What was?'

'He set us up. He told Chloe to say what she did. It was his idea.'

'I don't understand.'

'When we had the fight, after you went around to his flat. He 'phoned Chloe. It was Jay.' Becky turned grey, like the ground, like the sky, and I shut my eyes, letting a tear escape.

'Are you okay?' She put her hand to my face, wiping my cheek. I opened my eyes, and there was colour again.

'Are you coming home, Becky?' My voice was an unattractive whisper, not a voice for selling anything.

'I brought some stuff up on the train, it's in my flat.'

Her flat.

But she put her hands around my waist, an experiment. 'I went into your place, to see Fat Cat, you don't mind, do you?'

I put my arms around her, looking over her shoulder, looking at the church. 'Did he recognise you?'

She laughed softly into my ear. 'Yes, I think he still remembers who I am. He's pretty smart, you know.'

I looked at stained glass, at some Saint I didn't know. I haven't touched a bible since I was at school. 'He missed you.'

'I missed him too.' I could feel her breath, warm and full of history. 'Have you got any cigarettes on you, Tiger?'

I pulled back and looked at her. 'I quit. Why?'

She laughed. 'Funny. All this shit made me *start* smoking.'

I shook my head. 'Dirty habit, Becky.'

'I know. Are we going to head back, then?'

'Yeah.'

I took her hand, and we walked away from the funeral, back towards the bus stop.

Becky has something on me, something she can use to draw blood. The mistake I made, the lie I told. I hurt her, and now she has a weapon. She could use it at any time; it might feel cheap, but it will prove irresistible. I also have a weapon, I also have a plate to throw: Becky was the one who left. Power is essential for a relationship. Maybe her cards are better than mine, but at least I'm holding something in my hand.

We went to her flat. We had tea and buttered toast; cold afternoon food. Fat Cat seemed smaller with Becky in the room, but I could tell he was pleased to have her back. We watched television, a black and white film, war propaganda. The message was real, even if the bullets were not. We sat on the sofa, Fat Cat sharing our laps.

'Is your tea all right, Becky?'

'Mmm. Lovely.'

'Sorry there wasn't any milk. Busy day and everything.'

'It's fine, Roger, I understand.'

'I could pop out and get some, if you like.'

'Roger, it's fine.'

'Right.'

It must have looked very domestic. It must have looked cosy, even romantic. But what had happened sat with us on the sofa; silent, but impossible to ignore. I left the flat at five o'clock, to go to Buddies. To watch the rehearsal. To see Jay.

34

Human Resources

During decline a cohesive structure may be seen
as a critical defence against an aggressive environment. Organisations face difficult decisions
concerning retrenchment and withdrawal from
markets which are ingrained in the culture of the
organisation.
In some situations the difficulties of adjustment
can be so great that the company's directors
choose to sell out to another firm, which may
then be able to instigate radical changes.
– *Business Strategy in the Twenty First Century*

JAY:
The strangest thing. I tried some threeplay at
Marianne's funeral. I tried myself on a bleached
blonde with a black soul. But without success. Is
there guilt? Is that it? Oh please, not guilt. I really
don't have time for that nonsense.

There's nothing more to say about the funeral. It
was typical; grey, full of nervous glances and tired
smiles. Nothing out of the ordinary; we were all on
our best behaviour.

But I was guilty. No one knows the part I played,
although there's no need for a dirty confession. I
shall never tell. It will remain inside of me – a growth,

a weed – sending out green shoots, tentacles around my heart. Guilt, it's not something of which I have experience, it's not a road I have travelled. Roger, for once, is light-years ahead. And Alasdair – guilty of nothing, of being his pathetic self – leads the way, forging a path that I have only begun to follow. It's strange for me to be behind a trend, instead of setting it.

Theatre used to be my constant; reassuring, soothing my furrows. I leant on my Buddies crutch, trying to keep from falling. I have to stay upright; if I were to lose my footing, I might never hit the ground. It's a bottomless pit, a lift with no basement. But even Buddies lacks its usual strength. The Fringe approaches, promising bloody revolution. There are six days to go before Week Zero, with its do or die press nights, advertising frenzy, and acute fear of the general public. The period of artistic endeavour is over; subtleties of face and voice must stay as they are. Better or worse, we can't waste any further rehearsal time smoothing over the rough edges.

Now it is a case of ensuring the actor finds his words, finds her light, come on from the right side, at the right time. There are no sound effects in our *Dream*; no notorious gun-shots fated to go off ten seconds late, leaving the performers standing, turning murder into hilarity. The final props arrive – on hire, on a promise – and the actors handle them, get used to their texture. And the costumes have their final fittings – a nip here, a tuck there – the sound of scissors, the sight of bare flesh, goose pimples in the frigid dressing room. Ah, theatre is a business, it runs on money just like any other. Don't be fooled by the sights and sounds, the glamour and *trompe-l'oeil*. The bacon must be brought home, and this is achieved by making damn sure the actors and techies are in the right place at the right time.

Tara has moved into my residence. That heap of deleterious rags, she kept the keys and threw a fistful of toiletries into my bathroom cabinet. She has torn her way into my life, and we are playing by her rules. My home has lost its balance, its clarity of style. The bedroom has become infected with Tara's bitch scent, no amount of fresh air will alleviate the stench. The kitchen is malignant; cluttered with her weight-watching products, her jagged cans of Diet Coke.

There is no escape. At Buddies she makes it clear to everyone that we are together. There is no time, no room, for me to play with the actors. Tara is everywhere; she is constantly watching over the playground, making her wishes plain.

'Post-rehearsal cocktail, Sarah? I know the most delightful place. Very chic, very intimate. We could discuss your motivation, the whys and wherefores of your character.'

'Sorry, Jay. A girl has to get her beauty sleep.'

'Come now, Sarah, you look very well rested to me. You look positively radiant.'

'Sorry.'

The women are under her warped control, I have lost the ability to adjust their vision. The graceful art of manipulation; I've no idea who taught her these skills.

And you will have heard by now, I'm sure, about Rebecca's return on the Edinburgh scene. Is Roger happy? I'm sure he *thinks* that he's happy, I'm sure that he thinks that life is just rosy pink. He does not understand, you see, that greatness in life cannot be attained by playing second fiddle to a woman. This I know, this I teach. I tried, as long as I've known Mr. Brown, to help him understand the finer points of the human condition. But he is stubborn, unwilling to rise above the intellectual cattle. He is branded, he is ordinary. It is a failure of threeplay, I know that, but this one disappointment does not mean that the entire system is at fault. I'm a victim of circumstance, orchestrated by Roger's aversion to playing by the rules. Well, really, where did he get this sudden passion from? People shouldn't change, it shouldn't be allowed.

The evening after we buried Marianne under the earth, Roger strode into Buddies and ordered me into the office, crashing a rehearsal, gross misconduct. Right then I should have taken the reins and made it clear that I would not tolerate such rude interruption of the creative process. But Roger's shining eyes, the bit between his teeth, let me know that it was better to avoid a public scene. I called a smoke-break and followed him out of the auditorium.

I walked into the office and sat behind the desk. Roger stood by the tatty sofa, unwilling to sit down. I took the silver cigarette box out of the drawer but Roger shook his head.

'We have to talk,' he said.

'Yes,' I replied calmly, reaching for Peter Stuyvesant, lighting him up. 'Cigarette?'

'Becky came to the funeral.'

'I saw. Someone should let her know that Levi 501s are hardly the correct dress for such a solemn occasion.'

'She told me what you did. She told me what you got Chloe to do.'

I inhaled, filling my lungs, filling them up. 'Are you sure you won't join me in a cigarette? I'm sure you'd feel better for it.'

Roger glared at me, trying to stay angry, trying to

stay on track. 'Why did you do it, Jay? I thought we were friends, you told me we were best friends.'

I smiled, gracious to the last, despite such empty accusations. 'Indeed we are, dear Mr Brown, and that is why I'm rather surprised that you should take the word of a common tart like Chloe over mine. I'm a victim of blackmail, Roger, plain and simple. Anyway, what I did was purely in your best interest.'

'What? Are you nuts? You broke us up, you put me through hell. Jesus, all that time, never saying anything. Pretending to be sympathetic, when it was your doing, when it was all your fault. If Chloe hadn't admitted what she'd done, you'd still be sitting there feeding me a line of shit!'

'Oh come on Roger! If you hadn't made up that ridiculous affair in the first place none of this would have ever happened.'

'It was your idea,' Roger protested, aware of how weak his argument was as soon as the words left his mouth.

'I seem to remember that I suggested homicide and AIDS as well, but you didn't take me up on those fine options.' I tapped Peter with finesse, and Roger gazed at my cigarette with hilarious longing.

'You're missing the point, Jay, and you know it.'

'I'll tell you what I know, Mr Brown. I know that you were in a total mess with Rebecca, I know that you begged for my assistance, and I know that I did you a big favour, removing that girl from the picture. Face facts, Roger, she's simply no good for you, you were far better off without her.'

Roger's voice, sharp and grating; he was judging me, putting me in a box. 'You weren't helping, Jay, you were fucking everything up. Okay, so I made a stupid mistake, but there was no reason for you to keep adding to it, week after week, piling on the lies. What you did, that was just crazy.'

'So please forgive me for trying to help an old friend in distress.'

'Stop, Jay, it's over. Stop telling me all this crap. You were playing with my life, just for the hell of it. God knows what else you've been doing behind my back. Christ, Becky and me, we're human beings, you can't go around treating people like that.' He held out his hands, as if he had something new to offer, as if he has the power to save me. Don't bother, Roger. Whatever you're trying to sell, I'm not buying.

I stubbed out Peter and stood up, adding height, adding presence. 'It's Becky and *I*, you illiterate prole. And you think I was playing? You fool, I was trying to save you from yourself. You think that Rebecca is going to make you happy, but you're so wrong. She's a woman, and she'll leave you in the end, she has too, they can't help it. Women leave men, and you should have bumped her for good when you had the chance. Now you're the one who'll end up with egg on your face, and don't come running to me when it happens.'

Roger looked at me, a different expression on his face. He looked sad, embarrassed, and suddenly I knew what was coming. If I'd had a gun, I would have shot him there and then, just to stop the hateful words from being voiced.

'Becky isn't your mother, Jay.'

I leaned forward onto the desk, weakened. I looked at Roger with new eyes; a monster, an uncaring beast, to hit so low. I had to say something, and what else was there to say?

'You're fired, you virulent scab! Now get out of my office!'

'No,' said Roger, the calm, cool Chimera. 'I'll stay

until the end of the Fringe, and then I'll quit. Between now and then I'd appreciate it if you only spoke to me when absolutely necessary.' Then he turned, opened the door, and walked out of the office and out of Buddies.

I whipped out from behind my desk and ran to the side entrance. 'I make the decisions around here, shit! Not you, me, you shitty shit!' But he didn't stop, just kept on walking, and then he was gone. I walked back to my office and collapsed onto the tatty sofa, my heart burning, my eyes on fire. I reached into my pocket for my cigarettes but my fingers were made of stone.

A knock on the door, and Tara's voice splintered through the wood. 'Everything all right? Are we starting again?'

'Five minutes,' I said, shaking, trying to pluck Peter from his case.

'I heard shouting, are you okay?'

'Fine, fine. Five minutes, Tara, just give me five.'

'Right.' Feet clumped away, back into the auditorium, and I lit the cigarette, a wild flame, making it smoulder, blackening the paper, with those stone fingers that surely didn't belong to me. They shuddered, they quivered, they just would not do what I told them to. Breathing in, breathing out, I tried to regain control of my hands. Five minutes later I was better. After five minutes I could hold Peter in my hand without him falling to the floor. Small victories. I am reduced to the smallest of victories.

No blood, no slaughter. The days have passed and now we are in the present, the final few days before Week Zero. Roger and I have to talk to each other; unfortunate but unavoidable. In one months time I will be rid of him. I shall start afresh with a loyal producer; one who understands the rules of the game. Every day we sit in the office – a room that feels too cramped, too close for comfort – and discuss business matters. Then we take our turns on the stage: I, with my precious performers, showing them the difference between comedy and farce, teaching them how to be amusing without laughing at the joke; and Roger, ensuring the stage is flame-proof, checking that the bills have been paid. We do our jobs, director and producer, brushing past each other, careful not to push.

'Say, Mr Brown. How is our small predicament regarding the Fringe central booking office?'

'I called them this morning, Mr Wellesley. Everything's sorted out.'

'Well done, Mr Brown. Another excellent piece of work.'

The actors and technicians are silent when we are both in the auditorium; waiting for a flare-up, waiting for a fight. But there will be no blood. We are prisoners, Roger and I, working out our time. With good behaviour release will come sooner.

Roger and I sit in Negociants between three and four o'clock. Sitting at the same table, where the damn fool waitress has put us, we stare at the walls, examine our hands. One of us should leave, there's no longer enough room in the bar for such emotional toxicity. But this is my place, I will not go in search for another, not this late in the day. And Roger, with his new-found stubbornness, his arrogance born of second-rate sexual intercourse, will not leave either. The people who know me, who know Buddies, they steer clear of our table, sitting outside, hiding in dark corners. They don't want to taste our failure, fearful that some may rub off on their lips. We are strangers to the rest of them, just two men sitting quietly. Old friends, they might think, if they bother to consider us at all. They pass by, uninterested, ignorant of the illfeeling that sits heavily in the air, unaware of the toxic belligerence. So we sit there, looking everywhere but at each other, creating migraine and indigestion. And every so often one of us gets some more drinks: Roger with his ridiculous Highland Spring; Jay with his Cabernet, his Merlot, his tasteless vin du jour.

'Your round,' I say.

'Fine,' he says gruffly. 'Bitter Lemon?'

An old joke between two old friends. We've tried every drink in Negociants over the years, except the Bitter Lemon. Because it sounds bad, it sounds like something no one could possibly enjoy. But as Roger walks over to the bar, wallet in his hand and bad feeling in his stomach, I understand the Bitter Lemon. I realise that I deserve one. I *am* one. Biting and worn out, malignant and shattered, I have nothing left to give except caustic comments regarding the human race. Human *Race*. As if anyone is actually going to win.

I watch Roger stand at the bar, ordering the drinks and paying the barmaid. But it isn't just a matter of ordering and paying. They exchange hellos, howyadoin's, even a joke.

'Hi, Slim,' she says. 'How's the diet?'

'Hi. All going according to plan. I'm hardly worth harpooning at all. I think you can take me off the At-Risk Register.'

She giggles, an outrageous flirt.

'You're one skinny whale.'

I can't do that sort of thing anymore. I'm scared, these days, I'm scared of people, I'm scared of the damage I might do. Why should I be wary of a barmaid? She's earning peanuts, bar snacks, for

God's sake. But the words and smiles roll out of Roger's mouth. How does he do that? How did he get so relaxed? And I resent both of them for a few violent seconds, jealous of their trivial interaction, their simple respect. I lost that somewhere along the road, the misery superhighway.

Bitter Lemon. That's what I am, and I know it, as I sit in a hangover cloud with only my toilet tongue for company.

Marianne, dead in the ground but still in my life, dragging me down to the earth, soiling my clothes. I do not want to believe that I had a hand in her suicide. I do not want to turn myself in. I see her in the street, in the theatre, in the mirror, pointing at me with rotting fingers. Threeplay is a sport, it is not life and death. Threeplay is a game I play; how could I have foreseen such dramatic consequences? It is Alasdair who should be suffering. What did he do to her, to cause so much damage? Instead he is living it up, dancing with poetry, flirting with art. Events are not evolving the way I expected them to; everything is being turned on its head.

Oh yes, I know you and your bland advice. You think it would be better if I changed; if I made myself like everyone else, made myself like you. The world would look less bleak, you maintain, if I would just accept my limitations, accept that I was all too human. But I have no time for such frailties. I don't want to lower myself into the animal mainstream. My destiny, it is volcanic; good or bad, something meteoric will happen with myself at its core. I will not slink away, willing banality. I shall charge ahead, full speed, pedal to the metal. I will not shirk my responsibilities. I have lived – constant, unchanging, unbending – since I was a child, since my mother left.

My form has protected me against the inferior population, with it's petty jealousies and venomous scheming. Now, with problems growing, squabbling for attention, I will not adjust my behaviour. My pride, battered and bruised, will nonetheless remain intact. There will be no compromise of integrity. I will not bend. My father is coming, to see the show, to take me to lunch. I will ask him for guidance. I will ask him to show me the way.

35

Arthur's Seat

ALASDAIR:
Life goes on.

The days, weeks, a month after a successful suicide attempt, there is very little difference. I do the things I did before, the essentials remain unchanged. Late at night my body betrays me and I fall into sleep, undeserving. I eat – cereal, bread, potatoes – it passes through me, fuel for thought. And I don't want to think all that much. I pay bills. Money trickles in and out of my Royal Bank of Scotland current account: rent, gas, student loans. I settle my Mastercard, renew magazine subscriptions. I use my Switch at Scotmid, which leads to food, which leads to sleep, which leads to tomorrow.

Skin sloughs away; I shave and scrub, and new layers are formed. But I've given up on moisturisers, on alphahydroxies. I no longer replenish and tone last thing at night and first thing in the morning. These creams and potions, there's something about the smell. It is artificial, abrasive, it makes my eyes water. I haven't thrown all the products away; they hide in the bathroom cabinet, furtive and scheming. I keep my toothbrush and razor on top of the cabinet and the unscented soap lies on a plate on the windowsill. It's everything I need; I don't spend much time in the bathroom anymore. An occasional brief glance at myself in the mirror lets me know that my skin has not altered. The blemishes remain, neither better nor worse. My face is the same, but I am saving money.

I played tennis with Erika on Saturday. She was worse than Mari and I wasn't able to play badly enough to let her win. Not a good idea, tennis. Erika stood at the other end of the court, shorter and scrawnier, unwilling to run and reach. We spent the afternoon walking after tennis balls, bending down and picking them up, walking back, holding them aloft, a sign of disinterested intentions. One shot, one miss, and the cycle began again. We didn't shout jokes at each other and when we swapped sides there was no contact, no sporting insults. Erika couldn't keep score and I lost count so we ended up making feeble attempts at rallying, forehand to backhand, but our aim lacked precision, the court had never looked so big and impossible. Erika only agreed to play because I had appeared so desperate, but she couldn't pretend to enjoy it. She isn't any good at humouring me; she isn't any good at sport. After forty-five dead minutes we gave up and trudged back to my flat to sit in front of the blank television, dry and un-exercised, while Veronica flitted in and out.

'Coffee, Erika? Oh, you don't drink coffee, do you?'

'No, Veronica, but thanks anyway.'

'My pleasure. So what do poets drink?'

Erika blinked. 'What've you got?'

'Everything,' Veronica said.

'Thanks sounds nice,' Erika replied. 'I'll have some of that.'

'Ice and lemon?'

'Absolutely.'

I glared at Veronica. 'Don't you think it's a bit early to start drinking cocktails?'

'Christ!' Erika cried. 'It's never too early!'

Veronica squealed with delight. 'Cool! I think Erika is going to be a very good influence on you, Ally.'

'Oh, God,' I whispered. 'Okay, let's do it. We have nothing to lose but our livers.'

I leaned back and sighed. Veronica is used to Erika. Everyone is used to Erika except me.

So on Sunday we went for a picnic on Arthur's Seat. This is what Erika likes: to sit on the grass, watching over Edinburgh, her city. It was a clear day, we saw for miles and miles, sifting through a rucksack of home-made sandwiches and warm chardonnay. I don't like to drink in the afternoon but I make compromises these days just like Erika does. We test each other out, with tentative demands for the other to bend, synchronise. This must be what happens in a relationship. I don't want to change her, and I am immovable, static. But we can make small adjustments to our rhythms. The little things that let us get along. The lights.

We were not alone on this lump of rock, giving the impression of being a mountain, but in reality only eight hundred feet above sea level. Four million visitors every year to this mass of stone and soil. Groups of tourists, lost or intentional, scattered themselves around us, along with local families who know the perfect spot, the perfect route, the perfect time. Joggers, straying from the path, eroding, causing damage. Students too, clambering up, wearing black, wearing tired expressions; it's a torrid initiation during matriculation, to come up here late at night, protected from the cold by cheap lager and badly rolled joints. Finally there were other couples attempting romance, trying for intimacy in a northern exposure. I looked at these boy-girl teams and wondered which ones were just starting out, trying each other for size; which ones were used to each other, comfortably bored; which ones were approaching the end of their relationship tether, making one last attempt at reconciliation, or seeing things off with a final shivering bang.

Erika and I passed the bottle of chardonnay back and forth, anything to take away the taste of Bernard Matthews turkey-ham and Hellmans low-calorie mayonnaise. Low fat, low enjoyment; Erika said that next time she would make the sandwiches. I didn't tell her that this was my first try, my first clutch at the romantic picnic.

'It's supposed to be *fun*, Alasdair,' she said. 'Where's the *fun* food?'

I reached inside the rucksack. 'Bananas are fun,' I said hopefully, hopelessly. 'Good for energy, too. Bananergy.' I offered her the bunch.

'No thank you.' She sniffed, pushing her sunglasses (justified for once in the sunshine) up the bridge of her nose. 'There's nothing the slightest bit fun about fruit. Where's your sense of extravagance, where's the smoked salmon, where's the caviar?'

'Sorry.'

'Where are the creme eggs,' she said, 'the jelly beans? You didn't even bring any fucking Nutella.'

'Sorry.'

'And don't say sorry, you're always saying sorry, I'm sick of all your sorries.'

'Sorry.'

'Alasdair!'

I put the bananas away. 'It won't happen again.'

'There's no need to get snotty about it.'

273

'Oh you,' I said. 'Sometimes you're such a scabby old hag.'

A pause. We looked at each other, then burst out laughing. At least some things are in synch. At least we can make each other laugh. I may not know much, but I do know how important humour is. We laughed – hard, messy, making tears – our private jokes grow and prosper with each passing day.

Erika reached under her sunglasses to wipe away her tears. Then she rolled onto me and gave my ribs a friendly poke. 'Well, go on, then.'

'What?'

'Give me one of those fucking bananas.'

I took them back out of the rucksack, and broke off a piece of fun. 'You know what I like about you?' I said, passing her the banana.

'What, my sweet?'

I waited until she had started on her banana. 'You turn even the most basic request into sheer poetry.'

'Umph! You cunt.' The second poke in the ribs was markedly less friendly. 'You critic. You lousy fucking hack.'

I smiled, then I kissed her; a quick peck, full of daring. 'Show some respect, witch. My review will do wonders for your show, and you know it.'

'Haven't you heard?' said Erika. 'No one reads reviews anymore, especially not in *The Scotsman*.'

'True enough.' I kissed her again, cool breeze and sunshine, and then I remembered Marianne. It comes from nowhere, this sudden realisation. Sometimes I'm surprised at its ferocity, but mostly I can barely believe that I managed to forget her for even a moment. I gently pushed Erika off and stood up, knees crackling. I'm an old man, middle-aged, caught between *naïveté* and wisdom. I'm stuck in the middle, and I'm still too young for this. I stood, watching the smug tourists, the crabby families, and felt that dull ache that is similar to indigestion. No theatre, this feeling, just pain.

I walked past The Merlin last Thursday and imagined I saw Marianne sitting at one of the tables. Looking out the window with a Marlboro Light in her right hand, cradling a mug of hot chocolate in her left. I thought I saw her face, I thought I saw her laugh. The woman who wasn't Mari, who wasn't anything like Mari, saw me watching her and gave me *such a look* before turning away, with . . . with what? A tired resignation? She thought I was ogling, she didn't know that I had seen a ghost.

And my love, my love cuts a hole in my heart. I never wanted to feel this bad, I never wanted to feel this much. It truly is a physical pain that attacks me, this grief. I hate it, then I hate it again for I know one day I will recover, I will survive this, and Mari will still be dead. A day will come and I'll feel completely alive and happy, and in that instant forget her, betray her, reject her.

But still there is Erika. She is still here, holding my hand, showing me how to sleep. I am grateful. I try not to take her for granted, I try not to be annoyed. I try not to make comparisons. Erika on Arthur's Seat, her eyes with tinted vision. She wore no make up. She has vanity, but it is more artistic than physical. I shouldn't think of Marianne, with her eyes and mouth, perfect shape, perfect tone. She is history, she has dispersed; there is nothing for me to betray, really, is there? She can't be hurt anymore, she is beyond feeling.

I would not find the idea of an afterlife a comforting one. Instead it is this nothingness, less than numb, less than empty, that lets me get up in the morning. I don't want to care so much, I want to

275

leave it all behind. I want to think about *The Scotsman*, about Erika, about poetry and theatre. I know it can be dangerous, to blank Marianne out like this. But the other way hurts too much. I'm not strong enough to face her ghost, not yet. This is what I need for my own survival: Marianne and the art of dispersal.

So I stood on Arthur's Seat and Erika got up and held me from behind, holding me tight, gently nuzzling.

'A good idea, this picnic, don't you think?'

I smiled. 'Of course. It was *your* idea.'

'Right answer! Really, Alasdair, you're a very fast learner.'

She isn't what I thought a poet would be; there's so much image, it seems, to being an artist. At first sight she is stand-offish and aloof, behind her shades, behind her words. She is seriously ironic or ironically serious. But I've gone beyond that first layer, just as she has with mine. We're peeling each other away, two steps forward one step back, looking for the centre, intrigued and apprehensive at what we might find. No matter what your parents might have said, it's better to be someone other than yourself for most things. Don't let them see all of you straight away, because if they scoff, if they scorn, then you're left with nothing. Erika has managed two amazing things: she is a poet who actually finishes her poems, and she is a poet who people want to read. *The Sugar Bowl*; it sells, a river heading out into the Atlantic Ocean. Anything could happen after the Fringe, the final chapter of her UK promotions. America beckons, its streets paved with abdomenizers and sacrament. Perhaps she'll let me go with her, take me on board. We will travel first-class and I'll forget myself.

'Okay?' asked Erika, looking over my shoulder.

'Yeah,' I replied.

'What're you thinking about?'

'Usual stuff. Past, present , future.'

'I see. Any brainwaves?'

I smiled. 'No. I'm not much for that sort of thing, you know me.'

'Do I?'

I turned to face her. 'Yes. Well, more than anyone else.'

She looked at me. 'I guess I do. It's hard work opening you up, Alasdair.'

'Yeah. Sorry.'

'Don't be sorry. It's what I like about you. Almost impenetrable, but underneath you're full of magic.'

'Am I?' I tried to work her out, to see if she was kidding. She always seems so honest when we're together, but you never can tell with people. 'I don't think there's anything magical about me.'

Erika put her hands to my face, stroked my fucked up skin. 'Fishing for a compliment, sweetpea?'

'No,' I said, embarrassed. 'I'm just not special, that's all. I can't imagine . . . why do you like me, Erika, why do you stay?'

She laughed. 'Because you're you, sugar. You're you. What else could I ask for?'

'Lots.'

'Alasdair, you do me good, there's no need to act so unworthy. I've never met anyone who was so easy to be with. You understand me.'

'Yes.' I didn't tell her that she was a mystery, that her continuing presence was baffling. I didn't tell her that I was still in love with the dispersed Marianne. It was unrequited love at first sight with Mari: as soon as I set eyes on her I knew, deep down. Of course she was untouchable. Of course she was never going to return the favour. Or course it was hopeless. But it

277

was still love. I can't commit myself to Erika and I don't know what she wants. Does she really like me? She must do; a review in *The Scotsman* isn't worth all this threeplay, all this sex. Is it getting serious? I don't know how I feel. I don't think I love her, not yet at least. I should ask her where we are going; I don't have experience, it's my first trip. But kissing her, the sun beating down, standing on top of the world, I decided to put the question off for a later date. Right now I would let it be. Right now I would go with the flow.

'It's almost hot.' Erika reached into the rucksack for the sun lotion. 'Burn, baby burn.'

She put some on her face and neck, and then her arms. It glistened, white smears on her skin, then it was absorbed, becoming an invisible shield. Mari always used UV protection; a tan would have been bad for business. Something they have in common, this desire to stay white. But I should stop making comparisons.

36

The Climbing Machine

ROGER:
Seven days until my birthday. Seven days until I am twenty-six years old. My, how time flies when you're in the middle of the Edinburgh Festival Fringe. The shows at Buddies, the shows that aren't *A Midsummer Night's Dream*, they put up their sets and then they take them down, oblivious of the strained atmosphere, too excited and exhausted to notice the killer vibes between Jay and me. These six theatre companies renting our venue, our position on the Fringe, they work around *The Dream*'s scaffolding, they add scraps of paper and card, plus the two lights they are allocated as well as our own lighting rig. The Buddies lighting guy guards the tech box, slapping away any potential outsiders, choosing to take the cues and do the spots and fades, the music and effects, for them. All included in rent; they get a pretty good deal, these dramatic tourists, all in all.

The company that's proving the most troublesome is a bunch of students from Newcastle who somehow managed to get the money needed to buy the six o'clock slot. They arrived in Edinburgh, wearing black, wearing me down, armed with rolled cigarettes and some screwed up Balzac, intending to paint the theatre red. Literally. I was most sympathetic to their cause, and said no. Then the day before press night hell, they tried to drag a Renault 5 through the side entrance and onto the stage. Oh dear. But it's only the chassis. Oh dear. But the play won't work without it. Oh mercy me. As I listened to their director's argument, I remembered how mad, in a quite tedious way, most students are.

'The car, you see, is like a traffic metaphor. I mean, we're talking industrial conspiracy. We're talking, man, this thing is totally global, you know. We're spreading a message here, you have to see that. You have to let us have the car.'

University: I'm well out of that nightmare. I stood there listening, shaking my head, and Jay came outside to take in the scene. We exchanged glances and he immediately knew the score.

'My heart bleeds when I see artists faced with the terrible prospect of compromise,' Jay said. 'How they suffer in the face of bourgeois theatre owners. I think I may cry, I think I may just die with grief.'

'Were we ever this stupid at university?' I asked him. 'Were we ever this fucking mad?'

We smiled at each other, and just for a second everything else was forgotten. Crises like these, they really help to bring people together. The Renault 5 is still out there, half on our property, half on the pavement, looking ridiculous, looking like a fire risk. If it's not gone by this time tomorrow, I'm going to lock the stupid bastards out of the theatre and keep their fucking money.

There is success, however. A local company is doing a production in our four o'clock slot and it's listed in the Fringe for Schools programme. It's a fun-size, ninety minute version of Macbeth (no, I'm not superstitious), very sleek, very exam-friendly. Groups of forty or fifty school kids arrive every afternoon; time out of the classroom, they're euphoric, on their best behaviour. I'm more than happy to see the mass of Heriots blazers and those from further afield; the show is selling out with ease. A low ticket price was part of the deal, but we've never had a full auditorium in the four o' clock time before. I watched the teachers, haggard and smoking, as they traipsed into Buddies. I don't know why they looked so unhappy; surely watching Shakespeare is more fun than actually teaching. It was my idea, by the way, to book this company. Success for Mr. Brown, but Jay isn't about to give me a standing ovation. Yes, I've done a good job, and I''m still doing it, twenty one days before I leave Buddies forever.

Looking for work, looking for the way ahead. More theatre, you might suggest; same game, different venue. But I don't want to start all over again somewhere new, getting to know people, getting them to like me, with Jay gloating from afar. I want something fresh, I want a clean taste in my mouth. And besides, I'm not sure I want drama anymore. I think I may be getting too old for artistic ventures.

I sat with Becky on her sofa, Fat Cat prowling in the kitchen, looking for mice, looking for scraps. Becky's flat is the same shape as mine, but somehow it manages to be so much nicer. She does things with the walls, the floor and ceiling. There's room to move, room to breathe, and there's a lot of exhaling going on here. Sunday morning; we sat in our nest of colour supplements and croissants, trivia and honey.

Becky flapped through the television listings, then flipped the newspaper onto the carpet. 'So what're you going to do?'

'I haven't decided. I mean, I'm not really sure.'

'Tick-tock, Tiger.'

'I know.'

'Do you want to get something through the agency?'

'Very funny.' I looked at her. 'That was a joke, wasn't it?'

Becky shrugged. 'Mostly. But we have some good I.T. stuff going. You're clever at computers, you could get a short-term contract, just while you decide, just to keep you in Kibbles.'

'It all sounds a bit desperate,' I said, eyeing her Benson & Hedges, which she's cut down to five a day; four at work and one after dinner, a five minute collapse when I pace outside, thinking about healthy lungs, not thinking about cigarettes.

'Nothing wrong with I.T., Tiger, the shape of things to come and all that.'

'Fair enough, but I'd rather do something more interesting than plonk away at a computer all day. I'd rather sell accidental death-insurance, I'd rather put toothpaste into tubes.'

'Just an idea,' Becky said. 'You'll have to train for something new if you're quitting theatre altogether.'

I sighed. 'I know, it's just difficult to think about it in the middle of the Fringe, that's all.'

'Yes,' she said. 'I'm sorry, you're right. Perhaps you should have a little holiday, relax the old brain cells.'

'That'd be nice. Where do you want to go?'

'Sorry, Tiger. I used up all my time off in Hampstead.' And she patted my knee; friendly, not sexy at all.

Ouch. Bang. Crunch. There it was, there it is, there it goes. Our past stifles our future, I'm forever stubbing my toe on it. There's no going forward when we keep looking over our shoulders. There are moments these days when I think that this relationship is definitely not a viable entity. I wanted Becky to come back, but now that she's home I'm not at all sure how to deal with her. Before the Lie, before the damage, we strolled into each other's flats, bumping and grinding, slapping and tickling. But now we knock on doors, make appointments. There are kisses, don't get me wrong. There are hugs, massages, and of course, pats. But round my way, no one's getting fucked.

I have less sex now than when Becky was in Hampstead, because I threw my mental pornography away. I stuffed it into black rubbish bags, to be collected on Monday and Thursday. I washed my self, my bed, my toilet seat: I cleaned up my act for the return of the Beckster. But now that she's back we're careful not to turn each other on. Our hands stay in international waters, careful never to stray, slapping ourselves back from the edge. Only our words are in danger of causing friction; unintended pain, the association of what has gone before.

Early days, I'm sure. Absolutely right. Absolutely fabulous. And if Becky's punishing me, I'm punishing her, because it's definitely not one-sided, this lack of sex. If she was to throw herself at me, toss her filofax to the wind, then I wouldn't know what to do, or rather I would know what I couldn't do. We've forgotten how we played, how we came together. We're guests in each other's homes, on our best behaviour, wary of overstepping the mark, anxious not to overstay our welcome.

We sat there on the sofa, probably friends, potentially lovers, and I looked at my watch.

'It's nearly eleven,' I said, stretching my arms above my head. 'Time to do some good.'

'Okay,' said Becky, 'burn some calories for me.'

'Sure thing.' I got up and walked to the door.

Becky looked over her shoulder. 'Maybe I can do a long weekend sometime.'

I nodded. 'See how it goes.'

I opened the front door, armed with my bag of tricks, armed with good intentions. Yeah. We'll see how it goes.

Twenty minutes later I arrived at the Pleasance. I walked into the University Sports Centre, flashed my membership card, and clicked through the turnstile into a world of bodies far more attractive than my own. I get a special deal, being a graduate, so it's a cheap entrance into burning lungs and acidic calves. Such a bargain, this fitness game. Such a smart move.

I swapped jeans for shorts in the second changing room, the one that's a little further along the corridor, the one neglected by toned squash players and bulging weightlifters. I have no desire to meet these people in the shower and I expect the feeling is mutual. Face to face, the chalk and cheese, what would we have to say to each other? Naked, I look twenty years older than these shining undergrads; my belly, their abs, my blubber, their biceps. Who would be the most intimidated? Probably them, to be honest. To me, these sculptured bodies are an alien student lifestyle that no one ever told me about, while to them I represent potential future. I am a fish supper from The Central, ten pints of McEwans Export, twenty Regal King-size. One false move and they could be me. One false move and they could be in a world of hurt. But it doesn't go the other way. I'm never going to look like them. They are unattainable, an exercise too far. Instead, as I walked up the stairs to the circuit-training gym, I thought of my objective in all this punishment. To breathe with lungs instead of broken glass. To run for the bus instead of falling in front of it. And most of all, the

284

crunch-factor, my aim of aims: to be able to see my dick.

It wasn't crowded in the gym. Just a few pieces of straining Lycra dotted around the steps and mats, bars and machines. It appears that even fit students have hangovers on Sunday morning; a marginally comforting thought, as I lumbered over to the mats. I try to pick the quiet times at the Pleasance; as I said, it's less traumatic for everyone concerned. So I was able to warm up alone, safe from the chattering mass of hormones that hog the mats in the late afternoon, trying to get noticed, trying to score. Stretch, relax, stretch, relax. Five minutes of popping and crackling and I lay down, looking at the ceiling, looking at the lights. Edinburgh is almost humid these days and the old windows had been cranked open, letting in cool air, sucking out the smell of sweat; fresh and stale, but always righteous.

The first part of my little regime is the cycling machine. Round and round, taking the strain, I'm glad there are no mirrors; I really have no desire to find out what I look like during this ten minute onslaught. An elephant on a child's tricycle, no doubt, but I dream of better things. Some people prop books onto the handle bars and read pulp while they cycle. Others have personal stereos, treating their neighbours to the bang of the big bass drum and the crash of electronic cymbals. I, however, use neither distraction device. Instead I think about my muscles and fat, willing a change, trying to speed up my progress through sheer will power. If it can work for cancer patients surely it can work for me.

When the going gets really tough (and this doesn't take very long) I close my eyes against the stinging perspiration and draw a mental picture of myself. In my mind I am not fat, not weak, not clumsy and bumbling. I'm not begging for a miracle. All I want is average. All I want is everyman. That's not so much to ask, is it? There I am, standing straight, standing slim, and Becky is in the background, promising treasure. My new job is there, with its vague sense of worth and fulfilment, salary and perks, shop-talk at dinner-parties. Everyone is impressed and delighted; my mum and dad, my friends and colleagues, Barclay's Bank.

Legs roaring, I clambered off the bicycle and wobbled back over to the warm-up area, for push-ups, bent-knee sit-ups, and far-reaching pain. Back and forth, side to side, my thoughts turned to the frightening possibility of unemployment. Before I started going to the gym I thought that fitness training would be a chance to empty my mind of trash for an hour three times a week, to clean out my head. But it doesn't work like that. Instead, with only repetitive exercises requiring my immediate atten-tion, my mind goes into overdrive and I sprint through all problems, all my dreams. I think about Becky, Jay, Alasdair, and my family. This morning I thought about dole cheques and breadlines.

I couldn't survive signing on. I don't really believe that it's a possibility, but I also know I couldn't handle being without a job. During my summer breaks at university there were plenty of students who went home to England to lounge about for sixteen weeks, living off their parents, living off dole cheques. I never understood the attraction of all that, and besides, I'm not sure that my dad would have let me skive all summer in any case. My holidays were spent doing crappy jobs during the day and doing crappy plays during the night. Working in kitchens with free meals and smoking cooks, then stage-managing and producing the university theatre shows with free Pro Plus and smoking actors. I worked harder in those months than I ever did during term-time. Of course I did; I've always been better doing business than studying it.

I see the unemployed. In the winter, which is most of the year in Edinburgh with its slicing wind and soaking rain, the bludgers hide away, watching television, watching the days roll by, safe in their cardboard tenements. But when the sun finally arrives, ready to burn fair skin and scorch the grass, they emerge from their homes, romping over the Meadows, mocking the rest of the world. Mocking me, when I made the mistake of jogging through Bruntsfield Links, bouncing along, the ultimate target for footballs and Frisbees. What did they think of me as I loped past? Not much, ya fat fuck, not much at all. I am average, I am a link in the chain.

But I couldn't live their life. Lying in bed with grimy lovers, eating out of the tin, scraping together money for pool, pints and lottery tickets. That is not something I could do. I rely too much on the opinion of others to risk society's tut-tutting. I want to be able to look Edinburgh in the eye and say here I am, doing my bit, making you proud. I work around the clock, I pay my council tax, so don't look away, I'm one of you. So pushing and pulling, clicking and grunting, I decided something in the university gym: I decided not to fail.

Circuit-training. The name isn't a trick. Training is definitely involved, and it is done in a circular fashion. My first day at the gym was spent under the terrifying tuition of a fitness instructor, a lean machine who was almost certainly bullied at school. Nothing else could account for his aggression, his determination to remove the excesses of an overweight world. I walked into the gym, and he let out a heavy sigh.

'Roger Brown?'

'That's me.'

'Well, taking your hands out of your pockets would be a good start.'

He must have thought I was grotesque, and that was certainly how I felt. But he didn't wave a white flag or shoo me out of the building. He knew there was hope; perhaps he's dealt with even more desperate cases than mine. But this hope wasn't like a shining light or a cloudless sky. It was aerobic hell.

As we went through the recommended block of exercises I wanted to shout out, Christ! have mercy, it wasn't me who flushed your head done the toilet, I swear I didn't take your dinner money. But instead I heaved and gasped, proving something to both of us. I was a marvel that afternoon, grinding through the instructor's assault course, gaining a tiny nod of approval, and I was proud, fit to burst, until he said, 'Right, now do it all again.'

I coughed with great care, concentrating on keep my lungs in the right place. 'Again?'

'Again,' he said, emphatic. Big nod. 'Three sets make the circuit.'

'Three,' I whispered. 'Right.'

We stopped after two. By that time I was beyond actual speech, and made my feelings known via a set of shaky hand gestures, mainly pointing to the throat and chest. The instructor looked me up and down, left and right, then put a hand on my shoulder.

'Three next time.' And there was no arguing with that.

So I went the whole hog this morning, like I do

three times a week. I'm a good dog; I may not be a puppy anymore, but I can still learn new tricks. I went through the sets, increased the reps from ten to twelve, and my lungs stayed in my throat. I look better these days. These days, I look a little like you. I did some final stretching on the mats and then padded downstairs to the showers, chuffed and glowing.

Dinner with Becky. It was fine; no shouting, no crying, no custard pies thrown in my face.

'So where did this come from?' she asked, prodding the food with a dubious fork.

'Scot-Mid.'

She blanched.

'Hey, no, it's all right, really. Alasdair's shown me where all the good stuff is.'

'That couldn't have taken very long.'

'No, seriously,' I said. 'There's some real gems in there, you just have to know where to look. I'm a shopping expert, these days.'

We wander through the grey, looking for the light at the end of the tunnel. Tick-tock, Tiger. Then a few 'phone calls to Buddies; they don't need me on the premises now. The show's run is out of my control and there's no future for me to organise. It's only the other shows that I have to help out, it's only money that I have to play with. And *A Midsummer Night's Dream*. Do you really want to know? Buddies, I'll miss the place before too long, I miss it already, the old days anyway. But it's not me anymore. I have bigger things to worry about, theatre no longer occupies my daydreams and night-time fantasies. Becky and Becky and Becky; this fitness is no longer for her. Instead it is so I can cope if the worst happens. If she leaves again, even when I don't tell her lies, even when I act with honour and dignity, at least I'll be able to look at myself in the mirror and know that I will survive. So I shall leave the drama critique to Jay. The highs and lows, the make-up and trapdoors, he can have the lot. Jay can have it all.

37

Lunch

JAY:
There is one aspect of my life that shines like a sapphire. Has Roger told you about it? I bet he hasn't. I strongly suspect that he has neglected to let you in on this piece of success. *A Midsummer Night's Dream.* Word has gotten out, Edinburgh has gotten wind of my directorial triumph. Shakespeare is alive and well at Buddies. In my theatre, Shakespeare is having a riot.

Tara's Helena is stunning; venomous, hysterical, hilarious. An actor who actually learns from directions. I made her, I kept my promise and made her a star. She is the talk of the Fringe Club, she is the talk of the town. Despite everything, despite her ingratitude and dismissive attitude, casting her was worth it. For the sake of the show, at least.

We sell out every night; the auditorium bumps and grinds on a Tuesday and the rest of the week just gets busier. I walk past the queue – the clerks and tourists who didn't have the sense to book ahead – and smile as they are turned away. Try again tomorrow, ring the box office. Give us your credit card, give us your soul, and perhaps we will let you in.

Mr. Brown let Alasdair into Buddies, to do some cretinous damage. Sneaked him past the box office

291

manager when her attention was elsewhere. So the critic tried to draw blood the way he knows best: instead of merely slating *The Dream*, he pretended to be kind, and after dusting his column inches with light praise, called the production *unexceptional*. Oh really, Alasdair, haven't you heard? No one listens to critics anymore, no one has the slightest interest in what you have to say. *The Dream* is above you, above *The Scotsman* and the rest, you cannot touch it. Put your pen away, it is the end of the century, and your words mean nothing. It is word of mouth these days, it is what we see and taste. You are a dying breed, Alasdair, and the sooner you realise that the better. Give up gracefully, before you really embarrass yourself. Go home to your nest and take desperate advantage of the scheming Erika, before she finally squeezes you dry and moves on to her next hapless victim.

How dare he be happier than Jay Wellesley? How dare he upset the balance like that? We are living in strange days, and the nights are getting shorter. Alasdair and Roger, Tara and Chloe, they think they can simply turn the world on its head. They charge ahead without a care in the world, trampling over my plans and desires. I am the director, but they refuse to do what they're told. *How happy o'er others some can be.* But I'm not feeling sorry for myself. Salvation is at hand, to lift me from the temporary depths to which I have sunk. My father arrives in Edinburgh today for a fleeting visit; lunch, *The Dream*, then away once more, chauffeur-driven, pouring money into the city. This is how the world works, and I am gladdened by it. No, don't misunderstand me. I don't believe that my father can make everything as it was before, I don't claim that he can make everything all right. Rather, I feel supremely confident that he will show me the new path, a way to bigger and better things. Ah yes. Things can only get better.

I arrive at Pullingers ten minutes early. I always like to be there before my father, so I can see him walk in, so I can see him *arrive*. I also like to check for any major developments in the menu, the decor, the clientele. Pullingers is exclusive, of course. They don't have to advertise, and unless you already know about it, you will not get a reservation. No festival tourists hobbling in by accident, no middle-management shop-talkers looking for inexpensive *à la carte*. Such are the benefits of class. Such are the benefits of selective breeding. I walk through the door and I know that we shall talk, my father and I, without interruption from the cheap and the sordid. This is where I want to be; this is what I need.

'Mr. Wellesley, good to see you again.'

Well, *of course* it is. 'Good to be here, Richard. Let me tell you, I'm absolutely parched. A cocktail moment, don't you think?'

'Absolutely, Mr. Wellesley. This way, if you will.'

Ah, you see? Everyone knows our name, they all know their place. Service, it truly is a lost art. The Americans claim to have mastered it, but I really do not care for their attitude. I have been to New York, I have been from East to West, and the waiters and bellhops, they are not my cup of tea. The Billys and Donnas, they want to be your friend, they want to warm your heart, but it's all for dollars, it's all for fifteen to twenty per cent. And that can't be right. This crude ingratiating, it sullies the form, it takes away the grace. England is my country. A land without tipping, where the waiters in the common eateries are honest and surly, while in the prestigious establishments the staff are true ladies and gentlemen. Plain faces and excellent manners, they take your order without pissing in the soup. They see your class, and they love you for it. To serve with their highest ability, that is enough, that is more than necessary to keep them satisfied. In a place like Pullingers money is everywhere, but at the same time it is so far away. Edinburgh is not England. But believe me, it is close enough.

A jacket – linen, light, full of summer – is taken, hung with love in the cloakroom. A young man – all poise and vigour, a keen intelligence in his eyes – is led to the best table in the house, away from doors, from kitchen hustle. The looks of other guests are upon him, and they wonder at his grace and manner. He is life itself.

'Here we are, Mr. Wellesley. I'll have your drink brought straight away.'

But this is a little strange. 'Richard, we appear to have an extra chair.'

'Your father informed me that it would be three for lunch, sir. Is something wrong?'

'Fine, Richard, everything's fine.'

And he glides away, polished shoes on a polished floor, and I am left alone to ponder this curious development. It has always been just the two of us, without fail. There are possibilities – a business partner, an extended family encounter – but today is supposed to be father and son; only nuclear, just the nucleus. My aperitif arrives courtesy of a new face, young and respectful, and I sip and consider, caressing the menu, straightening my tie. Feeling the need for meat, for base cruelty, I decide on *Blanquette de Veau à l'Ancienne*. Meat is murder, I couldn't agree more, and the craving for blood illustrates the human condition more than adequately.

Now it is time, and I hear my father being welcomed into the restaurant. I practise my smile, then lift my face and look as he walks towards me. There is a woman with him, and for a brief moment I think impossible thoughts. I stand up and reach out, then we are shaking hands.

'Father.'

'Hello, Jason.'

'The journey?'

'Flew by.'

Still holding hands, we simultaneously glance at the woman by his side, and she smiles at me, holding a secret to her chest, about to burst, I think, with excitement and nerves. Impossible, though, the ideas that spring to mind. Salvage, salvage, you can do anything you want with this.

I give the woman a polite half-smile, then turn to my father. 'You didn't tell me you'd hired a new P.A.'

They laugh, releasing their pent-up tension into the air, and I suck it up, becoming stiff as card. I blush, I am seven-years-old, and the cold snow is numbing my fingers and toes.

'No, Jason,' he says, 'Helen isn't my secretary.' Now they are holding hands, and I touch the back of my head, searching for the off switch. 'I would have told you before, but I thought, well, a special occasion, why not do it in person, hmm?' His voice is light, bouncing along, and I notice now that my father looks younger, and his eyes shine with vitality. 'Jason, I would like you to meet . . . my fiancée.'

He is not nervous. Where is the tremor, where is the shaking hand? How can he look me in the eye with such confidence? Watching them, man and woman, holding hands, breaking me apart, these are the moments that the strong handle with grace, with esprit.

I hold my hands at my sides. 'I want to talk to you outside.'

He is genuinely bemused, he has no idea. 'Sorry?'

'I have to talk to you in private.' My voice is low, there will be no scene.

Such confidence. 'Helen is part of the family now, Jason. This *is* private.'

The very mention of the woman and my father acquires a wistful look. He is thinking only of her, he is thinking only of sex.

I push back my chair. 'You see, Father, I want to ask why you're getting married, I want to ask you why you're doing such a thing, when you told me . . . when you've been telling me all my life that women are all bitches and whores.' I walk past him and out of the restaurant.

Rose Street is too busy; full of summer, full of tourism. I stand outside Pullingers, surrounded by ugly human beings, wishing that my cigarettes weren't in my jacket, wishing that my jacket wasn't in the cloakroom. A minute passes, and it occurs to me that perhaps my father actually expects me to go back in. I glance towards the entrance and he walks outside at that moment, looking strained, but not as much as he should.

He looks at me, as if he never understood, as if he was truly confused.

'Now I'm not angry, Jason. I just want to know why you said such a strange thing in front of Helen.'

'Because it's the truth. And you might not be angry, but I'm mad as hell.'

'Bitches and whores? I never said any such thing.'

'Christ, but you didn't have to say it, did you? It was implicit, it was under your skin, it was every-where. What did you think, that I was expecting this to happen, that this was a normal thing for you to spring on me?'

He laughed, he couldn't help himself. He has no control, my father.

'I'm not springing anything on you, Jason, this isn't really anything to do with you. I simply want to be happy, and Helen is my chance at achieving just that. I admit it might be a bit of a surprise,' – I snorted, incredulous – 'yes, fine, quite a big surprise, but I thought you'd be happy that I'd found someone, that I'd finally gotten over what happened with your mother. I'm ready to move on, son, we should be celebrating, not standing arguing in the street.'

'I was seven years old.'

'I know.'

'Seven!'

'Let's sit down.'

'I don't want to.'

'Come on, Jason, let's take the weight off.' He walks over to a bench, and I stay where I am, clenching, hating, bleeding. Then I follow him over to the bench and sit down. More people, more tourists, drinking in the street, dancing to music, slaves to the rhythm. We sit together, father and son, backs to the restaurant, and I look straight ahead.

'Seven.'

'Jason—'

'I came back home for Christmas and Mother was gone. She was gone, all of her, and you spent two minutes telling me why.'

'I'm sorry, it seemed like the best—'

'We never talked about it. You let me know that we could never talk about it. Twenty years, saying nothing. It was my whole world, that night in the drawing room, you . . . you have no bloody idea the damage you did.'

297

I look at my father, willing him to say something, anything, so I can tear him apart. He is defenceless; I can kill him right here, there is nothing he can do.

'It was so messy,' he says, 'while you were away at Sheppertons. Things were very difficult. I really thought it would be best if we made a clean break, if we started afresh. You were so young, I just wanted to make it easier on you.'

I laugh, a bark, it sounds grotesque.

'Your mother and I, we really didn't want to hurt you, please believe that.'

I ask the question I have always needed to ask, although I know that the answer will not help, it will hurt more than anything. 'Why did Mother leave?'

'You know she was younger than you are now. You have to appreciate that.'

'What happened? What did you do?'

'Nothing. Rather, we were just living, but it was too much. Married too early, she was pregnant, we wanted to do the right thing, and we worked so hard, and we were very fond of each other, but it wasn't enough. Oh Jason, we worked so hard, but our life, it wasn't what she wanted, it wasn't what she could do.'

I listen, I hear the story unfold, and I realise that I never needed to ask. It was obvious, all along, there was only one reason for her leaving.

'She said she needed to get away. In November she left, packed a few things, went back to her family. After a month we spoke on the telephone, and it was the time away that did it. She knew then that she could never come back. So I forwarded all her things, got the lawyers moving. The divorce took a long time, because no one was at fault, exactly, it was simply . . . we simply didn't love each other.'

298

I look at my hands with blurred vision. I must need an eye-test, I can't see as well as I used to.

'What about me?'

'I . . . she, she was very fond of you, Jason.' This is difficult for my father to say, but I am without pity. 'She simply wasn't the motherly type. I'm afraid we made an awful mess of things.'

'She didn't love me.'

'Oh Jason, it wasn't you, it was . . .' He searches for the right words, the softest blow, but he has no script. After twenty years, he still doesn't know how to tell me. 'She wasn't meant to have a family, to have children. It wasn't what she wanted. Everything happened so quickly, you see, and she tried, we tried, but it wasn't any good.'

I am a victim. My parents, they flirted and screwed, unconcerned. I am a product of weakness and casual sex. Upper class fuck, I am a victim of threeplay. I say something, but I do not hear myself.

'Oh Jason.' My father wipes my face with his handkerchief, and it is now that I realise that I am crying. I am seven-years-old, I am a child, I am a broken family.

'Come back inside. We can talk about things inside.'

I stand up, back away from my father. Jerky movements, I am very afraid of losing control in public. 'I have to go.'

'We shouldn't leave it like this, Jason.'

'The theatre tickets are in my jacket.' I walk away, pulling out my wallet, feeling my money. I walk along Rose Street and up towards Princes Street, looking for a taxi, looking for a way home.

Now it is later. In bed, on bed, with Tara. Too close for comfort. But she doesn't want me. She knows that

I am damaged beyond repair. We lie together, to each other.

'I have to leave now,' Tara says.

'Not yet, love, not yet.'

'You know I can't be late.'

'Stay, love, stay.'

'There's no time.'

'Take a taxi, love, there's cash in my wallet.'

'Have to get a wriggle on. Kiss. Lovely. See you at the Fringe Club.'

I close my eyes, and things look a lot worse that I imagined.

I open my eyes, and the door clicks shut. 'Love?'

You have been expecting me to fall for some time, I know. You waited, growing impatient, while I remained standing. You anticipated the explosion, the fracture, the blood, the carnage. I understand. I also have been waiting for my own end. And now we have arrived. Perhaps you blinked, you missed it if you did. It only took a second, it only took a flicker of light. I deserve all this. It's my own creation, it's my own theatre. Marianne, forgive me, you got it all wrong. I'm the one. I'm the one who is supposed to be dead. Come back, you weren't the star attraction, you were only a spear holder. Get out of the spotlight, and back to the shadows where you belong. Get back to the land of the living.

Everything has changed. Everyone is changing. I am left in the wings, obsolete. If I wasn't a director I would let the world dispose of me as it felt proper. But I've seen too much drama, too much choreographed love and hate, to just let myself crumble quietly into nothing. There must be one more fling, one last attempt at threeplay. I think I still have the energy for one last go. Of course, perhaps nothing will happen, perhaps no one will notice. I am so diminished, after all. But in the final act, I must do my best to achieve a climax, to satisfy the audience, to gain closure. I know that this is my life, and in reality most phases of our existence end in a wet fart rather than a mushroom cloud. But I am a professional to the final curtain, and I shall endeavour not to disappoint. I am alone now, so what damage can I possibly do?

38

Assembly Rooms

Poetry comes to Edinburgh in dramatic style courtesy or Erika Cameron at the Assembly Rooms.

Cameron uses the stage to full effect during her performance. With video and slides ranging from the banal to the horrific, pictures fill the theatre, a story-board for her verse . . .

Saving the starkest poem for second-to-last, all the lights are faded out, leaving only the obligatory emergency lighting. A story of betrayal and manipulation, the poem is entitled, inevitably, 'Fire Exit' . . .
– *The Scotsman*

ALASDAIR:

I am busy these days. So many plays, venues, hype. I don't have the time I used to. I can't spend precious seconds, minutes, hours, worrying about my life. Instead I just do things. It's not impulsive, hardly rash. I consider my options, then I make a decision based on a strange mixture of art and economics. I'm relieved to say that there is no space in my diary to let myself agonise about skin, sex and suicide.

These days, I'm too tired to lie awake at night. I need all my energy to get through the day, I survive on hot chocolate and breathing exercises. I'm sure, yes yes, that coffee and cigarettes would be far more effective in boosting my stamina, if not for the fact that drugs don't work with me. Something in my make-up means that caffeine makes me sweat and nicotine makes me shake. I am ultra-sensitive, I'm like a caged bird down a mine-shaft, I'll drop to the floor at the merest whiff of an additive. As for Jay's kind of drugs, the amphetamines and designer pills, a brief teenage flirtation with them taught me that the morning after was not worth the night before. Insomniac university time was not spent lurking in Pollock Halls but at the Boots Pharmacy counter, stuttering requests for Sleep-eze, Doze-eze, blackout-eze. Shortly before Finals, when sleep just wasn't interested in rescuing me from my life-phobia, I tried half a bottle of Bells Whisky and half a bottle of Veno's Cough Syrup. Half-measures, half-witted; even at my extremes I wasn't brave enough to go all the way. It worked, though, if you're curious; I slept through the night. It was Veronica rattling on my door, begging bus money, that finally woke me.

'Ally, please Ally. Fifty pee, I'm desperate.'

'Huh?'

I fell out of bed, stumbled incredulously across the room, and opened the door.

'Veronica? What times is it?'

'Fifty pee, Ally, I'll miss my five o' clock at this rate, action stations!'

Money. That lived in my wallet. My wallet lived in my jacket pocket. My jacket lived on the floor. I bent down and fished around, my hand coming back with a pound coin. I flicked it to Veronica.

'There you go. What time is it?'

'Great! Thanks, you're a star. You look awful by the way, have you been in bed all day?'

I stood up, and by the time my bedroom had stopped spinning Veronica had gone. I looked at my alarm clock.

'Oh, *God*.'

I spent the rest of the day, a very short day, stumbling around, trying to find my brain, trying to swallow.

But now I am normal. Now I have a job, a girl-friend, stories to tell at dinner parties. Now I can get to sleep, satisfied with my mediocre lot. See me, I am still alive. It was my decision, and I'm glad I made it. Yes yes, I am easily satisfied, it only takes what everyone else has to keep me going.

I've seen Erika's show twice since it opened; once for *The Scotsman*, pen in hand, already knowing what I was going to write; and once with Roger, who actually asked if he could come. I owed him a favour, after he let me review *A Midsummer Night's Dream*, but I wanted him to come anyway. I wanted him to see, I wanted everyone to see the family fun that is The Sugar Bowl.

'How're you and Jay getting on?'

'Don't ask.'

'Okay. How're you and Rebecca getting on?'

'You know I feel, with Jay, I feel like I lost my best friend, then I realise that I never had one. It was all a great big farce, I was so thick not to see what he's like. It's perfect theatre that we should end things with *The Dream*.'

We sat in our seats, getting a sneak preview of the assembling set before the regular patrons were allowed into the auditorium. Men in Iron Maiden T-shirts, putting up the back screen, ready for projected images, ready for moving pictures. 'I hope you don't think my review was too harsh,' I said.

Roger shrugged. 'Not harsh, exactly, but not right either. I mean, unexceptional is not the word I would use.'

'Nothing jumped out at me, Roger.'

The men in black plugged keyboards into amplifiers, wiring up the sound, the background rhythms.

'Look, you got it right from an artistic viewpoint, even more so as it's selling out so easily. But you weren't there during rehearsals, you didn't see how close it all was to collapsing. Every night I see *The Dream* I'm on the edge of my seat, waiting, just waiting for everything to collapse. It is exceptional, in the sense that it survives all five acts in one piece. A victory for Buddies, for the crew, for Jay and me. We got there despite ourselves.'

He smiled sadly, and I knew he would be sorry to leave the theatre, even after all that had happened. But there was the future to think about.

'And Rebecca?'

Roger sighed. 'Don't ask.'

'Got it.'

'I tell you, this isn't how I thought things would turn out. If you'd told me all this three, no, even two months ago, I would've laughed in your face. Becky and me, we're not doing the sort of thing . . . we're not . . . okay, we're not shagging. It would just take one of us to make a move, and we'd be all over each other. But it's too frightening, I'm too scared to try, because if it doesn't work, then what? I'll never finish wiping egg off my face. Fuck!'

That used to be too much information, far too much hot gossip, but I care about such things these days. Now I'm on the other side of the fence, and a thought, true and bold, came to me. Roger looks better these days, he's been sweating off the fat. 'You're really losing weight,' I said. 'You lose some brain cells at the same time?'

'Eh?'

'Tell me something. Have you told Rebecca that you love her?'

Roger looked at me. 'Oops.'

'Isn't this what caused the problem in the first place?'

'Kind of.'

'Kind of?'

'Well, yes.'

'So?'

He smiled. 'Black and white, this stuff, isn't it?'

I nodded. 'Sure is.'

The technical crew left the stage and the musicians arrived on the stage, plucking at their instruments, checking the harmony. It was this sound that met the audience as they walked into the auditorium, taking their seats to music that had already begun but wasn't quite ready. They were young, these buyers into The Sugar Bowl. They were international, they were global. I was in, ha ha, I was in with The In Crowd.

Roger shifted in his seat, looking anxious. 'I hate this bit.'

'Isn't this the exciting part?'

'*Too* exciting. I'm always so nervous for everyone. Techies, performers. I pray, please God, let the lighting cues go at the right time, let the props be in the right place. The stage, I tell you, it's an accident waiting to happen.'

Then everyone was there and the houselights went down. 'Oh God, I totally hate this.'

'You're better off out of the theatre, Roger. Now be quiet.'

'Sorry.'

Silence, no pins to drop, and the back-screen was illuminated by a hive of bees, layer upon layer, everywhere, furious. I could hear a few hundred people's skin crawl, and seeing it for a second time didn't help a great deal. Then there was sound; no insect effects, but instead radio static, searching for a station, looking for popular culture. A pause, and Erika came on stage, walked down to her micro-phone. She didn't wear (as I imagined madly, for a split second) black and yellow stripes, there were no waving antennae. No special costume, she could have walked off the street; she was normal, ordinary against a backdrop of the extraordinary.

She breathed into the mic. 'This one is for my honey from *The Scotsman.*'

Roger snorted violently, drawing stares from the surrounding punters, and Erika gave a flicker of a smile. Then she began.

'Sugar bowl
Like a honey pot all grown up
With the fun taken out
We measure life in cubes these days
No more getting caught red-handed, no more
    sticky fingers'

Roger turned to me. 'So are you going to translate as she goes along, then?' he whispered.

'Stop pretending you don't get it, it really doesn't suit you anymore.'

'Okay, but I'm going to buy her a rhyming diction-ary from James Thin.'

'Fuck you.'

He grinned, a Cheshire cat.

'We're in hot water
Crumbling into nothing
Dissolving into hips
Disposable, down throats, down kitchen sink
    dramas

307

We're in the fifth cycle (don't touch! don't you
    know where we've been?)'

That was Erika up there; my poet, my lover. How did
this happen? No, I won't question what has come
before, I'll do my best to enjoy the present. We are
recycled, human beings; all these thoughts and feelings, they are nothing new. And that is the beauty of
it all. I'm sharing now, I'm one of you, I'm getting it
in Technicolor with surround sound.

'But it's better to be older
Pooh had no clue
Only an ass could fail to see the big picture
Let's bounce sacks of Tate and Lyle off the
    flowered walls
Spring forward, fall behind, until we are
    identical'

Roger had been right, back in James Thins the
night of the book launch. Jay would say this sort of
thing. But Erika and Jay, they're poles apart all
the same. Jay's time is over, he's the end of an era, at
least until the next cycle of destruction comes into
focus. But for Erika, for us, we're at the start of
something. It's something special, and it's only just
begun.

'I don't want any more mess, baby
Keep the milkshakes thick, and the chips
    grease-free
Keep the serviettes flowing, we can use them,
not afraid to be clean
Let me know your next mistake, because
    spontaneous attraction is the last thing I need'

I sat back in my seat, waiting for the rest, for the end and the beginning. There was light and sound, the white flash, and the big bass drum. Marianne should have been there; she would have enjoyed it, she would have belonged. But Mari was a victim of the time before, she was a victim of threeplay. It's up to me to play on, in spite of, because of, everything. I sat back, and I knew there would be applause. This felt good, believing in the inevitability of positive action.

39

Mutatis Mutandis

. . . for it may be that the action required is outside the scope of the paradigm and the constraints of the cultural web, and that members of the company would therefore be required to change substantially their core beliefs.

Desirable as this may be, the evidence is that it does not occur easily. Managers are much more likely to try to cope with the problem by looking for what they can comprehend and deal with in terms of the traditional paradigm. Managers will typically attempt to reduce the extent to which they are faced with ambiguity by looking for that which is familiar.

– *Business Strategy in the Twenty First Century*

JAY:
I relieve the pressure on my bladder at nine o'clock. I have ceased worrying about the dark yellow urine I produce these days. It is the colour I deserve, let's leave it at that. I flush the toilet, listening to the waves crash around the bowl, then close my eyes and imagine a waterfall that could flush out the poison that consumes me, the toxin that is dissolving my heart.

Bitter Lemon. Damaged goods. Second hand, not

given a second thought, a second glance.

The waves in the toilet subside, so I kneel down and splash the water with my hands, to drown out the waves crashing in my head.

'Hey,' I whisper into the bowl. 'I need some help up here. Anyone down there? I need a little assistance. Is there a doctor in the house?'

No answer, only an echo.

'Seriously now, I think I've got a significant problem. Any psychiatrists in the cistern? That thing you can see just around the U-bend, that's my life. Could you fish it out for me?'

Nothing.

Ah, let me tell you, I feel mild disappointment at the lacklustre response. Feel the waves chuckle around my head. Feel silly. We are now entering the old manic phase, I tell myself, calmly enough, until I realise that I've said it out loud. I pick myself off the floor and wipe my wet hands on my face, just to prove how much I hate myself.

'You had every advantage, Jason.'

My father is speaking from his mobile 'phone. His voice is tinny. His voice is artificial.

'Except a mother.'

'The best education, the best holidays.'

'You never wanted me.'

'We gave you a theatre, we gave you what you asked for.'

'You never loved me.'

'You're all grown up now, Jason. It's time to take responsibility for yourself.'

'I am the victim, here. You never gave me a thought.'

'Please come to the wedding. It would make Helen very happy.'

'I am the victim.'

I walk from the unwashed bathroom, along the un-vacuumed hall, and into the uncleaned kitchen. I open the fridge door and retrieve the vodka bottle from it's nest. I contemplate getting a glass, then decide against it. There aren't any clean ones any-way. I walk from the kitchen, along the hall, and into the bedroom. In my sock drawer, underneath the layers, is plastic and powder, chemicals to enhance the mood. A mirror, my Switch card, it's a simple operation. I hunch over my reflection, swiping and chopping, we have all done this before. It runs up my nose, although it is the back of my mouth that is left with a bitter, gulping aftertaste. Absolut, to seal the envelope, as it were.

That's better. No, that's worse. Hang on. It's not so bad, I think, just very quick, just a little disconcerting for my heart to beat quite that fast. Ah yes, now I have it. Yes, that's better. Yes, that's much much worse.

I wear my Versace shirt to Roger's birthday-bash, but my clothes are clearly low on juice.

The evening starts well enough. I pick my girl, then pin her down with a barrage of character assassina-tions regarding other people at the party. But five minutes into our one night stand, the Girl realises that I am very drunk indeed. She tries to slink away, but I never take my eyes off her. I follow her to the bathroom and wait outside the door, daring the girls in the queue to comment, to say anything. I get worse as the night wears on. Feel worse. Look worse. The Girl smells my failure and peers around me, silently appealing for a rescue team to take the loser away. I feel the Girl sniff out my character, and knowing the game is over I insert more coins anyway. I move to the next level. And get worse.

'It's hard to be bitter for a sustained length of time. Something nice always comes along eventually, to shake the blues away. Trust me on this one.'

I grin at the Girl, and the Girl looks back with anything but trust in her eyes.

'Trust me on something, for Christ's sake!'

I think I may be talking too loudly, feeling the world slip away, making yet another attempt to retain it in my grasp.

'It's clear to me now,' I whisper. 'I wasn't sure before, but now I've got things sorted in my head. This is nice. It's nice to be clear.'

The Girl just smiles, having finally attracted someone's attention; SWAT Team, SAS, it doesn't really matter.

'It would be nicer,' I say, 'at least I sometimes think it would be nicer, if we all had little computer chips with our personality on them. Then if you met someone at a party you could spend ten seconds booting up data instead of wasting a whole evening finding out you hate each other. Because that's always such a disappointment, don't you think? And I really would like to know what you think.'

'I think you've had too much to drink,' says The Girl, loud enough for the regiment to hear, loud enough for them to understand that she needed rescuing, definitely needed saving from the clearly insane gentleman in the horrifically out-of-date shirt.

'Of course I have! But what about the idea? What about the chip?'

'I think you should go home.' The Girl's voice is calm yet authoritative, she is probably a nurse in Real Life; outside the madness of the party. But even here she knows better than to try to deal with a deranged patient by herself. Indefatigable, The Girl waits for the reinforcements to move in.

'The chip! The motherfucking chip!' I take a small step toward her, my arms outstretched in emphasis, and the battalions are on their marks, most definitely set, and just waiting for the starting gun.

'Do you do this when you're sober as well?' asks the Girl, with what appears to be genuine curiosity.

'What?'

'Talk rubbish.' The Girl can say that, because she has back-up now.

'This is gospel,' I say, with shining eyes. 'You think people lie when they're drunk? No, they just tell the truth a little louder than other people.' I place a hand on the Girl's shoulder. 'And the truth is, you whore from Babylon, is that despite your constant whining and limited intellect, I'm still willing to sleep with you tonight.'

And with that line, the cavalry charge, and I find myself outside, on my knees, with a button missing from my Versace shirt. Now I am truly bleeding: I have been grazed, cut, wounded to the core. The future is now, and it is filled with violence.

40

Turning

This production, directed by Jason Wellesley, is full of drive and visual attack but, at its heart, fails to establish a through-line that pulls the various plots into a whole. The young lovers' stories are clearly explained, the ongoing battle between Oberon and Titania is accompanied by gymnastic and choreographic fairies, and the Mechanicals come and go with their theatrical preparations until they perform the 'Pyramus and Thisbe' tale, but to what end?

Do we learn anything from the chaos of the opening wherein a man threatens his lover with death? Are the mortals' foibles instructive to the spirits who oversee the events and, eventually, help to restore order to the Athenian realm?

If, by the play's end, characters have grown through experience, as indeed they do, when do the changes occur and how do the two worlds- mortal and spirit- comment one on the other?

This is what is lacking in the current offering and what, in spite of considerable invention, contributes to a pleasant but unexceptional evening.

– *The Scotsman*

ALASDAIR:
One more week of dreams and sugar bowls, then

Edinburgh can get back to normal. A city holding its breath for a month, squeezing in as many people as possible. Then they leave, for home, for the next venue, and Edinburgh exhales, exhausted, full of money. Now we can get back to normal, wait for the days to get shorter, for the wind to get colder. Now we can prepare for hibernation.

Rebecca asked me to help her organise a surprise birthday party for Roger. She didn't want to contact his friends at Buddies, afraid of getting Jay on the end of a mistaken telephone line. So I called them up, invited them along, then bussed along to Scotmid, for Budweiser and sausage rolls. Don't ask me if Roger was surprised. He looked it, he looked absolutely gobsmacked, but then again, Roger is a man of the theatre, for seven more days at least.

Erika wasn't able to attend such a prestigious social event due to the small matter of the Sugar Bowl; every night it is a little different, every night she laboriously prepares for the unexpected. So I arranged to meet her afterwards at the Fringe Club, then went over to Roger's flat, to hang streamers, to blow up balloons.

I mingled, I asked and answered, I laughed and cringed. I did what everyone else did.

'So, Alasdair, where's that famous girlfriend of yours?'

'Not that famous, not yet. She's performing tonight, I'm meeting her later.'

Grins all round. I think, quite possibly, they were actually happy for me.

'So what's it like?'

'Sorry?'

'What's it like, going out with a famous poet?'

'Oh, *that*. A blur, a media circus. Drugs, sex and country music. A riot.'

Laughter. And I realised I didn't care whether they were happy for me or not. As long as they were just a little bit jealous. For once, I thought, let them be fucking green with envy.

These days, the fabulous present, I'm a social chameleon. I was still there at one o'clock, out-rageously late, party animal, then decided to leave for Bristo Square. I sneaked out of the living room and squeezed past slithering bodies into the kitchen, looking for refreshment. The cat, the fantastic feline, was sitting by its empty food bowl. It looked very unimpressed.

'You don't need feeding. No you don't, oh no, not you, hmm? Oh no.'

I found the can-opener and doled out a tubular slab of Whiskas.

There was noise from the living room; shouting, grunting, two bodies rolling down the stairs and into the street. The cat looked up, then decided it was safe to start eating.

'I'm not doing you any favours you know,' I said, and opened the fridge door to retrieve a bottle of mineral water. There was an impressive bunch of flowers drowning in a vase on top of the fridge. Roses. Red. You know what they say. I walked over to the kitchen table and sat down, placing the bottle in front of me, contemplating the screw-cap. I re-alised that I needed a glass, which suddenly seemed like a pretty tiresome point. I gave up on the water and watched the cat eat.

'Wolf it down, wolf wolf wolf. You're just a little wolf, aren't you, hmm? Yes you are, yes you—'

'Everyone talks to Fat Cat.' Roger walked into the kitchen, out of breath, examining his hands.

'Hi.'

'Hi, Alasdair, taking a break?'

'Yeah. You bleeding?'

He looked up, smiled. 'Oh no, it's all right,' he said, waving his hand. 'It's not my blood.'

'That's okay then. I fed your cat, I hope you don't mind.'

'No sweat. What doesn't kill Fat Cat will only make him stronger.'

'I see. Nice flowers, Roger. Yours?'

'Thanks. I Interflora'd them for the Beckster. It's amazing what you can sort out over the telephone these days.'

I grinned. 'You're just an old-fashioned boy, aren't you?'

'Oh no,' he replied solemnly. 'I'm a modern breed. I'm the next generation.' He pointed at the Highland Spring. 'You need glasses for that?'

'Need is perhaps too strong, but I suppose it would make things easier.'

Roger got up from the table, fetched two glasses and filled them with ice. 'There we are.'

'Thanks.' I poured us both a generous measure of Highland Spring. 'Happy Birthday, Roger. Skol.' I drank, tasting the fizz, and then the chill. 'So was that Jay I saw you throwing out?'

Roger nodded. 'He was being a little antisocial with the unconventional vegetarian.'

'Who?'

'Oh, Elizabeth. Someone I met, sort of, a little while back. I didn't think I was going to ever see her again but she popped up in Negociants the night before Mari's funeral, so I got her tickets for *The Dream*.'

'Small world,' I said.

'But I wouldn't want to paint it.'

'Mmm? Oh, absolutely, hell of a job, that.' I took a

sip of water. 'So I assume Rebecca didn't actually invite Jay to the party.'

Roger grunted. 'Unlikely, but the Buddies grapevine, it's difficult to keep anything secret for too long, especially amongst actors. Christ, and I'll have to face him all over again in the morning.'

'I didn't see Tara anywhere,' I said, 'are they not . . .'

'No idea, it's not something I've been keeping tabs on. You know I can't believe how much I thought of Jay, I really thought he was an amazing guy.'

'Don't worry,' I said, 'I think we were all pretty envious of him.'

'You weren't jealous of him, were you?'

I smiled. 'I'm jealous of most people. I actively cultivate my jealousy, it's a valuable character trait. I'm jealous of the sky for being so blue, and for being so close to the sun. To be honest, I could resent the ocean.'

Roger laughed. I wasn't joking, of course.

'Jealous or not,' he said, 'I'm well shot of him after what he did to me and Becky.'

'Talk of the devil.' Rebecca wandered into the kitchen, and catching sight of Roger, wobbled over and planted a wet kiss on his lips. 'Let's dance, baby.'

'You wouldn't rather sit down?' Roger asked her.

'Or fall down?' I suggested.

'Piss off, Alasdair. C'mon, c'mon, right . . . now!' and she pulled Roger up from his chair with surprising force.

'Little help?' said Roger as he was dragged out of the kitchen.

'Sorry,' I said, 'you're on your own, I have to get to the Fringe Club.'

'Okay, well . . . ow! Have a good one, and don't drink too much water, that shit is bad for you.' And then they were gone, sucked into the hallway, sliding into the noise and heat of the living room.

I walked down Middle Meadow Walk, through the crowd of late-night Festival-goers. I walked with the tourists, and I felt proud of my city. The Edinburgh Festival Fringe. It is my work, my life, my love.

My old life? I stole feelings from people, stolen moments. I saw their tortured soul and reached into it, clutching their anguish to my heart and bleeding it dry. I cut myself off from my own fears, so I looted theirs instead. A cynical form of empathy, a professional foul. But I couldn't guard against Marianne. She broke me down, she made me care. Life's a bitch, and then you turn thirty? No. Life's a bitch, and then you turn. Turn over. Turn the channel. Turn on the light. Move on. Do you think we can just move on now please?

My new life. Erika and poetry. Is that all? It's a lot, but is that all? Mari has gone, dispersed, a casualty of art and commerce, of greed and threeplay. I am left with sex and work, an old flatmate, an old job. Same newspaper, same city. Anything can happen. I have decided that anything can happen. Too much potential, I'm not checking out early, so it'll take tomorrow's ironic bus to break my bones and stop my heart. Touch wood. Touch down.

Promised myself I'd run from this. Run away from this when I've finished writing about it. So I'm going to take a holiday. Somewhere hot, somewhere easy. I asked Erika and she's coming as well. She has a week free, before New York City, before the rest of her life. This is good, I need someone to help me function. Besides, I like Erika a lot. There's even more to her than I first thought. I scratched beneath her soft milky surface and discovered hidden depths. Perhaps, who knows, our futures may have something in common.

I walked, a brisk stroll across the Meadows, two minutes away from the Fringe Club, two minutes away from Erika. Talking business with peers and strangers until Rock Steady Security throw us out into Bristo Square. I walked, the faint ghost of Marianne haunting my soul. Walking, overwhelmed by the things I once knew. Sitting tenant, I'm a psychological squatter. These feelings don't belong to me anymore; I've no right to have them, no capacity for dealing with them. I shall move, take my emotional baggage to the south of France; maybe it'll get lost during the flight.

41

Falling On In

ROGER:
> Rebecca
>
> Do you ever find yourself feeling happy and then
> forget what you were feeling happy about? I had one just
> a moment ago. I suddenly thought, damn, what was it,
> what was that wonderful thing? Do I have a party to go
> to, is it pay day, did I get mail this morning?
> Then in a flash I remembered.
> It was you.
> I love you forever.
> Roger

I'm getting better at all this. Oh God, I'm absolutely
fantastic. Want some advice? Go on, ask me something, I might know the answer.

My heat skipped a beat as the bus steamed through
the traffic lights at Tolcross. To love someone, now I
knew how that could feel. To dive in, to love myself
in the flood. Without limits. Without rules. Magnifi-
cence, life dressed in silk and smelling of jasmine.
Carried away? Fuck you, I won't do what you tell me.
I got off the bus and ran (yes, ran!) the last few streets
home, stopping only to buy a bag of donuts (hey, one
step at a time, okay?) from the inimitable Crawfords.
I walked up the steps to my flat, allowing myself

the forbidden luxury of undressing the Beckster in my mind. Tick-tock. I opened the door, walked into the darkness and fumbled for the light-switch. In the split second after about thirty mouths took a deep breath, I made a pretty good guess as to the situation.

'Surprise!' The lights clicked on and I squinted against the brightness, recovering to see about thirty pairs of eyes smiling at me. Becky jumped from the shadows and to my side, planting a big kiss on my cheek.

'Happy birthday, Roger!'

I put my arm around her waist and smiled as I felt her sway slightly. Her face was flushed; it appeared as though she had started partying before the official starting date. I removed my arm from her waist long enough to shift the pole between my legs with one hand and hold up the paper bag with the other.

'Anyone for a donut?' Laughter, and the party had begun.

It was a good party. Birthdays, I knew they had to be good for something. There was only one problem, only one potential disaster, threatening to lay waste to all I had worked for. Who else? Well, indeed.

I walked from the bathroom back into the living room, post-piss, post-hair check, post-gargle, to find Elizabeth on the verge of being assaulted by Jay Wellesley. I say assault. Of course, Jay looked incapable of anything too violent, looked incapable of affecting anything. But it was my party, and I could define a given situation any way I wanted. My birthday prerogative, thank you very much. Elizabeth – the unconventional human being looking all too ordinary at that moment – waved at me, lighting flares, an embarrassed smile on her face. I walked over, passed bemused onlookers, then made serious inroads into Jay's personal space.

Standing at the door of my building, with the sun having finally gone to bed, I looked at Jay. Standing at the curb, under the bright moon, Jay looked at me.

'You damaged my shirt. That was an expensive shirt, Mr. Brown, you have absolutely no respect for today's fashions. Besides, you didn't give me time to fetch my jacket. I'll have to go back up and retrieve it.'

His eyes were dancing, they were pinpricks, tiny bullet holes. 'I'll send it on, Mr. Wellesley. Time you went home, time you hit the hay.'

He looked at me, pleading, speeding. 'I'm in charge, Roger. Please, let me be in charge.'

I gave him my Buddies smile, cold as ice. 'Go home, Mr. Wellesley.'

'And where is that? Fuck—' With a sudden burst of energy Jay ran at me, probably just trying to get back inside, probably not wanting to hurt me at all. But as I said, it was my birthday. This was my party anecdote, and he wasn't going to remember anything in the morning. Such are the newly-discovered advantages of sobriety. A fist of self-defence (because you can't be too careful in the dark streets of Edinburgh) made sharp contact with Jay's face, nose cracking, putting blood on my hands. He wiped his nose on the sleeve of his shirt and looked up at me.

'It wasn't like that at all,' he said, the words rattling in his throat. He sat down on the pavement, looking out into the street with blinking eyes.

I am not a monster. I am not a shit. But I define this night, I can tell you anything.

'Go home, Jay, please go home.' I looked down at him, and I knew he wasn't listening to a word I said.

The Beckster stopped short of the living room. Put her hands to my face. 'Tell me a secret, Tiger,' she whispered, caught in a moment of sobriety, a moment of clarity.

'What kind of secret?' I asked, admiring the deep brown colour of her polished nails as they explored my face.

'The kind I know already.'

'Okay,' I said. 'I'm naked without you, little fawn.'

'Really?'

'Truly.'

'So what were you wearing when you sent me those roses?'

'A determined expression.'

'Huh?'

'My face. I looked . . . very keen, I was made of steel.'

'You're on form tonight!'

'You'd better believe it. Now let's dance.'

Everyone's getting drunk tonight. Everyone's getting high. Did you notice? Everyone's doing drugs except me. Tonight, I've never been more sober.

The music played. One thousand watts of power sent fat shapes of bass into the floor, bounced sharp cuts of treble off the walls. Music played and people danced. Too loud to talk. So dance. Or make out. Or both. But don't try to talk. Rebecca and I danced. I swayed, Becky's arms around my neck to stop me escaping, and to stop herself falling over. Becky hung around me like a necktie tried first thing in the morning, before you've woken up. Like a confused pendulum on a grandfather clock. A pendulum that failed the swinging exams: *Too low. Too much to the right. Try again. No, no, that's no good. Come on, it's not that difficult, swing, for Christ's sake!* My neck ached as I supported most of Becky's weight. At least for most of the time. But that's not so bad.

Happy Birthday, Roger.

It was a good party. Because I had a hold on things. At least, there was certainly hold potential. A surprise birthday party, it's not such a bad thing, is it? Look how happy Becky was to organise all this. Why? Because me being happy makes her feel happy. This is good. It's good to be better. And of course, above all else, it's better to be good.

The music went on. Modern music is awful, everyone agrees. But modern dance, that's the best. Because anyone can do it. Even I can do it. I swung and swayed, and Becky hung. Let's not overcomplicate matters, here. I've never really liked parties. But despite the strain in my neck and upper back, this one was pretty good.

But wait. Becky's mouth is open. She's speaking. Louder. The music, it's deafening, We can't hear. Speak up, Becky, this might be important!

'What?'

Becky pulled my head down to her mouth and screamed in my ear. 'I love you!'

I heard it that time. Sounds nice. Let's hear it again.

'What?'

'I . . . love . . . you!' A real yell this time, and I felt the words, really tasted them that time, vowels and consonants crashing into my head, with no concern for the havoc they might wreak. Why do the words sound so nice? Is it really the meaning, the connotations, or is it the sound? Let's be grand. It's the sound of sacrifice. It's the sound of absolution.

I smiled as the words rushed through my mind. They tickled, in a nice way. They rhymed with my heart, they skipped rope with my soul. I took Becky's head in my hands and kissed her. Not her lips. No, I didn't want to get lost, not yet. Wanted to stay on the periphery, looking in on the scene, seeing its beauty before I dove into the whirlpool.

'I love you!' shouted Becky again, her head in my hands, her heart in my domain.

'Yes, but will you respect me in the morning?' I asked with a smile.

Becky was drunk, but as I already knew, drunks don't lie. They just tell the truth louder than other people. I felt . . . bigger. As if I had a new layer of skin. A protective film. I could, and would, do anything. She shouts three words, and I am happy. That's all she did. But of course that's not all. The words are just the final part. They're just the beginning of the rest. I kissed her face. Her nose. Her cheeks, flushed, full of life. Her forehead, her neck, her ears. Then the highlight. No, not the mouth, tasting of alcopop, tasting of Hooch. The eyelids. I kissed Becky's eyes, and she gasped, then lifted herself up to me. She wrapped her legs around my waist and tested my back to the limit. I laughed, and Becky put her mouth to my ear again and said one more thing:

'Tiger, take me to bed.'

Feeling her body weight fall into me, I staggered back and then shifted weight, taking her in my arms.

'Your timing's fantastic, Becky.'

I carried Becky through the throng of either amused or oblivious guests, then walked down the hallway and into the bedroom, depositing her gently on the bed. Fat Cat sat in the doorway, his tail twitching nervously.

'Nothing to see here, Fats.' He remained in the doorway, looking into the room with wide eyes.

'Hey man, trust me, everything's A-okay. Go find a mouse.'

Fat Cat gave me one final look, then turned and padded back down the hallway.

42

Infected

JAY:
Welcome to the lowest ebb. Welcome to the highest fear.

Welcome to Marianne's bridge.

It's not the tallest bridge in Edinburgh, but it's tall enough. Obviously, she chose a bridge that wouldn't leave her in a hospital bed with egg on her model's face. Did she have enough time to have second thoughts? Did she have time to have any thoughts at all? I bet she did. Time must slow down, when you're falling through space. Time must really crawl along the curb, when you're falling to your death.

There's hardly anyone around tonight, two o'clock at Marianne's bridge. She chose one close to home. Leith, the dead zone, not a place to be caught reading a street-map. I look down to the street below, and wonder if she came here often. Doing her research, out in the field. Working out the direct approach, planning her final nose-dive.

I look down to the street, and I think that jumping wouldn't be hard at all.

'Hey.'

A voice – young, female and local – interrupts my morbid curiosity. She's standing right beside me, how long has she been watching ? Perhaps she thinks I'm a jumper, perhaps she's Leith's lone Samaritan.

I turn to face her. 'Yes?'

'Have you got twenty pee for the 'phone? I need to call my friend.'

She's so young. Face plastered with makeup, a tiny joke of a skirt, she can't be more than sixteen-years-old.

I have no sympathy. I have one or two problems of my own.

'Why should I give you anything?' I ask coldly.

But the girl isn't intimidated.

'Good karma, man,' she says. 'Looks like you could use some.'

I remember my nose. I touch it, and the dried blood that I have yet to clean up brings thoughts of Roger Brown flooding back.

The girl clears her throat. 'Were you in a fight?'

I try a contemptuous snort, but it hurts too much.

'Not at all. Merely artistic differences.'

I reach into my trouser pocket, fingers moving past money and more money. Paper and metal, it's one thing that I can still rely on.

I hold out twenty pence. 'Here. Now go away.'

She snatches the coin, then smiles, and I wonder if I'm being softened up for an accomplice, waiting in the shadows. I shiver, then start walking to the steps. She trots after me, high-heels on concrete slabs, and my back feels terribly vulnerable.

I quicken my pace, but as I jog down the steps, the girl comes alongside me and tugs at my shirt.

'You got a fiver? I don't think my friend can pick me up, I think I need to get a taxi.'

She can smell my cash. Despite my nose, she knows I have money to burn.

At the bottom of the steps I reach back into my trouser pocket. I know the shape of banknotes. I

know them blindfolded. I pluck out five pounds and
hold it out to her.

'There. Now piss off. Go home, I'm busy.'

The girl grins, then starts to walk away. But as I
stand underneath Marianne's bridge, she stops and
turns around.

Looking at me appraisingly, she says, 'I'm Libby.'

I shrug. 'So?'

'So what's *your* name?'

Quick as a flash. 'Roger Brown.'

Even now, I keep my sense of humour.

Libby walks back and takes hold of my hands.

'You know, Roger, I'm a great fuck.'

Of course she didn't say that. I need to get my
hearing tested, I need to have them syringed.

'Pardon?'

'I'm a great fuck,' she said again, without a hint of
a schoolgirl blush.

'Go home.'

'Thirty quid. Come on.'

'Go home, Libby.'

Hands on my crotch. 'Come on, Roger, you look
lonely.'

'Please . . . please don't.'

Her mouth in my ear, her voice is a whisper.

'Right here, baby.'

'*Ah.*'

I pull money from my pocket. I am blind, it could
be anything, it falls from my hands and into the
street.

Libby pounces, scrabbling on the ground, collecting her winnings. She transfers it to her own pocket
and her face is triumphant, but I hear my zip coming
undone, my trousers falling down, and this is no
sting.

I hold on tight, thinking of the condoms in my

jacket, the jacket I left at Roger's flat. I should ask if she has protection, before my mind fills with buzzing insects, with honey bees.

But she laughs, and when I look down I see that the question is purely academic.

'This isn't going to work if you're not hard, Roger.'

'Shit,' I whisper, blushing, distraught. 'Speed, it does this to me. Speed's no good for sex.'

But Libby misses the point. I stand under Marianne's bridge, trousers around my ankles, and she strokes my face.

'Don't be embarrassed, it happens to every guy now and then. We can take it slow if you like, you *are* sweet.'

Stupid girl. She has no idea, she thinks I'm ordinary. She doesn't know my history.

I pull my boxer shorts and trousers back up.

'It doesn't happen to *me*, you stupid little whore. It never happens to me. Christ, don't you know who I am?'

Libby takes a step back, sensing trouble, sensing a premature end to her pot of gold.

'Hey, Roger, take it easy.'

Of all the names to call me. It's the only one she has, of course, but my vision is tinged with pink. Pure rage. And let's face facts, here: she's asking for it.

'My name, you fucking cunt, is *Jay Wellesley*.'

I swing my clenched fist and hit her lying mouth. I punch all the way through, and she falls to the ground.

'Fuck! Oh fuck, please!'

She curls up, crying for mercy through blood and broken teeth.

But this is theatre. This is the finale. I send my right foot into the small of her back and she opens up, screaming.

'No, *fuck, please, Jesus fuck!*'

'Oh. Oh, you cunt.'

Our voices together, a *stretto*, we are an orchestral climax, we are so much more than sex. Life and death, mine and hers. I am killing us both.

I kick her ribs with Italian shoes, and she gasps, winded.

I have had precious little experience of violence on the street, but I have read countless scripts. I know the stage directions, I know exactly what to do.

I kick her in the head.

Click.

A tiny noise in the back of her throat, then silence.

I step back, take a look around. Leith is deserted, Leith is dead.

Libby lies under Marianne's bridge. Someone should have told her what a dangerous place this is. Someone should have taken her under their wing.

I look down at her. Dead or alive? Well, really, does it matter? Either way, she has taken what was left of my life. She has stolen my sex, and now I have nothing.

It's cold. The knuckles of my right hand are bleeding. Now I have the virus. Now I am terminal.

I run. These days, so much more than before, I seem to spend my time running away from women. And here's something I've discovered about the opposite sex. Despite Tara and her ferocious survival tactics, despite my mother's crippling disappearing act, women are far more dangerous when they're dead. I run, gasping, and blood drips from my nose into my open mouth. Racing oxygen, tongue on fire, I taste an infection, I savour an incurable disease.

There is nowhere to go. But I run for my life.

43

Rubber

ROGER:

The cool, dark bedroom was a distinct relief after the bright heat of the party. I could sit here for a while. Sit there in the darkness. The party would go on without us. Nice to sit in the darkness. I am hers, she is mine. I'm ready. I'm ready to kiss her lips and fall on in. Ready to fall in love. This is what people do. Night. Party. Drunk girlfriend.

'I'm not drunk,' said Becky, reading my mind.

I looked down at her. 'Not much.'

She swallowed. 'I do feel a little bit sick, though.'

'That's okay, I'll look after you.'

She sat up, back against the wall, more sober than she had been acting, after all. 'And why would you want to do a thing like that?'

'Because I love you, Becky, that's why.'

'I see.' No fireworks. Really very ordinary, this business of love and madness. 'So . . . we were about to have sex, weren't we?'

I nodded. 'Think so. You up for it?'

Becky snorted with laughter and leant forward, reaching for my belt. 'Anything you can do, Tiger.' Then she looked up at me, frowning. 'Do you have any condoms?'

Oh shit.

'Maybe, I mean probably, oh I'm sure I do.'

Definitely not. Definitely no chance in hell.

'Hang on.' I turned to my beside drawers and hunted around, frantic, under money, between scripts. Everything was in that drawer. Everything and an old cigarette. Everything but a condom.

'Fuck!'

'Problem?'

'Yes, a little one, a minor setback. Do you have any in your flat?'

'Nope.'

'Bloody hell!'

The Beckster looked at me, bemused. 'Just go and borrow one from someone, it's no big deal.'

'What? Why don't *you*?'

'Are you kidding? That's the tiger's job'

'Since when?'

'Since you didn't have any. Now hurry up, before I fall asleep.' Becky, the bitch, she lay back on my bed and closed her eyes. 'I'm so-o-o-o tired,' she murmured.

I stood at the door.

'I'm yawning, Tiger.'

I cringed, paling at the thought.

'I'm snoring, Tiger, snore snore snore.'

'Okay, fucking hell!'

I leapt out into the hallway and raced into the living room, to my certain doom no doubt, no doubt at all. Who to ask? Where was that perfect person, that benevolent stranger, with sealed lips, never to be seen again? Really, it was worth a run to the BP all-night garage, surely, to avoid the utter humiliation of it all.

Then I saw it. Ignoring friends and Buddies people, I eased my way over to the spider plant and picked up Jay's jacket. I reached inside and found his wallet. Sure enough, good as gold, I knew he was useful for something. Jay Wellesley, protecting himself against the Edinburgh low-life, protecting the family blood. I replaced the wallet and raced, three-legged, back to the bedroom. I raced back to the Beckster. And as this was my birthday, and I called the shots, she was still awake when I got there.

Becky and I. We shall look out for each other. Whatever happens, we shall have each other. There is both good and bad up ahead, there are things so bad that I can't even imagine them. It is grey, vague and mysterious, but I understand now that we cannot predict the future. There is no point in playing it safe; even that strategy – especially that strategy – has its own inherent dangers. But nothing is impossible.

Jay was in the morning. A new job was in the morning. Cleaning the flat was in the morning. I lay beside Becky, and we lost each other in our skin and souls. Then we slept. I dreamed of symmetry that night. I dreamed of parallels and straight lines. I dreamed in black and white, because those colours can only exist in dreams, but we need them all the same.

THE END